What Lies Beneath

Rane Williams

Dedicated to my grandmother Marilyn who is always my constant source of inspiration and drive. And to the forgotten people of the world, this one's for you.

Hey there! Before you dive in, I want to give you a quick heads-up. This story touches on some heavy themes that were important to the journey these characters go through. That includes mentions of cancer, addiction and overdosing, death, abuse, sexual harassment, and references to sexual abuse.

Contents

Prologue

You'd think the days that completely change your life would stand out *before* the news hits. But the day my mother went missing was just... typical. I did ordinary things, went through ordinary motions, right up until everything changed. There was a before, and then there was an after. A clear line in the sand. The truth is, the days that change your life the most are often the most typical, until the turning point makes them unforgettable. You're probably thinking that had to be the worst day of my life. Would it shock you if I said... it wasn't? Don't get me wrong it's definitely in the top five. But the worst? No. Not even close.

Chapter 1

I cram myself into the middle seat, silently cursing for not paying extra for a window. With a frustrated huff, I resign myself to the fact that comfort won't be part of this flight. A three-hour layover has already worn me thin, and my mood is hanging by a thread. Still, I know there's no point in stewing over it. No matter what choices I made—or didn't make—I'd be irritated right now. Hell, I could be in first class with a crisp glass of wine, and I'd still be a very cranky woman. Quitting your job of three years and uprooting your life to move back to your tiny hometown will do that to a person. The stranger next to me elbows me, and I make a vow then and there: I will *always* reserve a window seat, no matter the cost. I throw on my noise-canceling headphones, take a deep breath, and close my eyes. Despite the discomfort, the mood, and the elbows, I know one thing for sure: I'd sit in a hundred middle seats, quit a thousand jobs, and get elbowed into oblivion if it meant being there for my grandmother.

When my grandmother tried to casually mention she was sick during our weekly call, I knew better. I know her well enough to tell when she's not telling the whole truth. The next day, I didn't hesitate to put in my notice. Yes, I loved my job at *Ink Ever After*. After three years, I'd worked my way up to Associate Editor and was even in the running for Senior Editor. But I made the decision to move back to Summit Grove, Missouri. Population 2,018—soon to be 2,019. My grandmother raised me and she is the only person in the world I would do this for. She is the closest thing to a saint in this world and has done everything for me. Everything except moving with me when I got my job in New York. I cringe thinking of the memory. One of the few times we really disagreed.

3 Years Ago

I run upstairs, heart racing, a grin stretching across my face.

"Grandma!" I shouted, taking the stairs two at a time until I tripped at the top and went sprawling.

"Sloan, please slow down," she called from the kitchen table, not looking up from her paper.

"They called!" I gasped, scrambling to my feet and rushing toward her, breathless.

She lowered her newspaper and raised an eyebrow. "Who called?"

"The magazine! *Ink Ever After!*" My voice was practically squeaking.

"Sloan, I'm right here. No need to yell," she teased.

"Okay, sorry," I said, trying to pull myself together, though excitement still fizzed under my skin.

"Which one is that?" she asked, genuinely confused.

"They're a smaller magazine based in New York. They said I can start next month. I can't believe it." Her smile faltered, just for a moment, before she masked it with warmth.

"That's great, honey," she said, placing her hand gently over mine. "So… what other jobs are you waiting to hear back from? When will you make your final decision?" She got up to refill her coffee like this wasn't the biggest moment of my life.

"Oh, it doesn't matter. This is it. I'm taking the offer. It's the only one in New York that's made me an offer, and it's a magazine I actually believe in. They feature artists and writers from all over the world."

She froze mid-pour. "So… you're moving," she said softly. The room fell silent.

"Yes," I replied, hesitation creeping in. "That's something else I wanted to talk to you about…"

"You're a grown-up, Sloan," she said abruptly. "You can move." Her tone was firm, even a little harsh, but when she looked back at me, she smiled and shuffled back to the table.

"I know," I said. "I just wanted to ask… move with me."

She paused mid-sip, eyes fixed on me. "Sloan… I can't leave here."

I sighed, frustrated, because she *could*. The magazine was covering the move. We could both go, start fresh, live a big life in the big city. "They're paying for everything," I said. "We could finally see New York together, like you always wanted."

She set her cup down and cleared her throat. "Sloan, I'm sorry. I can't. You know I can't."

"I don't want to go without you," I said quietly, trying not to let the moment sour.

"There's always the *Summit Gazette*," she offered. "Didn't they offer you something?"

I scoffed. "Grandma, they want me in the obit section. I wouldn't even be writing."

"I can't stay here," I added, "not while he's still around." She gave me a look filled with quiet sympathy.

"Honey, that pain will pass if you stick it out."

"It will pass," I said, cutting her off, "*if* I leave." I stood, pushing my hair out of my face. "I don't understand why you won't come with me."

"You *do* understand," she said. "The same reason you want to leave... is the reason I have to stay. You're running from something, Sloan. I can't run. I have to stay, just in case she comes back."

My hands hit the counter before I could stop them. "She's not coming back! If she wanted to, she would have by now."

"Sloan..." Her voice trembled. The hurt in her eyes hit me like a weight. Something inside me cracked, but I couldn't take it back. I threw up my hands, exhaling.

"Fine," I said, my voice lower now. "I'm going. I'm leaving in a month."

"I'm proud of you," she said softly as I turned away. I cried as I walked downstairs to my room, knowing I'd just hurt the one person in the world who would do anything for me.

My stomach grumbles, dragging me out of the awful memory and reminding me I haven't eaten all day. The last thing I wanted was to shell out twenty bucks for stale airport food after quitting my job. I hear the crackle of the intercom. "Folks, welcome to Columbia, Missouri." I sigh and open my eyes just in time for someone's bag to smack me in the face.

Welcome indeed, I think sarcastically.

CHAPTER 2

I finally find my luggage and trudge toward the exit, knowing I still have to figure out how to get to my grandmother's house two hours from here. I opened the Uber app, and of course, no one wanted to accept a ride request from Columbia to Summit Grove. My grandmother offered to come get me, but I told her no. She shouldn't be driving two hours one way for me. I'm supposed to be here to make things easier on her not the other way around. I sigh, already preparing myself to pay an astronomical amount for a cab. I try searching for the nearest service, but of course, my phone picks now to lose signal. Another sigh escapes me as I start heading for the information desk, hoping to grab a number for a cab company.

"Sloan!" someone yells. I look around, but I don't see anyone familiar. I must be hearing things. Between the flight and the hunger, I wouldn't be surprised. I keep walking, the squeaky wheels of my suitcase dragging behind me. "Sloan!" Okay, that was definitely someone calling me—or someone else named Sloan. I turn around again, feeling my annoyance grow. A man is walking toward me. I squint, trying to recognize him as he comes closer. My heart stops and instantly I'm sweaty, my mouth goes dry and I feel my breath hitch. He waves at me like this is totally normal like it's the most natural thing in the world to run into me here, of all places, on the day I've come home. Why won't my legs move? I'm frozen. He reaches me, arms open for a hug, and the me that was once frozen hugs him back.

What am I doing?

"It's good to see you," he says, still wearing that dumb smile.

"Hey, Nathan," I say, staring down at the floor. I know if I keep looking at him, I'm either going to cry... or scream. "What are you doing here?" I ask, surprised he's not more shocked to be running into me *here* of all places.

"I'm here for you," he says. I look up sharply, squinting at him. *What is he talking about?* I must look annoyed because he adds, "Your grandmother didn't tell you?"

Of course she sent someone to pick me up. Of course it had to be Nathan Reed. I would've gladly spent two hundred bucks on a cab just to avoid this. "She didn't," I say flatly.

Silence falls between us, and it's deafening. He's looking away now, probably trying to ease the tension neither of us knows what to do with. I let my eyes drift up to him, just for a second, but it's enough. Three years has done a number on him. The stubble along his jaw is new—a little rugged, a little older—and it suits him in a way that makes something twist in my chest. His arms are more defined now, the sleeves of his shirt stretched just enough to make it impossible not to notice his biceps had grown.

Those damn eyes. Still that impossible shade of green, even brighter somehow, like moss after rain. I remember how they used to look at me—

No. Don't do this.

I didn't come back to get swept up in nostalgia. I came to take care of my grandmother not to revisit the past I spent three years trying to outrun. "Should we get going?" he asks, reaching for my suitcase. I take a step back.

"I got it," I say, a little too sharply. He raises an eyebrow but doesn't argue. "Where are you parked?" I ask, trying to keep my tone neutral.

He gestures toward the lot, and I follow, my arm already aching from dragging the suitcase I stubbornly refused to let him carry. Pride is a heavy thing and so is this damn bag. We reach his car, and I toss the suitcase into the trunk myself. He doesn't offer to help again, which somehow annoys me more than if he had. Then I pause at the passenger side, debating. Do I really want to sit in the front next to him for two hours? Sitting in the back would feel weird—*childish* even—but the idea of being that close to him makes my skin buzz with unease. Also, I get carsick in the back seat. With a quiet sigh, I reluctantly climb into the front. A moment later, he slides into the driver's seat beside me. The car feels too small. The space between us, not nearly enough. I stare out the window for the first thirty minutes.

"Sooo," he says, dragging the word out, clearly trying to break the silence. "How was New York?" I scoff before I can stop myself. It just slips out sharp, automatic. Of *all* people, why does he care? The question hangs in the air between us like smoke, and I can feel him glance at me, waiting for an answer I don't feel like giving. I stare out the window, jaw tight.

"It was fine," I mutter, knowing he doesn't deserve more than that. My stomach growls—*loudly*—betraying me for what feels like the millionth time today.

"You hungry?" he asks, glancing over.

"Nope," I lie, straight through my teeth. I can feel him looking at me, but I keep my eyes locked on the passing road. There's no way I'm accepting *anything* from him except this ride. Not food. Not small talk. Nothing. We continued the drive in silence, only the hum of the road filling the space between us. A dull headache starts to pulse behind my eyes, definitely from the lack of food, maybe from the emotional whiplash of seeing him again. I lean my head against the window and close my eyes, just for a minute. The motion of the car, the quiet warmth, the exhaustion pulls at me. I feel myself drifting, slipping into that blurry half-sleep.

Then—

"Yeah, can I get a number two combo? No lettuce, large fries, and a sweet tea with extra ice." The speaker crackles loudly, yanking me awake. I startle upright, my heart jumping.

"What are you doing?" I ask, rubbing my eyes, blinking at the drive-thru sign outside the window.

He doesn't even look at me. "Ordering food."

"I said I wasn't hungry." He glanced at me then, one eyebrow raised.

"I know you. You're starving and too stubborn to admit it." I fold my arms and sink into the seat, jaw tightening. I hate that he's right. Instead of being grateful, I'm *annoyed.* He got my order right. Down to the no lettuce and the exact drink. Of course he did. I stare at the bag in my lap, my stomach growling again, louder this time. I hate that he remembers. My hunger was so rampant that I begrudgingly tore into the fries. They tasted like heaven. I hadn't eaten out much in New York, the cost was always too high, and it had been forever since I'd tasted the salty greasy comfort of fast-food fries. Each bite was a small rebellion against my stubbornness, a guilty pleasure I couldn't deny. I tried to keep my expression neutral, but inside, a part of me was silently thanking Nathan for this small kindness no matter how much I hated admitting it. "You and those fries should get a room," he says, laughing.

I freeze mid-chew, cheeks flushing hot. Great. Now I'm moaning while *inhaling* fries. I glance at him, trying to look annoyed but fail miserably and let out a laugh, unable to help myself. "Well, it'd be the first 'room' I've gotten in three years," I say, still chuckling.

I stop mid-chuckle, my smile fading as I realize what I just said. *Seriously? Did that plane ride come with a side of temporary brain fog or something?* Admitting I haven't had sex in three years to my last serious relationship—and we both know that was *when* we were together—was not exactly my smoothest move. The air between us thickens, heavy and awkward. He goes silent, and I clear my throat, hoping to fill the space before it swallows me whole. "Do you want some?" I ask, tipping the bag of fries toward him.

He shakes his head. "No thanks. Your grandma fed me before I left." I cock my head, confused. He went to her house *before* picking me up? Maybe it was just a polite thank-you?

Before I can ask, he says, "I have to stop and get gas real quick." I curse inwardly. We were only thirty minutes out, and already the forced proximity was getting to me in more ways than one. We pull up to a gas station, and I quickly inhale the rest of my food, not wanting Nathan to watch me continue stuffing my face. I gather the empty wrappers and cup, not in the mood to get out, so I twist around and lean into the backseat to drop the trash there. Just as I shift forward, Nathan slides back into the driver's seat a little too fast, and we end up face to face.

Close. Too close.

We both freeze. My heart stumbles in my chest, and I'm suddenly hyper-aware of every breath I take—fast food breath and all. *Did he just lean in a little more? Or did I?* I can feel his breath on mine—warm, close, pulling me in. I lick the lingering taste of salt off my lips, and that's when I realized he was definitely leaning in. The space between us vanishes, inch by inch, until we're one heartbeat away from touching—

HOOOONK!

A car blares its horn behind us, and we both jolt apart like we've been caught doing something we shouldn't. I straighten in my seat, forcing my tone back to neutral. "We should go."

"Right," he says, sighing and quickly starting the car.

By the time we pull into the driveway, I'm thoroughly exhausted. I step out of the car and stretch, the crisp country air wrapping around me like a half-forgotten memory. It smells like childhood—grass, dust, and something faintly sweet. I head to the trunk, ready to grab my bag so Nathan can be on his way. But just as I lift it out, I hear the car door open. He's getting out. "Oh no, I got it," I say quickly, dragging the suitcase out with more force than grace. "You can head home now." He ignores me and keeps moving, closing his door like he's not going anywhere. I let out a sigh, barely keeping the edge out of my voice. *Has he always had a listening problem? Or is it just conveniently selective now?*

"I'm coming in," he says, like it's already decided. No room for argument. I still grab my own suitcase; *I'll be damned* if I let my guard down around him again.

The screen door creaks as I open it, familiar and loud, the same one from every memory I have stored in my bones. I step inside and call out, "Honey, I'm home," I yell jokingly.

"In here," my grandma calls from the kitchen, her natural habitat, where the air always smells like something baking, simmering, or frying. I've always loved her cooking. That hasn't changed. If history's any indication, I'll gain *at least* fifteen pounds while I'm here and love every bite of it. The scent of something warm and buttery drifts from the kitchen, wrapping around me like a hug I didn't know I needed.

I can feel Nathan behind me. His presence is like a shadow I can't shake, silent and unmistakable. My shoulders stay tight, still wired from what almost happened in the car... and everything that *did* happen when we were together. My grandmother looks up at me and smiles with everything she has. She turns off the burner beneath a pan of what looks like fried tomatoes and comes over to wrap me in her arms. I hug her back tightly, trying to blink away the sudden sting behind my eyes.

I'd only visited twice since I moved, quick trips for the holidays, both rushed and far too short. Now, holding her, I notice how much smaller she feels in my arms. That realization cuts straight through me and I feel like I might tear in two. "Why are you up?" I ask as I pull away from the hug. "You should be resting."

She shoots me a look. "I'm making you dinner." I open my mouth to argue, but she's already turning back to the stove. "All your favorites," she adds. "The potato salad is done, the chicken's in the warmer, just finishing these." She gestures to the skillet of fried tomatoes.

She looks tired. I can see it now, in the way her shoulders sag just slightly, in the way she moves a little slower than I remember. Guilt tugs at me, sharp and sudden. I glance over at Nathan, annoyed—mostly because I'd already stuffed my face in the car and now she's gone through all this trouble. He just shrugs, like he's not the one who let her go to all this effort. "Well, I'm *starved*," I say, forcing some lightness into my voice. "Let me just go change. I feel gross from the plane and the car ride." Without waiting for a response I head toward my room, knowing she hasn't changed a thing.

"I'm sorry the magazine didn't work out, Sloan. They were fools for firing you."

I pause, glancing back at her. "Thanks Grandma," I say softly, giving her a small smile before continuing down the stairs.

Calling it a basement is an understatement, it's mostly redone warm and lived-in. My bedroom is down here, along with a guest room, and I've always loved having it all to myself. It was my sanctuary growing up, and even now, it still feels like the one place I can truly exhale. I reached my room and stopped short—my suitcase was still upstairs.

Of course it is. I sit on the edge of the bed, elbows on my knees, head in my hands. I take a few deep breaths, trying to steady myself. The scent of freshly laundered sheets drifts up around me, clean and comforting. I hear footsteps creaking down the stairs, looking up to see Nathan standing in the doorway, my suitcase in hand. "You forgot this," he says, setting it down just inside the room. I nod, not trusting myself to speak. Everything in me feels zapped—emotionally frayed and too thin. He doesn't move. "You lied," he says quietly.

I lift my gaze, eyebrows knit. "What? I couldn't exactly tell her I already ate after she slaved away in the kitchen." I roll my eyes and hope that is the end of it.

He shakes his head. "Not about that." I stare at him, confused. "You didn't get fired, did you?" My eyes drop, the weight of the words hitting me like they've been waiting just beneath the surface. I stare at the floor silently. "Why didn't you just tell her you wanted to move back? That you came to take care of her?" Nathan asks, his voice low but steady.

I snap my eyes up to him. "You *know* why." My tone is sharper than I intend, but I don't back down. "She wouldn't have let me. She would've insisted I stay in New York and would have told me not to worry about her." I take a breath, my voice softening but no less firm.

I loved my job. I did. But I love her *more,* and I owe her every-thing. She raised me, gave me stability when no one else did. So no—no one else is taking care of her while she's sick. Not if I can help it. I'd be damned before I let anyone else try. He knows I'm right. He's known her his whole life, having spent so much time here as a kid—dinners, holidays, whole weekends. Hell, he even spent the night sometimes. Or... sometimes he came in through my window.

Sloan, stop. Focus.

Now is *not* the time to revisit that particular highlight reel. I stand, brushing my hands on my jeans. "If you don't mind, I'm going to change."

He steps back quickly, almost startled. "Right. I'll... see you up there." *Huh.* So he's staying for dinner? She must've invited him as a thank you.

I quickly changed into sweats and a T-shirt, because really who am I trying to impress here? I pull on my fuzzy socks, knowing the floor down here is always impossibly cold, like it's been storing winter for decades. As I reach for the door, I freeze. A tiny, nagging voice in the back of my mind makes me second-guess my outfit. *Is this too casual for dinner?* I shake the thought off immediately. No. No way. I'm not falling back into *that* trap. I am not going upstairs trying to impress Nathan. I reach the top of the stairs and spot Nathan helping my grandmother set the table, both moving with a quiet ease. They look up as I enter, and something nags at the back of my mind.

"Let's eat," my grandmother says, settling slowly into her chair. I notice she doesn't have her glass of water yet, so I grab one for her. She only drinks from a specific glass, with a precise amount of ice. I set the glass gently beside her. "Thanks, sweetheart," she says with a soft smile. I take the seat to her right; Nathan sits to her left. He starts eating before I do, immediately breaking the silence with a compliment.

"Marilyn, this is delicious—*as always.*"

We eat in a comfortable silence, and even though I'd already devoured fast food earlier, I manage to finish every bite on my plate. When I look up, I catch Nathan staring at me. I want to snap and ask him what the hell he's looking at. I refrain, not wanting to be rude in front of my grandmother. Instead, I just meet his gaze and hold it for a moment before turning away. "I'll help clean up," Nathan says, standing up from the table.

I'm *so* over him sticking around like this is his house too. I plaster on a polite smile. "No, Nathan, it's okay. Really."

"Thank you for driving me from the airport, but I can handle the cleanup. You can head home now." The words come out sweeter than I feel.

My grandmother looks up from her plate, confused. "What did you just call him?"

I blink. "Nathan," I say, equally puzzled. "That's his name."

She gives me a soft, curious look. "Honey, are you tired? When have we ever called him Nathan? You know he goes by Nate." I nearly scoff but swallow it down.

The guy who broke my heart was Nate. "Nate" belongs to a version of him I don't want to resurrect. I just nod at her, forcing a small smile, and begin gathering the plates. To my annoyance, *Nate* continues helping. We walk to the sink together, arms full of dishes, and once we're close enough, I whisper sharply, "*What are you doing? Will you leave already?*" He blinks at me, caught off guard. "I'm trying not to be a bitch to you in front of my grandmother," I hiss, "and you're making it *awfully* hard."

From the table, my grandmother calls out, "Nate, don't forget the new lightbulb for your room before you head downstairs."

I freeze. *Your* room? I turn slowly to look at him, and of course—*of course*—he's smiling.

"Oh yeah," he says with a smirk. "Did I forget to mention? I'm living in the extra room next to yours."

CHAPTER 4

I lie in bed, staring at the ceiling, after what feels like the longest day of my life. I definitely didn't expect Nathan to be living here, but then again, I never asked. I just showed up, ready to take care of my grandmother and avoid stepping on any emotional landmines. Apparently, his mom passed away last year. The house—just three doors down—was under a second mortgage, and he lost it. So, my grandmother, being exactly who she is, insisted he move in. Said he could help around the house while saving money. When I asked her after dinner why she didn't tell me, she just patted my leg and said, *"Honey, you know why,* and I didn't want you thinking you weren't welcome home. You *are* welcome here."

Even though I'm exhausted, I'm all too aware of Nathan in the next room. I wonder if he's awake, wonder if the thought of me is keeping him up. I scoff at myself. Of course it's not. I sit up in bed, eyes adjusting to the familiar shapes of my room. Everything's the same, but it all feels... louder somehow. Memories drift in before I can stop them, Nathan and I in here, back when he was *Nate* to me. The blanket forts we built as kids. The nights we studied side by side, sharing snacks and secrets. The times we made out in this very room...

Sloan, seriously? Get a grip. Frustrated, I throw off the covers and get up, pacing for a second before settling at my old desk. It looks recently dusted. Now I'm wondering if the clean sheets and tidy surfaces weren't my grandmother's doing after all. Maybe it was Nathan. I open the top drawer and pull out my journal, flipping to the back where I know the page is waiting. There it was an old, faded missing person flyer, glued in place like a piece of me. I know the missing person flyer by heart. Scarlett Mercer. Frozen in time at twenty-seven.

> **Missing: Scarlett Mercer.**
> *'Last seen leaving the Highway Four Motel on June 17, 2000. Last seen wearing jean shorts and an oversized black jacket. Brown eyes. Brown hair. 5'2". 152 pounds. Tattoo of a cross on her right wrist'*

I run my fingers lightly over the grainy black-and-white photo. Scarlett Mercer—my mother—still missing. I close the journal and slide it back into the drawer, pressing it shut like that might keep the memories from spilling out. Scarlett is the reason my grandmother never left this place. She still believes she's coming back, and she wants to be here—*needs* to be here—when she does. She even kept the landline, because Scarlett knew that number by heart.

Scarlett was never mother of the year. Even when she *was* around, she was up and down, hot and cold, love and chaos. When the days were good, they were *really* good. But when the bad days came... they were bad in that way that left the whole house tense, tight, and echoing with things you wish you could unhear. She made sure everyone felt it. She often went missing for days at a time, even before she was *officially* missing.

So, when she didn't come home one night, no one thought much of it. Not at first. Not until I showed up to school in the same clothes for a week, smelling like I'd been dragged through a sewer. That's when they called my grandmother, and because this is Summit Grove—where everyone knows everyone—they used that small-town courtesy to quietly hand me over to her instead of calling CPS. That's when I finally told them Scarlett hadn't been home in five days.

When my grandmother asked why I hadn't called her sooner, I broke down crying. I told her I didn't want my mom to be mad at me. Because Scarlett *hated* when my grandmother knew her business. Even at that age, I understood the rules of her silence. I followed them, right up until I couldn't anymore.

I can hear Nathan moving around in the next room, and I still can't help but wonder what he's doing. I force myself back under the covers and let my eyes close. Thankfully, I drift off into a dreamless sleep.

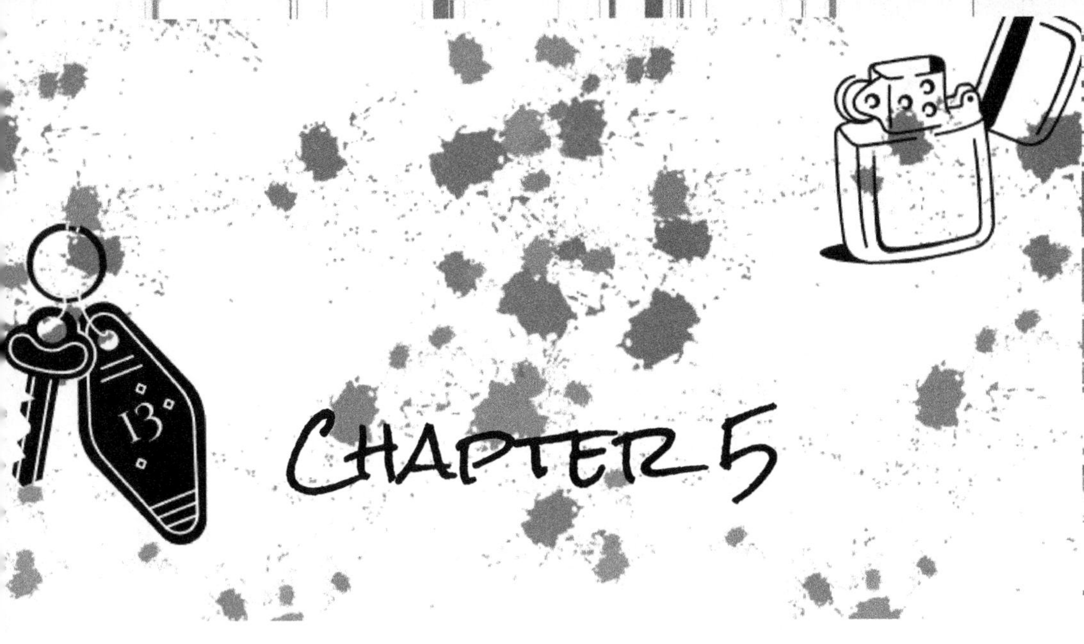

Chapter 5

I wake to a knock on my door and, without thinking, say, "Come in." The door opens, and I shoot up realizing I hadn't asked who it was before I said it. *Of course. Lucky me.* It's Nathan. I quickly pull the blankets up over myself. Partway through the night, I'd gotten hot and kicked off my sweats, and now I'm all too aware of it, especially with him here, even with the blankets hiding me.

He stands in the doorway, trying to look at anything except me. I can feel my hair sticking up in every possible direction just the cherry on top of this humiliating morning. "Your grandmother wants to know if you want breakfast," Nathan says, still avoiding eye contact. I lower my head with a sigh. Of course she does. That woman will never rest.

"Sure," I mumble, waiting for him to take the hint and leave so I can get out of bed *without* pants. But he doesn't move. His eyes drift to the end of the bed. I know exactly what he's thinking. It's where we had our first kiss. It was Sixth grade. We weren't together, not yet anyway, we were just two awkward kids checking the "first kiss" box like it was some school assignment. I cleared my throat looking at him silently asking him to *please leave.*

"Oh—yeah. Sorry," he says, snapping out of it. "I'll tell her you'll be up." He starts to close the door, then pauses, looking down at the floor, then up at me. "Make sure you wear pants to breakfast," he says, and winks, shutting the door as he leaves. I groan, flopping back onto the bed. I'm never going to get used to living in the room next to him. It's been three years since we've seen each other. So why does it still feel like it was *yesterday* when we were together? Why does it feel like *yesterday* when he broke my heart?

Three Years Ago

I was halfway through another job application, the weight of student loans pressing on my chest, when I heard a soft tap on my window. I looked up and smiled. Nate.

I opened the window and let him climb in like he had a hundred times before. As soon as he was inside, he kissed me long and deep, like he hadn't seen me in years instead of hours. Nothing compared to moments like this with him. He eased me down onto the bed, his lips brushing down my collarbone, making it nearly impossible to think straight.

"Nate," I whispered, breath catching. "I have to finish applying for jobs... I'm going to be dead broke if I don't." He didn't stop. Just kept kissing me like I was the only thing keeping him alive. My protest melted under the sheer intoxication of him. He pulled me down towards him, pressing his hand on my center. I gasped, arching at his touch.

"Do you want to stop and apply for jobs instead?" I bit my lip, knowing that if I said anything, it wouldn't be coherent. I wondered for what felt like the millionth time when my body would stop reacting like this to him. Not that I was complaining, although it did make it hard to get things done when he was around. My thoughts scattered like startled birds the moment he entered the room, every sense hyper-attuned to the shift in air, the sound of his voice, the way he smiled like he knew exactly what he was doing to me.

"Thought so," he said, kissing down my stomach, lower and lower, until I could see nothing but pure bliss. Right when I was about to lose it, he grabbed my hips and slowly entered me. If the house had been empty, I would have screamed right there. I bit my lip to keep from waking the entire neighborhood.

"Good girl," he said, and he began to pump faster, making the sensation all the more pleasurable. I dug my nails into his arms, and he grunted as he found his release too. He leaned into me, pressing his forehead gently against mine, and in that moment, I knew I could stay with this man forever, because no one had ever made me feel the way he did. No one had ever made me this happy. We lay in bed afterward, half-watching some mindless TV. I didn't get a single new application filled out, but he *thoroughly* made up for it.

"So, what jobs are you applying for?" he asked, his voice lazy and warm beside me.

"Oh, you know... the usual. Papers in the city, and even the one here—though I don't have high hopes for the *Summit Gazette*," I said with a sigh. "Even if they offer me something, I doubt it'll be anything I actually want."

He chuckled. "Well, everyone has to start somewhere." I grew quiet, unsure how to bring up the next job I applied for.

"I applied to one in New York." I say it softly in almost a whisper hoping he wouldn't hear me. He stiffened beside me, and I didn't look at him. Just stared at the ceiling and waited for his reaction, for anything. He sat up suddenly, looking at me like I'd just punched him.

"New York? Like... the *New York*?" I nodded, my throat tight, the words stuck somewhere between guilt and truth. He looked down at his hands, curling them into fists like he was holding something in. "So what have we been doing here, then?" he asked, his voice low and raw.

I flinched. I wasn't sure how I was supposed to answer that. "What do you mean, Nate?" I asked, my voice soft but tight. "We're together. We've been together. It doesn't change anything about us. It's just an application."

"It's not *just* an application, Sloan," he said, his voice rising with something between hurt and frustration. "It's the *intention.* If you get it... you'll take it, and with how good of a writer you are—you *will* get it."

"Even if I *somehow* got it, that doesn't mean I'd take it," I said, more defensive than I meant to.

He scoffed, rolling his eyes. "Right."

"What is that supposed to mean?" I snapped. He got up out of bed, pulling on his clothes with sharp, jerky movements.

"It means you've always made fun of how small and boring this town is," he said, not even looking at me. "Don't think I haven't noticed that you want out of here." He paused, running a hand through his hair, frustrated. "I get it, okay? It's small. It's quiet. I'd even move to Columbia if that's what it took. But you know I can't go to New York. My mom's here. I have to be close to her."

The room falls silent, and I look at him, feeling the weight of his hurt. Why was he acting like this? "I didn't ask you to go with me," I say quietly, trying to keep the edge from my voice. I had never seen Nate look so hurt. I never expected to be the one causing him pain. He stared at me like I was a stranger, like he didn't know me anymore. I knew what I said wasn't true, because the truth was, I was going to ask him to come with me. I was going to base my decision on him. I just applied for the New York job to see if I could get it. I didn't expect it to become such a big deal. I didn't expect him to be so mad.

"Good to know, Sloan," he says quietly, turning away. Without another word, he climbs out the window he came in and slams it shut behind him.

CHAPTER 6

I smell bacon as I walk up the stairs, craving the bacon, egg, and tomato sandwiches I love so much. My grandmother looks up from the pan and smiles at me. I glance at the table and see Nate staring out the window. I follow his gaze and spot the friendly neighborhood peacock perched on the back patio. "I can't believe that's still around," I say, amazed. It showed up about ten years ago, and no one's bothered it since. I guess that's why it stuck around.

I look back at Nate, feeling a blush rise to my cheeks as memories flood in. I really needed to let this go. We sit down and start digging into our food when suddenly the landline rings. No one ever calls the landline. We all freeze, and my grandmother jumps up to answer it. "Hello?" she says hurriedly. She immediately hangs up, her face tightening with frustration as she sits back down. "Telemarketer," she mutters. I exhale, realizing I'd been holding my breath. Sadness floods me, not for myself, but for my grandmother, a mother still missing her daughter.

I help clear the table, then start sorting through my grandmother's appointments and medications. From what I can tell, she has two treatment sessions a week, plus daily meds that need to be taken on a strict schedule. She catches me filling her pill organizer and walks over. "Honey, you can leave that alone. I can do it," she says softly.

"No, it's fine, Grandma. I want to help, it's the least I can do since I lost my job and you won't let me pay rent." She pats my shoulder and, for once, doesn't argue. "Please, go rest in your chair." She shuffles away, and I finish up quietly. Then I head to the living room to check on her, noticing she's struggling to pull the blanket over herself. I gently reach out, grabbing the blanket and covering her up.

"Thanks, sweetheart," she murmurs.

"I'll turn on *Dateline*," I say, reaching for the remote. I grew up watching *Dateline* with my grandmother, some things never change. I snuggle up on the couch, feeling that this is exactly where I'm supposed to be.

Suddenly, the roar of the mower breaks the quiet, and I jump up. "That's just Nate," she says softly, already half-asleep. "He takes care of the yard work." I look at her surprised. Oh, maybe he's not going to the gym after all, just handling five acres of land for the last year.

I glance out the window and see him—shirtless in the sun, mowing around the front patio. I can't help but bite my lip, feeling a flutter somewhere deep within me. I scold myself silently: *I really need to get laid so I can stop thinking about him.* I hear my grandmother mumble something under her breath. I lean in closer, realizing she's half-asleep, her eyes barely open. "What was that, Grandma? I didn't hear you."

She lets out a soft sigh, her voice barely more than a whisper. "I just don't know why you two couldn't work things out." I freeze beside her, my breath caught somewhere between a laugh and a sob. Of course she'd say that—at the very moment I'm telling myself to get a grip.

She drifts off to sleep, her head tilting slightly toward the armrest, and I quietly slip into the kitchen for a glass of water. I hesitate before turning the tap off, and against my better judgment I head to the front door and step outside. Nathan is out front, still shirtless in the sun, pushing the mower around the edge of the patio like it's nothing. Sweat glistens on his chest and shoulders, his skin perfectly sun-kissed. I wave him down, pretending this is just a casual gesture and not the result of me spiraling into a thirst trap flashback. He kills the mower and walks over, his chest rising and falling with every step. "Here," I say, holding out the water like it's not a peace offering for my inner turmoil. He takes it, nodding. "Thanks."

I tell myself not to stare at the way his throat works when he drinks, not to notice the muscles in his biceps flexing. I tell myself a lot of things. None of them work. I force myself to look away. I *really* need to get laid. Or exorcised. Possibly both. He hands the empty glass back to me, smirking.

"Like what you see?" he says, adding a wink that makes me want to throw the glass *at* him. I snap out of it, snatching the glass from his hand.

"Don't flatter yourself." I roll my eyes so hard I'm surprised they don't get stuck, then turn to go back inside before he can say anything else smug and infuriatingly attractive.

"Come on, Sloan. Get it together," I mutter, pacing the kitchen. No matter how hot he is, how good he was in bed, or even how sweet he used to be. It doesn't erase what he did. It doesn't undo the way he broke your heart. Stop getting soft just because he flashes that stupid smile or remembers your fast-food order. You've survived without him. Don't start slipping just because your heart conveniently forgot what your mind has never let go of.

Chapter 7

I spend the rest of the day penciling in my grandmother's appointments for the month. Most weeks have three days booked solid with treatments, check-ins, lab work, but the other four are wide open. The pattern is pretty consistent. I glance at my bank account that morning and wince. Maybe I should think about filling some of those 'free' days with something that pays. Something nearby. I open the paper, yes, the actual paper, my grandmother still swears by it. In a town like Summit Grove, it's probably more reliable than the internet. I skim through the ads, hoping to find something that doesn't involve cleaning stalls or frying chicken.

Then I see it. *The Summit Gazette* is hiring for the obituary section.

I drop my head onto the table and groan. Of course. Three years ago, this exact job was offered to me. Now here I am, broke and back home, with a degree, a mountain of debt, and the obituary section practically waving at me like an old friend I ghosted. The universe really does have a sense of humor. A dark, twisted one. I make plans to apply, telling myself it's temporary, just a steppingstone. My grandmother will get better, and eventually she won't need me as much. Maybe if things line up, I could still get a job in Columbia down the line. The rest of the listings in the paper aren't exactly inspiring. Fast food, bank teller and a cashier at the local grocery store. With a huff, I fold the paper shut. That's as good as it's going to get for now. It's just for a paycheck, I remind myself.

I decide to make my grandmother lunch before she drags herself into the kitchen to do it herself. I throw together a simple ham sandwich, add a scoop of leftover potato salad, and pour a crisp cold Coke into her favorite glass. Pleased with myself I carry the tray to her chair where she's slowly waking from her nap, still looking completely worn out.

She blinks up at me, eyes soft but puzzled, like she's not sure if she's dreaming or if I'm really standing there with lunch in hand. "Did I ask for lunch?" she asks, clearly unsure if she forgot.

"No," I say, laughing softly. "I just wanted to take care of you for once."

She gives me a tired, apologetic smile. "I'm sorry, sweetheart. I'm just not that hungry. I had a big breakfast." I furrowed my brow, because I was there; she barely ate half of it. I don't want to upset her, so I just nod and decide to put the plate away for later. "I will take the Coke, though," she says, leaning forward to reach for the glass. I move to meet her halfway, gently handing it over, but freeze when I see a small clump of hair on the headrest of her chair. I gasp before I can stop myself. She looks at me, concerned. "Are you okay, hon?"

"Yeah," I say quickly, forcing a smile. "I just remembered I need to go apply for a job I found earlier."

"Of course," she says, smiling again. "The keys are hanging by the door. Help yourself. I think I'm going to rest my eyes a little longer."

I nod, afraid that if I open my mouth, I'll fall apart. I grab my bag and the keys and wave at her as I slip out the front door. She's already nodding off again. In the dusty driver's seat of her old car, I lay my head on the steering wheel and start to sob. Why her? Why did it have to be her? She doesn't deserve this.

A knock on the window startles me mid ugly cry. I jolt upright so fast I nearly bonk my forehead on the sun visor. Fantastic. Just what I needed: a witness to my breakdown in the front seat of a dusty sedan like I'm auditioning for a melodrama called *Crying in Grandma's Buick*. I look up and—surprise, surprise—it's Nathan. I sigh. *Does he ever leave the premises? Is he part of the house now? An emotional support porch goblin? Of course he would be the one to catch me mid-meltdown.* I've been holding it together all day, but the moment I fall apart—*poof*—he materializes like some kind of sad-girl radar.

I roll down the window, wiping at my face in a way that probably just smears the tears around more dramatically. "Are you okay?" Nathan asks, leaning against the car with his forearm propped just right, perfectly angled so I can fully appreciate how defined his arms are. *Really, Sloan? You're emotionally unraveling in a dusty sedan and your brain decides now is a good time to thirst over his biceps?*

"I'm fine," I snap, a little too quickly. I'm more annoyed with myself than him. "Just... allergies. This car is dusty."

He nods slowly, not fooled for a second. I probably look like a puffy, mascara-smudged nightmare. "It's dusty because I run a lot of her errands," he says casually, like he's giving me a weather update. "Hate to be the bearer of bad news, but it also needs an oil change, and one of the tires is low."

I let my forehead thump against the steering wheel with a dramatic sigh. "Of course it does," I mutter, voice muffled by the faux leather and my despair. "Why wouldn't it?"

There's a beat of silence, and I swear I can hear him trying not to laugh. "If you need to go somewhere, I can take you," he offers, casually like he's not watching me fall apart in slow motion.

I hesitate, but honestly? I really do need to get out of here for a bit away from the house, from the weight of it all, I find myself nodding. "Yeah. I just need a ride to the *Summit Gazette*." I glance away, still mildly horrified by the words leaving my mouth. "I'm going to apply there." He doesn't say anything, which somehow makes it worse.

"Maybe a coffee shop after, if we even still have one? I can't remember if it survived or shut down." I shrug, trying to sound casual. I can feel myself start to ramble, words tumbling out, completely unchecked and I'm helpless to stop it.

Thankfully, Nathan cuts in. "Yeah, let's go. Just let me grab a shirt." Right. He's still shirtless and I definitely noticed.

I climb out of the Buick and slide into the passenger seat of his car. While I wait, I can't help but glance around—okay, fine, I'm being a little nosy. Or maybe just curiosity with a side of emotional self-sabotage. My eyes land on the cup holder. A few loose hair ties rest at the bottom. My stomach dips a little, just a quiet sinking feeling. I mean, why shouldn't he have moved on? It's been three years. I assumed he had. Assumptions are one thing, evidence is another. It stung more than I thought it would. I'm already on edge, already emotional, I feel the tears rising again. I blink hard, tipping my head back against the seat, willing them to stop. I'm not even sure what I'm crying for anymore. My grandmother, who's fading just enough to scare me. Or a relationship that hasn't been mine for years.

I wipe my tears away as I see Nathan walking up, a shirt finally on. He slides into the driver's seat and immediately blasts the AC. We drive in silence for a while, the kind that feels heavy but not unbearable. I fiddle with the radio, hoping a good song might distract me. Nothing. Just static and country covers. "So…" he finally says, breaking the silence, "the Gazette?"

"Yeah," I say, short, not wanting to talk about it.

"It's not the obit section again, is it?" he says jokingly. And that's all it took for me to completely lose it. Tears flood my eyes without warning, and my chest tightens like it's caving in. His face falls, and he immediately pulls over to the side of the road. "Sloan, I'm so sorry. I didn't mean it like that; I was just joking—"

I shake my head, sniffling, trying to breathe through it, trying not to completely unravel. "It's not that… well, maybe it is a little." I admit, my voice catching. "But it's everything. Being back here. Seeing my grandma like this. I saw the missing person flyer for Scarlett last night, and these stupid hair ties in your car, and—" I dropped my face into my hands, overwhelmed, embarrassed, and still crying anyway. "I don't even know what I'm crying about anymore," I mumble.

"Hair ties?" he asks, because of course that's the part he's going to fixate on.

"Nothing," I say quickly, brushing it off. "Can we just go? I want to get this over with."

Thankfully he lets it go and pulls back onto the road. It doesn't take long before we're pulling up in front of the *Summit Gazette*. I let out a sigh, staring at the building, dreading every part of this. Dreading walking in here to apply for a job I was offered three years ago under very different circumstances.

Then I feel his hand gently settle on top of mine and my heart jumps. "Go get it, Sloan," he says quietly. "It'll be okay."

"I know," I say softly. "I just... I didn't think I'd be using my degree to write obits."

He nods, keeping his hand there, warm and steady, and it feels like a slow burn or a spark about to ignite. "Tell them you can do more than obits," he says, so casually, like it's the simplest thing in the world. I almost laughed.

"That's all they have open, Nate. It's also the only thing close by with any flexibility." He looks shocked for a second, and it hits me, I just called him *Nate* for the first time in three years. Heat rises to my cheeks. I quickly pull my hand free from under his and open the car door. Without looking back, I start walking toward the entrance, trying to steady my breath and brace myself for what's next.

Chapter 8

I walk through the doors of the *Summit Gazette*. The air smells faintly of dust, and the dim lighting makes the place feel like time stopped somewhere around 2007. At the empty front desk, I ring the little bell. "One minute!" someone calls from the back.

I glance around, the sight of the place stirring something in me that makes me want to bolt. Before I can talk myself out of it, an older woman appears, walking toward me. She looks familiar, but I can't quite place her. "Hi, I'm Sloan—"

"Oh, Sloan! You're back? I didn't know!" she interrupts with a smile that says she absolutely knew. But of course everyone knows everyone in this town. It's the size of a thimble. "How's your grandmother? I was so sorry to hear about her cancer. Poor thing." I nod politely, waiting for a chance to speak. "She's a fighter, that one. Oh well, of course you know, she taught you everything she knows."

I keep smiling and nodding, because that's the Summit Grove way. "Yeah, she is," I finally manage to say, and then I wince, already dreading the words about to come out of my mouth. "I was just wondering... is there a job application I could fill out?"

She peers at me over her glasses, clearly surprised. "Really? You know we only have one opening."

"Yes, I know. I just need something flexible while I'm here helping my grandmother. She has a lot of appointments." I remember her now, Mrs. Bono, my high school English teacher. No wonder she looked familiar. I loved her class. She always gave me great feedback on my essays.

She nods slowly, her tone softening. "Well, I should warn you this isn't exactly New York. Most of our staff work from home now, and we only publish the Sunday paper. We stopped doing the daily about a year ago, it just wasn't financially sustainable anymore. These days, I'm mostly here to answer phones and help the occasional walk-in."

"That's fine," I say quickly. I just want to apply and get it over with.

She nods. "A lot of people submit their own obituaries. You'd be editing their work or writing them yourself now and then." I nod again, trying not to let my impatience show. "Well, if you're okay with all that... you've got the job."

I blink. "I'm sorry—I didn't even fill out an application."

She waves it off. "Oh honey, it's no big deal. I know your writing—it's excellent. Like I said, it's mostly editing and proofreading. We don't pay a ton, but hopefully it'll be enough."

I'm stunned at how easy it was, but maybe I shouldn't be. This could be the same position that was open three years ago. "Great," I say. At least I can work from home and be close to my grandmother. She gives me a few forms, the pay rate, a schedule, and a laptop. As I head toward the door, something catches my eye: an old cork board near the entrance.

I walk up to it, my heart skipping a beat as I see it.

> **Missing: Scarlett Mercer.**
>
> *'Last seen leaving the Highway Four Motel on June 17, 2000. Last seen wearing jean shorts and an oversized black jacket. Brown eyes. Brown hair. 5'2". 152 pounds. Tattoo of a cross on her right wrist'*

I stare at the paper, breath caught in my throat. I turn back to Mrs. Bono.

"I want to write more than obits," I say, louder than I intend.

She looks up from her desk, confused. "Honey, I told you that's all we have available."

"I know, and I'll do the obits. But let me write *something else*, too. A short article here and there. Just—let me write."

She sighs. "There just isn't enough funding for another section, Sloan."

"Then I'll do it for free," I say quickly. "Lump it in with the obits. I just... I *need* to write."

She stares at me a moment, and I brace myself for the let-down. "Okay."

Tears prick my eyes for the thousandth time today. "Thank you, Mrs. Bono. You won't be sorry."

She laughs. "Oh, I know I won't, and please call me Diane. You're not in high school anymore." I nod, beaming, and nearly skip out to the parking lot.

I'm full-on beaming when I slide into the car, practically bouncing in my seat. Nate looks over at me, clearly perplexed by my sudden mood swing. "I got the job!" I say, maybe a little too loud.

He raises an eyebrow, still looking more confused than excited. "Well… yeah. I figured you would. You got offered it before—back when you had zero experience."

"I *know*, I know!" I nearly shout. "She said I could write articles. I mean, yeah, I'll be doing obits too, but who cares? I can still *write* for a paper. I get to choose the topics, and the best part? I get to work from home. I'll be close by."

I'm rambling now, breathless. "I can help my grandmother get better, and once she doesn't need me as much, maybe I can take a job in Columbia. When I do, I'll actually have something recent to show for it." He's giving me that look again, the one that says he's trying to keep up, but I've lost him somewhere between 'articles' and 'Columbia.'

"Thank you, Nate," I say, catching my breath. "I wouldn't have asked if you hadn't suggested it." There it is again. *Nate.* Like an old wound I didn't realize was still tender, the name makes me flinch just a little. He notices. Of course he does. He leans in, and before I can stop myself, before my brain catches up to my heart, I'm meeting him halfway.

The kiss is soft at first, familiar. It deepens, and suddenly his hands are in my hair, and my hands are on his chest and it's like nothing's changed, like no time has passed. That feeling rushes in again—that terrifying, intoxicating feeling in my stomach that says *I could kiss this man every day and be the happiest person on the planet.* But …I remember the hair ties in his cup holder and what he did three years ago. I pull back, breath caught in my throat.

"We should go," I say quickly, avoiding his eyes. He looks stunned, like he has no idea what just happened, but he nods anyway, shifts the car into gear, and drives us home in silence.

CHAPTER 9

That night in my room, I was getting ahead on proofreading the pieces Diane sent me. I was trying not to think about the kiss. I *should* be thinking about what my articles are going to be about. What should I write? I've never really had total creative freedom before. An alarm goes off on my phone, it's the reminder for my grandmother's nighttime medication. I head upstairs to make sure she's awake and remembers to take it. Good thing I do, because she's fast asleep, and if I remember correctly, she's not supposed to miss any doses. I grab her meds and gently shake her awake.

"Grandma," I whisper. "Hey, it's time for your medication."

"Huh?" she mumbles groggily. Of course she's out of it, she's been sleeping all day, and now she's even more worn down.

"Your medication," I repeat softly. She tries to sit up and reach for the glass of water, struggling a little. I help her steady it in her hands.

"Thank you, Scarlett," she says. I freeze. My breath catches, and I don't know what to say. Everything I've read says not to correct someone in her condition when they're confused. So, I play along.

"You're welcome," I whisper.

"Let's get you to bed," I say, guiding her gently. "You don't want to sleep in the recliner all night." She nods without protest, letting me lead her to the bedroom. I cover her up, tucking the blankets around her.

"Scarlett," she says softly.

"Mhmm?" I respond, trying not to speak more than necessary.

"Make sure you take good care of Sloan."

"I will," I say, my voice catching in my throat.

As I turn to leave, she calls again. "Scarlett?"

"Yes, Mom?" I reply, and it kills me to keep pretending.

"I love you," she says. "I'm sorry I couldn't help you like I should have."

I turn away, trying to collect myself. Of course she'd still be apologizing to Scarlett, even now. Even after all these years. Even when she didn't do anything wrong. "It's okay, Mom," I whisper. "I love you, too." I kiss her forehead and move to turn off the light.

"Come visit more," she mumbles as I close the door. I sit on the couch in the dark and cry quietly, letting it all pour out. As I sit there with my head in my hands, it hits me.

Scarlett.

I'm going to find out what happened to her. I'm going to tell her story, and maybe I'll help bring some closure to my grandmother. Everything clicks into place, and it just feels right, *this is what I'm supposed to do.* I run downstairs and knock on Nathan's door. He opens it, and I brush past him without a "hello" or anything, sliding down onto his bed. "I need your help," I blurt out.

He smirks. "Hello to you too."

I'm still wired, probably looking like a hot mess with all the crying I've done today. He eyes me carefully.

"Were you crying again?" I decided not to lie.

"Yeah, I was. Grandma called me Scarlett." I let out a heavy breath. Nathan sits down beside me, keeping a respectful distance.

"Sloan, I'm sor—"

"Yeah, it's awful," I cut him off quickly, "but then it came to me." Nathan looks at me like I'm speaking in code. "What I'm going to write about. I'm going to write about Scarlett. And not just that, I'm going to find out what happened to her."

He stares at me, giving me a worried look like I've lost my mind. "Sloan, that's a tall order. She's been missing for a long time. People have looked, haven't they?"

I wave him off. "I'm her daughter. I haven't looked. Maybe I can see something no one else has—with fresh eyes."

He nods, clearly not wanting to argue with me today. "Okay, well good. I'm glad you figured out what you want to write about." I smile, realizing we've scooted closer to each other, and I quickly stand up.

"I might need your help. You've lived here the last three years; you have better rapport with the people in town."

He nods. "Okay, I'll help you. Just tell me what to do."

"Great," I say, heading toward the door. "I'll get you a list of people to talk to. Maybe doing this will help Grandma recover faster." He gives me that same confused look he gave me in the car when I mentioned her getting better.

"I'll see you tomorrow after her appointment."

"Wait!" he calls out, a bit louder than needed. "I'll go with you guys. You've never been there, and I've taken her a few times. It's a big hospital."

I'm taken aback by the offer. "It's okay. I can take her."

"But you've never been there," he insists.

"I'm sure I can use GPS. Or is this the only place in the world where we can't?"

"Look, Sloan, it's an all-day appointment. Just let me come and help. We can all eat afterwards too."

I feel myself giving in. "Fine, come with us if you insist."

"Good night, Nathan," I say as I walk out, catching that little frown when I call him by his full name again.

Chapter 10

We're all loaded in the car the next morning, Nathan insisting on driving. I give Grandma the front seat so she can have the seat warmers and extra legroom. Columbia's a two-hour drive, but it's the better option for her treatment or so I'm told. Her hospital bag is packed next to me, way fuller than I expected. They explained it's got activities, snacks, a blanket, and, of course, her meds just in case the trip ran late.

I noticed Nathan walk around and put something in the trunk before closing it. "What was that?" I ask as he starts the car.

"Oh, nothing. Just making sure we have everything if we get a flat or something." He doesn't look at me when he says it, but I let it go. We've been driving for a while when I decide to pull out my laptop and get some work done. Proofreading obits hasn't been as bad as I thought it would be, I'll admit. There's something oddly grounding about it. Having the side project, digging into what happened to Scarlett, makes it feel like I'm doing more than just filling space on a page.

Up front I hear Nathan and my grandmother chatting, their voices easy and familiar. I pause for a moment, listening.

They're talking about someone they both know, from church, maybe, or a neighbor. I can't quite make it out, but the way they laugh together makes me smile. I'm glad she's had him this past year.

Before I realize it, we're pulling up to the hospital. Nathan parks at the front entrance, hops out, and grabs a wheelchair without hesitation. I make a face, half-whispering as I step out of the car, "She can walk, Nathan."

I glanced at my grandmother, worried she might be offended. But to my surprise, she smiles softly and says, "It's okay, sweetheart. I'll take it," as she slowly lowers herself into the chair. I grab her hospital bag, still confused, watching as Nathan hands his keys to the valet like this is something he's done a dozen times. My grandmother has never been one to want to be carted around. *Ever.*

As if reading my thoughts, Nathan leans in close and whispers, "These days are long, the chair just helps her conserve her energy." I nod, suddenly unsure how to feel. He's right. Of course he's right. It stings a little, realizing he knows more about her day-to-day care than I do but then again, I haven't been here. I *left.*

I trail behind them as we approach a large check-in desk, watching as Nathan smoothly checks her into several appointments and grabs the paperwork. The woman at the desk is eyeing him like he's a slice of cake and she skipped breakfast. I feel my annoyance rise, this is a hospital for God's sake, not a brothel. I step forward, cutting into their flirty little exchange. "Nathan," I say, pointedly ignoring Miss Perfect Highlights and her overly whitened teeth, "shouldn't you be showing me what to do, so I'm not completely clueless next time?"

I can feel her eyes on me, trying to assess if I'm competition. I flash her a too-sweet smile and focus on Nathan. He stutters a bit, caught off guard. "Uh—yeah, for sure. So, we always start here. They'll check her in for all the appointments since everything's in the same hospital. Then they'll hand you a printed schedule with times and room numbers."

I nod along listening, but mostly just relieved I interrupted their little desk-side rom-com. We depart from the brothel—I mean, the front desk—and make our way to the first appointment: blood work. Easy enough. Grandma heads back alone, leaving Nathan and me in the waiting room with a stack of outdated magazines.

I pull out my laptop and start typing, trying to knock out the last of my proofreads so I can finally move on to the article that's been eating at my brain. Nathan watches me for a moment before speaking. "So," he says, dragging the word out, "did you make a list of people you want me to help you talk to?"

"Oh—yeah, I actually started one," I say, clicking around. "I'll email it to you really quick."

He checks his phone, eyes scanning the list. Then he squints at the screen, making a face. "Are you serious right now?"

"What?" I ask, suddenly nervous.

"Well, for starters, at least two people on this list are dead. I'm pretty sure a few others moved away years ago. Also... you want to interview Kent and Tammy?"

I groan. "I didn't even think about people moving away. Most people don't move from Summit Grove. They usually just... merge into the landscape."

He chuckles. "Yeah, but Tammy lives in Florida now, and Kent—well, good luck getting him to say anything without launching into conspiracy theories, being a total jerk, or trying to bum twenty bucks off you." I sigh, already opening a new tab to start revising my list.

"Well, maybe we can try to call Tammy or message her," I say. "She was one of Scarlett's best friends—they went on benders together all the time. Good for her for getting out, honestly. Hopefully she's clean now."

I pause, then add, "And Kent... that jerk. We *need* to talk to him. I remember hearing them arguing a few times when I was a kid. If it takes slipping him twenty bucks to get him talking, then so be it. For all we know, he did something to her." I sigh, the weight of my own words hitting me. I don't tell Nathan, but that's been my working theory for years. He'd been in and out of jail more times than I could count because of possession, domestic violence, just pick your poison. The guy was a walking red flag.

"I'll interview him on my own if you don't want to," I add. "I mean, this is my thing. You don't have to do anything you don't want to. I won't be mad or anything."

He stiffens and looks at me dead-on. "No way," he says, voice firm. "You're *not* going to see that guy alone. If you go, I'm going with you. You hear me?" I blink, taken aback by the seriousness in his voice. He's looking at me like I just offered to wrestle a live bear. I nod, swallowing back the heat crawling up my neck.

Trying to break the tension, I blurt, "You're kinda cute when you're serious." I let out a nervous laugh and instantly froze. Did I just say that out loud? He lets out a low laugh, clearly not letting that slip go.

"Well," he says, flashing me that infuriating grin, "you're cute when you're concentrating ."

I roll my eyes, trying not to smile but I can feel it tugging at the corners of my mouth anyway. "Right," I mutter. "Nothing hotter than emotional damage and hyperfocus."

The door swings open, cutting off our playful jabs, and my grandmother rolls out with a smile that doesn't quite reach her eyes. She settles back into her chair like this is all completely normal, like she doesn't have a body full of poison and appointments mapped out like battle plans. "Where to next?" she asks cheerfully, as if we're just running errands.

I glance down at the appointment sheet. "Looks like CT. Did you finish the contrast?"

She makes a face, her nose wrinkling. "Yes, I drank the nasty stuff. It's disgusting, no matter what flavor they try to trick you with. They could call it Piña Colada Paradise, and it would still taste like crap."

We head toward the elevator, and as we ride up to the third floor, I see her color drain a little. "Grandma?" I ask, frowning. "You okay?"

She gives me a tight, wary smile. "I'm fine, just feel like I'm about to blow chunks."

I immediately reach into the side pocket of her bag and pull out the waste bag I grabbed when we checked in. "It's okay if you do," I say gently. "I came prepared."

"No," Nathan cuts in quickly, and I shoot him an annoyed 'what now' look. He softens his tone, holding his hands up. "I just mean... if she throws up before the CT, they might have to reschedule."

My grandmother nods, clearly struggling but trying to power through. "He's right. I'm going to try and hold it down. Just, no running with my wheelchair, okay?" We all chuckle, but beneath it I feel powerless. Nathan knows all of this stuff, what she needs, what she can and can't do and I'm just... here. Absorbing new information like a student who missed the first half of the semester. Every fact feels like a reminder that he's been here, and I haven't. I should be grateful, and I *am*, but it still stings. Somewhere between the paperwork, the appointments, and the ease with which he moves through it all, it hits me—he hasn't just been looking after her. He's been *taking care* of her. Like I should have been.

And now I'm trying to reclaim that role, fumbling through care schedules and hospital routines, while he pushes the wheelchair like he's the Clark Kent of caregiving, effortless, dependable, and somehow always one step ahead.

He wheels her to the CT doorway, and they take her back inside. Nathan comes back and sits next to me. I can't even look at him, there's this tangled mess of shame and annoyance twisting in my stomach, making it hard to breathe.

"Hey," he says casually, nudging my knee with his. "Don't think I just magically knew not to let her puke before a CT scan. I learned the hard way, okay? The wheelchair? That wasn't always the plan either. First few times, she walked until she couldn't anymore." I finally glanced over at him. "And that hospital bag? We forgot half of that stuff the first couple trips. I only know all of this because I've messed it up before." He pauses, his voice softening a little. "You're not behind, Sloan. You're just new to this part. That's all." His words settle in my chest, stinging and soothing all at once. I stare out the window, a stray tear slipping down my cheek.

"Yeah, but you know all this because you've been here. I haven't. I left her." My voice is quiet, but the guilt behind it is loud. "If she knew I quit my job to come back, she'd flip out. I should've stayed three years ago—taken that job in Columbia, stayed close. I left because I couldn't be in that town anymore, around…"

I trail off, unable to finish the sentence. I don't need to. We both know why. "I just want to help her get better," I say, my voice cracking. "I wish I'd been here from the start. God—this woman raised me. She made me who I am... and I just left." He gave me that look again—the one I couldn't figure out, the one that was really starting to piss me off. What *did* it mean? "Sloan... there's something I should tell you—"

"I'm ready for the next appointment," my grandmother said, rolling up beside us, reaching for her bag.

Before either of us could say a word, she grabbed the waste bag and threw up.

Chapter 11

After she was done throwing up, we got her some water, gum, and a snack—per her request. We were headed up to the sixth floor now for the next appointment, and I could finally see why the wheelchair was necessary. These days were long, the walking was endless, and the waiting rooms all started to blur together. We sat in yet another one, waiting for the doctor's visit, the one we finally all go into together.

My grandmother turned to me, her face tight with something close to guilt. "Sloan... you don't have to go back with me if you don't want to."

I blinked at her. "Of course I do. If I'm going to help take care of you, I should be here." She glanced at Nathan, and I swear it was *the* look—the same one he kept giving me. What was going on with these two? Some sort of silent agreement I hadn't been looped into?

"Sloan..."

Before she could finish whatever she was going to say, a nurse opened the door and called her name. We were led back to a large, comfortable exam room. She lowered herself into the big cushy chair meant for patients, while Nathan and I took the standard ones off to the side.

The nurse began taking her vitals, all business, except for the way her eyes kept darting toward Nathan. *Really*? I sat there watching this unfold, annoyed. *Now* was not the time for someone to be mentally undressing him. Shouldn't these women be more concerned about, I don't know, their patients? I eye her as she walks out, hoping my look says what I'm too polite to: *Please just do your job and stop undressing people with your eyes. This is a hospital, not an audition for The Bachelor.*

"This day's gone pretty smoothly," I say, glancing around the room. "They don't keep you in waiting rooms long here." Nathan and my grandmother exchange another look the same loaded, secretive glance they've been tossing around all day. It's starting to make my skin itch. I can tell they both want to say something, and I'm this close to snapping. Just spit it out already, because being left out of the loop is not something I handle well.

Before I can, there's a knock at the door. The doctor steps in, smiling warmly, clipboard in hand, like he's about to deliver a weather report instead of a diagnosis. I looked up at him, he looked young for a doctor, maybe just aging well. He shakes Nathan's hand, then mine, lingering just a little longer than necessary. "You are?" he asks, scanning me up and down with a polite but slightly awkward smile.

He's caring for my grandmother; I should be nice. "Nice to meet you. I'm Sloan, Marilyn's granddaughter."

He glances at my grandmother. "Oh, so *this* is the famous Sloan you talk about all the time." I blush and let go of his hand.

"I'm Doctor Tucker," he says. "I've heard a lot about you."

I keep smiling, but I feel Nathan tense up beside me. "Okay," Nathan snaps, a little impatient, "can we get on with this? She's a little hungry and we want to take her out to eat after her treatment today."

Doctor Tucker clears his throat. "Oh yes, sorry. Let's get to it. I'm afraid I have some bad news though; I don't think we can do treatment today."

My eyebrows furrow as I glance at my grandmother, worry creeping in. What puzzles me even more is that no one else seems confused or concerned. He continues, "In fact, I'm sorry to say we need to keep her overnight for a blood transfusion. With the amount she needs, it will take about eight hours."

My face twists in confusion, what is he saying? She seems fine. "As you know, they take a while," Doctor Tucker continues, "and you'll be well cared for on the oncology floor, just like last time." Pressure builds in my chest. Why are they acting like she's been admitted overnight before? He keeps talking, but there's a ringing in my ears, drowning out his words. I shake my head, trying to focus.

"It's okay, Marilyn," I hear Nathan say softly. "I brought the overnight bag with everything, just in case." My grandmother nods, as if accepting her fate. Like this is all perfectly normal. I try to swallow, but my throat feels thick, clogged. Am I having an allergic reaction to something in the room? I want to ask what the hell is going on, but no words come out.

"Now, let's discuss this CT," Doctor Tucker begins, and I force myself to focus. I'm supposed to be present for this appointment—not having a breakdown. "So, as we expected, the tumor did grow," he says, and I blanch. *Expected to grow?* Is this doctor on actual drugs?

"But just a little," he continues, "which is good news—that was the goal here. We all knew it." I freeze. What is this nonsense? *Expected to grow?* Then he drops the bomb: "With stage four cancer and being on a clinical trial, this is good news. It means we've bought you some more time." My mind goes completely blank. Did I really just hear *stage four*? No one mentioned stage four before.

Suddenly, it all clicks. I finally understand those looks they've been giving me every time I mentioned her getting better—they knew she wasn't.

I stop myself from breaking down. I force my vision to stay steady, this isn't the place or the time to fall apart, not in front of her. "How long does she have?" I ask, as calmly as I can manage, because really, how else do you ask a question like that?

"Good question," Doctor Tucker says. "With pancreatic cancer, especially at stage four, the odds typically aren't good. The clinical trial she's been on for the past three months is helping—it's slowing the growth. She's getting more time than most. I'd say... six more months."

I nod. Not because I'm ok or because I understand, but because if I speak, I'll scream.

Three months. She's known for three months. Yet she only told me less than a month ago. No wonder Nathan moves through this place like he owns it, like every hallway and waiting room has his name etched into it. He's been coming here for three months.

He's known, all this time. I sit there as the doctor drones on about her blood work and the need for the transfusion, but none of it matters—nothing matters. Not when someone just stamped a ticking clock on her life. Six months. Who even knows how accurate that is? I glance at Nate. He's already watching me, his expression unreadable. I meet his gaze just long enough to glare before looking away.

"Alright," the doctor says, standing. "I'll go let them know to get your first-class room ready," he jokes, and I have to fight the urge to roll my eyes. What kind of doctor jokes like that?

He shakes Nathan's hand, then turns to me, clearly expecting the same. I reach out, robotic and tight-lipped, forcing a smile. His eyes trail over me again, too slow, too familiar and I suppress a shiver, pulling my hand back the second it's polite to do so. I plaster on a smile as Doctor Tucker leaves the room.

"Grandma, I'm going to run to the bathroom before they show us to your room," I say, keeping my voice light. She nods, maybe a little surprised that I'm not upset. How could I be upset with her? She's the one fighting for her life. I make it to the bathroom, barely closing the door before I lock it and fall apart. The sobs come fast, loud, and ugly like they've been waiting in my chest all day, just looking for the right crack to escape through.

Chapter 12

We get escorted to the eighth floor, and when we reach the room, Nathan excuses himself to grab her overnight bag from the trunk. I settle in while the nurses hook her up and I flip through the channels until I find the one she always watches. They bring in a dinner menu, but she nudges it aside, telling the nurse she's not that hungry.

"Grandma," I say gently, "you haven't eaten all day."

She looks like she's about to argue, but then she sighs. "Okay, hon. How about you pick for me?"

I smile and grab the menu. "Alright... how about meatloaf and mashed potatoes, side of corn, and—of course—chocolate cake."

She nods, smiling. "Perfect choice, my sweetheart."

I place my hand over hers and she closes her eyes for a brief moment. Then she opens them, and says, "You know, that doctor of mine sure is cute." I roll my eyes. Now? Really?

"You want me to ask him out for you?" I tease, trying to steer her away from where I know she's headed.

She chuckles. "No, silly. I meant *you* should go out with him."

I'm about to protest—because one, that's ridiculous, and two, any doctor who hits on his patient's granddaughter has questionable morals, but Nathan walks in. While I'm not mad at *her*, I *am* still pissed at *him* for keeping secrets. So, I egg her on a little. Let him listen. "Oh, Grandma, I don't think he'd be interested anyway."

She scoffs. "Of course he would. Look at you, and he never shook Nathan's hand as long as he shook yours." Nathan settles in the corner, pretending not to listen, but I see the tension in his shoulders.

"Well," I say playfully, "if he asks me out, maybe I'll say yes." From the corner, I hear Nathan grunt. Before I can call him out on it, or make an ass of myself, a nurse walks in, saving me from the moment altogether.

"Mrs. Mercer, I'll be your nurse until the night shift gets here. Do you need anything?" the nurse asks. My grandmother tells her what she wants for dinner and says she's fine otherwise. I can hardly believe she's not at home, tucked into her own bed.

I clear my throat. "I was wondering... can I get an extra pillow? I'm going to stay here tonight, and I just want something for the chair."

The nurse glances at the chart but doesn't look up. "Sorry, visiting hours end at nine, and overnight guests aren't allowed. It's not my rule, just hospital policy," she says in a flat tone, like she has this conversation every hour. I feel the air rush out of me. What am I supposed to do? Just leave her here alone?

Before I can protest, my grandmother gently pats my hand. "Sweetie, it's okay. You can go home and pick me up tomorrow."

"Go home?" I say, stunned. For one, we live two hours away, and now that I know she has six months... I'll be damned if I'm going far. I make a silent plan to sleep in the car before I even think about going home.

Just as the nurse steps out, Doctor Tucker walks in, smiling like he's got good news. Hell if I knew what there was to smile about right now. My grandmother nudges me, and I mentally roll my eyes. *She's not serious right now, is she?* Nathan looks up, equally shocked—like a doctor just doesn't casually drop by a patient's room.

"Did they set you up well?" Doctor Tucker says, checking everything the nurse just checked. Maybe he's just a thorough doctor?

"Everything's good, doctor. Just a little thirsty," my grandmother replies.

"Oh, I'll go grab you something," I say, jumping up, eager to escape this room before my grandmother decides to play matchmaker. Before anyone can argue, I'm out the door and at a vending machine, buying a Coke. On my way back, I ran into none other than Doctor Tucker.

"Sloan," he says, delighted.

"Doctor Tucker," I reply, matching his polite tone. He is her doctor, what else can I do?

"Oh, please, call me Eugene." I want to say, *No thanks,* because that feels unprofessional, but I hold my tongue. "You found the vending machine?" He asks, nodding toward the Coke I bought.

"Yeah," I say, gesturing.

He nods, silent for a moment, then says, "Look, I usually don't do this—" *He is not about to ask me out,* I think to myself, "but if you ever want to go out sometime…"

I glance over my shoulder and see Nathan stepping out of the room, walking this way. "Oh, well, really, Eugene, my grandmother and my job keep me pretty busy."

He nods. "Yeah, I get that, but if you change your mind, here's my number." He pulls out a slip of paper. "That's my personal number."

I nod, fluttering my lashes a little more than necessary. "If I change my mind, I'll let you know." He stands there, watching me, while Nathan draws closer, so I want to end this conversation. "Well, I better get back, duty calls," I say, holding up the Coke.

He nods. "Well, I hope to hear from you."

I walk away, deliberately not stopping for Nathan on my way back to the room.

CHAPTER 13

We stayed with my grandmother until they kicked us out for the night. She pretended to eat her dinner, taking a few bites and pushing the food around like I wouldn't notice. We walked out to the parking lot, waiting on the valet. "I'm not going all the way home," I told Nathan. "If you want to take the car, fine. I guess I'll just wander around the hospital all night, but I'm not leaving the area."

"Of course we're not," he said like it was obvious. "One, it's nine o'clock at night, and two, we're not driving two hours away from her."

I smiled but didn't really want to. I was still pissed at him. "Okay, so we sleep in the car?" I said. I'd pretty much figured that's what we'd end up doing.

He scoffed. "Not a chance, I did that last time, and it sucked. She could tell the next day when I picked her up; she wasn't happy." I wanted to claw at him again, reminded he'd lied to me.

"Okay," I say, annoyed. "What should we do then?"

"I got us a hotel room," he said like it was no big deal. I stayed quiet, not ready to say thank you just yet.

"Fine, let's go, and it better not be far."

"It's literally across the street," he said, trying to ease the tension. I get into the car wordlessly. There's nothing negative I can say; this is the best-case scenario. But I'll be damned if I compliment him right now.

We take the incredibly short drive across the street, and I trail behind him by three paces, still mad. He checks us in, and the receptionist says, "Room 113."

We're halfway down the hallway before it hits me. "Wait seriously? One room?"

He stops and turns, clearly trying to keep his cool. "Sloan, you can't be serious. One room was already expensive enough. This is a nice hotel—did you miss that part? I made sure to get two beds."

I glance around, realizing he's right. It is a nice place. "Then why stay here? Surely there was something cheaper."

"If something happens, we don't even need the car. We can just run over." I say nothing. Because damn it... he's right. And if I say anything now, I'll just sound like an ungrateful ass. He unlocks the room, and we pile in. Thankfully there were two beds. I notice he's carrying two duffel bags and hands one to me.

"I didn't know what to pack for you, so I kept it basic. Sorry," he says, looking almost guilty. "I was hoping we wouldn't need this."

I unzip the bag, grateful to have something—anything—that might help me wash this day off of me. "You can take a shower first," I offer. "You booked the room." He looks like he wants to argue, but either he's too tired or he knows better, because he just nods and heads to the bathroom. I walk over to the window, pulling back the curtain slightly. The hospital glows faintly across the street, sterile and quiet in the night. I wonder what my grandmother is doing right now. Is she asleep? Awake and scared?

I press my forehead lightly to the glass, still reeling. She's known for three months and so has Nathan. My blood starts to boil all over again. I can finally see red. My grandmother isn't here to yell at, to press for answers. Even if she was, I couldn't bring myself to be angry with her, not without breaking her already fragile spirit. Nathan is, and before I even realize what I'm doing, I march to the bathroom and yank the door open.

"What gives you the right?" I shout. There's a loud thud as he startles and smacks his head on something in the shower. Good.

"What the hell, Sloan?" he says, poking his dripping head out from behind the shower curtain, eyes wide with confusion. I freeze for half a second, realizing I've barged in while he's completely naked.

"You knew," I say, voice shaking with rage. "You knew she was sick. You knew for three months." He opens his mouth, but I don't let him speak. "To make it worse, it's terminal. Stage four. No one thought I deserved to know. I had to find out from some smug, pigheaded doctor who looked me up and down like I was dessert."

I'm breathless now, chest heaving, but I push forward. "So yeah, I was blindsided. You and my grandmother kept me completely in the dark. I can't yell at her; she's been nothing but good to me. But you?" I walk closer to him, not caring that he's in the shower. I jab a finger in his direction. "You—I can yell at. So, tell me, who gave you the right to decide I don't get to know my own grandmother is dying?"

He blinks, water streaming down his face, stunned into silence. Then he slowly reaches for the shower curtain, pulling it closed just enough to cover himself. "I didn't decide anything," he says, voice low but firm. "It wasn't my place to tell you. She made that call."

I cross my arms, heat rising up my neck. "And you just went along with it?"

"She asked me not to, Sloan." His voice sharpens, frustration seeping in, I open my mouth, but nothing comes out.

"She didn't want you to come back out of guilt," he continues, his tone quieter now, almost pleading. "She wanted you to come back when you were ready, because you wanted to, not because you felt obligated." My chest tightens. I glance away, trying to blink back the sting in my eyes. "She was trying to protect you," he says gently. "In her own way."

I feel the water rise behind my eyes. "You took that time from me," I say, my voice breaking. "You didn't tell me. You *should have*, Nathan."

He shuts the shower off, grabs a towel from the rack, and steps out, with it around his waist. "Sloan, I don't know how many ways I can say I'm sorry. You have to understand, she's as good as a grandmother to *me*. She took care of me when I was a kid. When my mom wasn't around—just like when *yours* wasn't." He looks at me, eyes earnest. "Or did you forget that's how we even know each other? Our moms ran around together. Went on benders together. So yeah, of course I wanted to respect her wishes. Do you want to know how many times I almost picked up the phone to call you? I lost count, believe me when I say I wanted to tell you."

I could feel myself wavering, because deep down I knew I would've done the same thing. And really, what loyalty did Nathan even owe me anymore? I leaned against the counter, crossing my arms tightly. "I don't want to lose her," I say, my voice barely above a whisper.

"I know," he says softly, pulling me into a hug.

I go to resist but the weight of it all crashes down on me, and I crumble, sinking into him as the tears come again. "I feel gross," I say quietly. "I just want to wash this day off me."

"Take the shower," he says, stepping back. "I'm done anyway."

He leaves and I step into the shower. I just stand there, letting the water run over me. I have no idea how long I stay like that, lost in thought, until the water starts to grow cold. I snap out of it and quickly wash up, eager to get out of the chill. I realized too late that I left my clothes on the bed. I sigh, bowing my head, of course I did. I grab the towel and wrap it tightly around me. Slowly, I creak the door open, hoping Nathan was already asleep. I hear the TV still on and hear a low whistle. I cringe. Of course, he's not asleep. He doesn't say anything, just watches for a moment longer before turning back to the TV. I hurry over to the bed, grabbing my clothes quickly, hoping to break the awkward silence.

"Thanks for not making it weird," I mutter, running to the bathroom to put my clothes on.

Nathan smirks without looking up. "You're welcome. I'm a professional."

I step out wearing the oversized shirt and sweats he packed. I glance at him and say, "Nice choice in clothing, you somehow picked my usual go-to. I'm slightly impressed."

"So... does this mean you went through my drawers?" I say, amused.

His cheeks flush a deep red. I gasp, "Nathan Reed, you went through my underwear drawer!" I laugh giving him a hard time. "Oh wow, just imagine what the town would say if they found out *scandalous!*" I joke, smirking.

"Oh sure, they'd be shocked," he said sarcastically. "I ordered a pizza," he said, changing the subject. "Pepperoni, light sauce, extra cheese."

I flushed, surprised. Does he really remember *everything* about me? "Thanks," I mutter, staring blankly at the TV.

"So, you also think that doctor is pig-headed too?" I snort at how blunt he is. "What? That guy was totally hitting on you," he says. "He's your grandmother's doctor, talk about a conflict of interest."

The thought of him actually caring if he was hitting on me made my heart race. "Oh, and all those nurses and admins today were any better?" I teased.

He rolls his eyes. "Oh, come on," I say. "They were and the only difference was none of them asked you out, although I think Miss Front Desk Highlights definitely wanted to." I scoff, remembering her annoyed glare.

"Maybe she would've if someone hadn't interrupted," he teased.

"Oh, you wish," I shot back. "I was just trying to make sure I understood the hospital routine. Sorry you couldn't pick up a date."

I was half annoyed, half curious if he really was interested. We hear a knock at the door. Nathan answered it, paid for the pizza, and called out, "Sustenance has arrived!" I yelled back, "Huzzah!" and was instantly transported back to our childhood every sleepover filled with the same silly ritual whenever pizza showed up. Our laughter fizzles out, and we eat in silence with *Dateline* playing quietly in the background.

I glance up to find Nathan watching me chew with my mouth full. "What?" I ask, wondering if there's something on my face.

"You're beautiful," he says softly. His words catch me so off guard, I don't even know how to respond.

"I'm tired," I say quickly, turning away. "I'm going to bed." I roll over and pretend to sleep, but inside, I'm silently crying, because no matter how much I want him, I still can't forgive what he did three years ago. Deep down, I'm not sure I ever will.

CHAPTER 14

Three Years Ago

It's been days since Nate last reached out. I didn't expect him to stay mad this long. I've been trying to figure out how to apologize, but he's been working every day, mowing lawns. And every time I stop by his house, his mom says he's not home.

I sigh and head out to the store for some groceries, needing something to distract me from Nate. I grab the list my grandmother made and the keys. At the local store, I pick up everything on the list—plus a little junk food to sulk over Nate with. At the checkout, the girl scanning my items looks familiar.

"Taylor, right?" I ask. She nods, looking bored.

"We graduated high school together," I say, trying to spark some small talk. "How's it going?"

She looks at me, still unimpressed. "Well, I work here, so what do you think?" she says, popping her gum obnoxiously.

I nod. "Yeah, I'm trying to find one myself, haven't decided yet." She rolls her eyes. I couldn't figure out why I was even trying to get this girl to talk to me, but it felt like a faucet I couldn't turn off. "So, what does everyone do for fun around here anymore?" I ask. "In high school, we used to have those bonfires out in the woods."

She snorts. "We still do those." I almost laugh, but then I see she's serious.

"Oh. But don't high school kids go to those too?"

She rolls her eyes like I just asked the dumbest question ever. "No, we have a different spot for the adult bonfire. Obviously."

"Oh, okay," I nod, trying not to sound like I think it's beneath me.

She finishes ringing me up as I pay. Then she looks me up and down and says, "We do throw them behind the Highway Four Motel. The night manager lets anyone crash there who can't get home. You know, safety and all." I wasn't sure if that was a jab about Scarlett, but I wasn't about to ask. I start gathering my things, ready to leave, when she calls out, "You should really come, it's fun."

I look up, surprised by how genuine she sounds. "Sure," I say, surprising myself by actually accepting. On the drive home, I decide to stop by Nate's house to see if he's home. I knock on the old screen door, hoping his mom doesn't answer again. Of course, it's Karrie who opens it.

"Hey, Karrie," I say, trying to look past her. "Is Nate here?"

She scoffs. "No, the boy's out working, trying to make money for the bills." I bite back the urge to roll my eyes. Clearly, Nate is the one covering most of the bills. Karrie could barely hold a job to save her life.

"Do you know when he'll be back?" I ask, anxious.

"I don't know," she says, taking a drag from her cigarette. "You two fightin' or something? This is the third time you've come by this week."

"No, we're not fighting," I say. "We just keep missing each other."

She scoffs. "Oh please, Sloan. You rarely come around here. You and your grandmother act like you're better than me. No wonder your momma hasn't come back."

I curl my fist, the disgust for this woman rising inside me. "Listen, Karrie, you have no right to talk about—"

She cuts me off, sneering. "That's exactly why you're trying to leave, right? You think you're better than this town, better than everyone. Just admit it. Everyone thinks so."

I feel my stomach clench. "Did Nate tell you that?"

She shrugs, blowing smoke in my direction again, putting me even more on edge. "He came home the other night, going on about how you're trying to leave, blah blah. I told him, 'Of course you are. She thinks she's better than everyone.'"

I roll my eyes, finally done caring if she likes me or not. "Karrie, that's not what I think. Just because someone wants to take a job in New York doesn't mean they think they're better than anyone." I huff, not wanting to keep this conversation going. "Can you please just tell Nate to call me?"

"Whatever," she mutters, flicking her cigarette out the door and slamming it behind her.

I sigh, walking back to the car, wondering why I even bothered. She probably won't even give Nate the message. I unload the groceries, and with nothing left to do, a restless feeling creeps in. Maybe I should go to that bonfire. I haven't been to one in so long and maybe it would take my mind off Nate. I get ready, throwing on my favorite pair of jeans and a simple tank top, and layering it with my black denim jacket. I toss my messy hair up and glance at the clock.

9:00 p.m.

Late enough. It should be in full swing by now. I head to my grandmother's room to tell her I'm heading out but conveniently leave out exactly *where* I'm going. If she knew I was going to a party in the woods behind the Highway Four Motel, she'd absolutely lose it. Adult or not, she'd still find a way to put her foot down.

"Hey, Grandma," I say, poking my head into her room. "I'm heading out."

She looks up from her book. "Where to, sweetheart? It's a little late for you to be going out," she teases.

"Oh, just to a friend's place—Taylor. We went to high school together. She invited me over."

Grandma nods, smiling softly. "Alright then. Have fun, honey."

She has no reason to question me, and I feel a little guilty for the lie. I park in the motel lot; no way I'm dragging Grandma's Buick into the woods and risking a flat. I head toward the tree line, following the sound of music and laughter echoing through the night.

As I step into the clearing, someone shoves a wine cooler into my hand. It's already open. "No thanks," I mutter, setting it down on a nearby stump. I scan the area, looking for something sealed. I walk toward a cooler, hoping there's something left inside. I open the lid and pull a wine cooler from the top, the condensation slick against my fingers. As I look up, I freeze. *Nate.*

He's not alone. Taylor, the girl from the grocery store, is draped all over him like she's done it a hundred times. She's whispering in his ear, and he's nodding. From where I'm standing, I can't tell if he's actually into it or just too tired—or too drunk—to care. The fact that he's letting her touch him at all is enough to twist something sharp in my chest.

I stay where I am, watching from across the firelight like I'm outside my own body. She leans in, starts kissing his neck. My stomach drops. He's not stopping her. Why isn't he stopping her? She says something else, too low for me to hear, and he nods again. Then she grabs his hand and leads him toward the motel.

I don't know what possesses me, but my legs move on their own. I follow, silent and stunned. My heart is pounding so loudly I'm surprised they can't hear it behind them. I can feel it echo in my ears, in my throat, in every part of me. Still, I keep walking. They reach the parking lot and head straight for a door marked *13*. It looks like she already has a key. My feet slow as they stop just outside the room. Nate leans her against the wall and kisses her like he really means it. I feel my heart tear in two, and just when I think it can't break anymore, the door to room *13* swings open, and they disappear inside, the door closing behind them.

Click.

That soft sound is the loudest thing I've ever heard. My stomach churns, my chest tightens. I don't need to see anything else. I'm not naive, I know what happens next. My mind does the rest, cruel and unrelenting.

Chapter 15

I wake with a start, tears already falling from my eyes. No matter how many times I had that dream, I still wake up with my heart broken like it happened just yesterday. I hadn't had it in a while, but being around Nathan must've triggered it.

I sit up, already in a mood because of it. I glance over and see Nathan still fast asleep in the bed next to mine, looking peaceful. That only annoys me more. I toss off the blankets and tiptoe to the bathroom to brush my teeth and get dressed.

Digging through the bag Nathan packed, I found a simple pair of black leggings and a t-shirt. I start changing; halfway through pulling the shirt over my head, the bathroom door suddenly opens. I spin around, mouth opening to scream, but it comes out as a strangled squeal. Nathan stands frozen in the doorway, eyes wide, staring at me in just my leggings and bra. After what feels like an eternity, I snap, "Do you mind?" and slam the door shut. From the other side, I hear a muffled, "Sorry!" I roll my eyes and finish getting ready, trying not to think about the fact that my face is still burning. I step out of the bathroom, doing my best to preserve what little dignity I have left. I avoid his gaze as I say, "Bathroom's yours."

"Thanks," he replies, his voice low and equally embarrassed. He's in and out quicker than I expect, and when he returns, he grabs his jacket and asks, "So, you ready to go?" I don't answer. Instead, I just snap my laptop shut and stand up, letting the motion speak for itself. He watches me, clearly confused by my mood this early in the morning. We reach the lobby to check out, and just as he grabs the keys, he turns to me.

"I'll go get the car," he says.

"Actually, you take the bags and get the car. I want to walk." I see him rear back slightly, puzzled again. "Just need some fresh air, is all," I say, already turning away and leaving him with the luggage.

The short walk to the hospital helps, a little. I stop at the café and order a latte. I sip my latte like it holds all the answers, but it doesn't. It's just overpriced caffeine with a fancy foam leaf on top. I tell myself *I can't be mad at Nathan today for something he did three years ago. Let it go. Old news, ancient history, dinosaur-level grudges.* But another, louder, sassier part of me chimes in—*Actually? I can be mad. I **am** mad. I'm the CEO of Mad. The founding member of the Grudge Club.* Frankly, no one voted me out.

I get to the eighth floor, the sun streaming in, and despite the fact that we're on the oncology floor, it's a pretty sight. I stand there in the glow of the sunrise, breathing in the sterile smell of the hospital, pretending—just for a second—that we were anywhere else but here. Maybe in Vegas. She always wanted to go there. She traveled some when she was young but never made it to Vegas. After Scarlett went missing, she stopped traveling altogether.

I feel a presence blocking the streaming sunlight, of course, as I open my eyes, it's none other than Doctor Tucker. He's walking toward me with that same ever-present smile. Good

God—he's not going to ask me out again, is he? I smile politely as he approaches. "Sloan, nice to see you this morning. Your grandmother is looking better."

My fake smile melts into a real one. "That's great news. So... she can go home now?"

"She sure can," he says. "We're working on discharging her now. Usually, I don't get around to discharge patients this early, but I thought I would for you."

He winks, and I force my smile to stay in place, because what am I supposed to do? Kiss his feet for doing his job? "Well, I'm sure she'll appreciate that. It'll be good to get her home," I say.

He nods just as I feel someone behind me, a hand resting on my shoulder. "Sloan, have you seen her yet?" Nathan's voice cuts in, and my shoulder burns under his touch.

I can practically feel Nathan shooting daggers at Doctor Tucker, the air between them thick enough to cut. "Um, no," I say, responding to Nathan's question, my shoulder now perpetually up in flames from his touch.

"Well," he says, voice tight, "we should really get her home, don't you think?"

"Yep." Wow, apparently, I can only speak in single syllables now. I turn back to Doctor Tucker and give him another polite smile—because, despite everything, he *is* my grandmother's doctor. "Well, thank you again, Doctor Tucker." I reach out to shake his hand, and he takes it prolonging it just a second too long, his eyes raking over me yet again.

"Remember, it's Eugene," he says, like that was ever going to stick. I force my eyes to stay where they are instead of rolling so hard, they get stuck. God, this guy is a walking HR violation.

Still smiling, mostly because I know I'm about to say something snarky if I don't walk away, I turn toward my grandmother's room, heels clicking purposefully down the hall. I can feel Nathan following close behind, radiating heat and quiet judgment like some kind of jealous space heater.

I walk in to find my grandmother sitting up in bed, looking noticeably better. Her whole face lights up when she sees me—and somehow gets even brighter when she spots Nathan behind me. "You ready to go home, Marilyn?" Nathan grins, rubbing his hands together like a kid about to unwrap a present.

"Yes, and please tell me you two didn't eat on the way here because I'm *starved*." Nathan and I glance at each other, exchanging a silent pact: we will *never* tell her we didn't go home last night—we'll take that secret, and the overpriced hotel bill—to our graves.

"Oh, we were just waiting to see if *you* wanted to eat," I say a little too cheerfully. "Good news, they've already started your discharge paperwork."

She furrows her brow. "Already? They usually don't bust me out until lunchtime." I force a smile, swallowing down the anger that bubbles up. Lied to or not, I'm not about to ruin this moment. Not when she's smiling. Not when she still looks like *her*.

"Uhh, I don't know," I say, feigning ignorance. I hear Nathan mutter something under his breath and shoot him a sharp look. "What was that?" I ask, practically daring him to say it out loud. What *is* his deal today?

"Nothing," he replies, too quickly. "Just... hungry." He turns to my grandmother with a tight smile. "I'll start gathering your stuff, Marilyn."

She nods at him, then turns her attention back to me. We talked about how she slept and what she might want to eat on the way home. I'm just about to suggest something when —

"Marilyn," a voice cuts in from the doorway. Of course. It's Doctor Tucker. I inwardly groan at his persistence. The man has the timing of a rom-com villain. "I just came to personally let you know you're good to go," he says with a smile that's a little too performative. "Hope you have a great drive home. We'll see you next week."

My grandmother smiles and nods, still looking a little confused. Before I can even fake a thank you, he says, "Sloan." He's looking straight at me now, slowly approaching, and I feel a flicker of panic rise. How many times was I going to have to shake this man's hand?

Before I can answer, Nathan crosses the room and extends *his* hand instead. "Thanks so much for the *class* A service, Doctor," he says, voice tight and just this side of sarcastic. "We're going to get her out of here and get her some much-needed food."

As thankful as I was for Nathan stepping in, I still worry the doctor will think we're rude. Again—he *is* her doctor. "Thanks, Doctor Tucker. Really," I say over Nathan's shoulder, forcing another polite smile. "We're just glad she's in good hands."

He nods. "Well, I hope to see you next week." *Finally*, he leaves the room. I exhale hard, shoulders slumping. Being hit on while my grandmother is lying in a hospital bed isn't exactly at the top of my bucket list.

"Let's get you home," I say, so glad this hospital trip is finally over.

CHAPTER 16

We finally make it home, all of us feeling bloated and achy from the long drive. Nathan helps my grandmother out of the car. She asks to be put in her recliner and requests to take a nap right away, and my heart sinks a little. Did the meal at White Castle and the drive really take that much out of her? She looked so good this morning, full of hope, and now it feels like every time she makes progress, we end up taking two steps back.

I make sure she's settled comfortably in her recliner, and head out to the back porch. The patio furniture still looks fairly new, a quiet contrast to everything else. I sit down and stare out at the backyard—the focal point of her property—a lovely little pond with a small dock.

I smile, thinking about how the pond came to be. My grandfather had it dug for my grandmother when they bought this place. Money was tight back then; they couldn't afford much, but she wanted that pond, and he made sure it happened. I hope someday I'll have a man who'd build or create something extravagant for me, the true definition of *'if they wanted to, they would.'* She used to keep the pond filled with fish every year.

Well, she *used* to, anyway. It's sad to see all the things she gave up to take care of me, only to get sick later in life. It was her pride and joy, something she cared for with so much love and patience. But lately, she hasn't been able to tend to it like she used to. It feels cruel, life owes her more than this.

I hear the back door creak open, and I turn to see Nathan stepping out, two drinks in hand. "Iced tea, extra ice," he says, setting one down in front of me. Suddenly, I realize I don't really need fresh air after all, I stand up, feeling the weight of the day. "Sloan, what's your problem? You're so hot and cold—I can't keep up," he says, watching me with that mix of frustration and concern.

I keep my face neutral and respond coolly, "Nothing. I've just got a lot of work to do on the article." I slide open the glass door to head back inside, hoping to end the conversation there.

Nathan speaks up behind me. "I got Tammy to message me back." I stop mid-step, grumbling under my breath because I know I can't ignore that. *Damn it.*

"Okay," I say, still not turning around. "Can you forward it to me, by chance?"

"Or," he says, raising an eyebrow like he's in a bad spy movie, "you could come to *my* room and discover what secrets I hold." I roll my eyes so hard I practically see my own brain.

"Great. Lead the way, James Bond." He springs up like he's been launched, I add, "Bring the drinks. I'll need hydration for the nonsense." We swing by my room to grab my laptop and end up in his room where he proudly reveals a laptop that looks like it's been through three wars and a house fire.

"Wow," I say, raising an eyebrow. "Does that thing still work?"

He waves me off. "It does what I need it to. Mowing lawns in town doesn't exactly scream *new laptop* money."

He's not wrong. Still, I can't help but think he could've moved on from landscaping a long time ago. Nathan wasn't dumb. If anything, it was this town that kept him rooted, like wet cement hardening around his feet. I curse myself for thinking that, because the truth is, if he *had* left my grandmother would've been alone before I ever came back. He had the perfect opportunity to get out after his mom died, but he didn't.

"Here," he says, turning his laptop toward me showing their back and forth on Facebook messenger.

Nathan: Hey Tammy. I know it's been a long time, but I was hoping you could help me out. It's about Scarlett.

Tammy: ...*Wow.* Wasn't expecting to hear that name. What about her?

Nathan: Do you remember the last night you saw her? I know it's been years, but anything you remember could help.

Tammy: Yeah, I remember. *Unfortunately.* That night stuck with me more than I wanted it to.

Nathan: What do you mean?

Tammy: She was at that bonfire behind the old motel, but she wasn't herself. Scarlett was usually loud and wild, always the one trying to keep the party going. But that night... she was quiet. On edge.

Nathan: Did she say anything to you?

Tammy: Not much. Just that she wasn't staying long. I asked why, and she gave me this weird look, like I was prying or something. She said, *"I've got somewhere to be,"* and walked off.

Nathan: Somewhere? Do you know what she meant?

Tammy: I don't. I assumed she was meeting someone. Her and Kent had just fought, but… that wasn't new. They were always fighting. I figured it'd blow over like it always did.

Nathan: Did she leave alone?

Tammy: Yeah. I saw her walk off toward the road. It was dark, and she didn't look back. I thought maybe Kent would go after her, but he never showed up. I didn't follow. I told myself it wasn't my business… and then a week later, everyone was saying that was the last time she was seen.

Nathan: Thank you. This helps.

Tammy: Look, I'm not mad you reached out. Just… I really don't like going back there. I've worked hard to leave that version of myself behind. I'm clean now. My kids talk to me again. I left Summit Grove for a reason. So please, just… don't contact me again.

I scoff at the laptop. "Well, this isn't exactly groundbreaking. We already knew she was last seen near the motel; it's right there on the missing persons flyer."

"Yeah," Nate says, "but did we know about the bonfire?"

I pause, realizing I hadn't thought of it that way. "I guess not. I just... didn't think they were doing those back then. It feels like one of those traditions that started after we were teens."

He shrugs. "Small town. Not much else to do. Traditions like that don't die easy."

"I still don't think this is helpful," I say, leaning back with a sigh. "I wanted something new, something for the article that would actually draw people in."

"You're smart, Sloan," Nathan says, his voice low but sure. "You'll figure it out."

I glance away, feeling my cheeks do their embarrassing little volcano thing. Seriously, how does he still have this power? One complement and boom—blush city. "Thanks," I say quietly, genuinely.

Back in my room, I sit at my desk, mentally willing inspiration to hit me like a freight train—or at least a mildly aggressive nudge. Nothing and then... everything. A sentence. Then another. Suddenly, my fingers are flying across the keyboard like they know something I don't. It's not perfect, but it's honest. And it's mine.

Scarlett Mercer: The Mystery Summit Grove Forgot

In a town as tightly knit as Summit Grove, mystery feels out of place. We know each other's routines, each other's families and—let's be honest—each other's business. But one mystery has lingered in the background for more than two decades: the disappearance of Scarlett Mercer. Scarlett was last seen over twenty years ago near the Highway Four Motel, not far from a bonfire gathering that has become a quiet tradition in our community. Since then, there have been whispers, theories, and unanswered questions—but little progress. For a town that prides itself on closeness, we've allowed Scarlett's case to fade into the past with surprising ease. We rally around small-town scandals and petty gossip, yet we've let a woman's vanishing go unexplored for far too long. Scarlett was more than a name on a missing persons flyer. She was a mother, a daughter, and a member of this community. Her story deserves more than silence. If you know anything about the night she disappeared or anything that might be relevant, no matter how small, please consider coming forward. You can reach me at **wheresscarlettme rcer@gmail.com***. Even the smallest detail might bring us one step closer to answers. It's time we remember her. More importantly, it's time we care.*

The Summit Gazette didn't exactly have a bustling newsroom. We were told to email our pieces to Diane, but it was heavily implied that after hitting 'send' there wasn't much editing—or even proofreading—going on. So, I read over my article one last time, attached it along with the week's obituaries, and hit send, hoping Diane wouldn't actually read the article too closely. Now I just had to cross my fingers and pray it makes it into Sunday's paper.

CHAPTER 17

Monday rolls around, and I'm more nervous than I'd like to admit. It's been a full day since the article ran in the Sunday paper, and I've been dreading logging into the email account I set up. My grandmother was too tired to read through the whole paper, which, honestly, was a bit of a relief—especially since I hadn't exactly told her what I was up to.

I finally sucked it up and logged into the email, waiting until everyone was tucked away in their rooms for the night. To my surprise, there are over a hundred messages waiting. I don't know what I expected, but it definitely wasn't that.

I start scrolling, heart racing, hoping for something—anything—useful. But with each click, my hope dims. One after another, the emails are less about Scarlett and more about me. Angry messages flood in, questioning where I get off talking about the people of Summit Grove like that. Some accuse me of thinking I'm better than everyone else. And worse some dismiss Scarlett entirely. *"Who cares where she is? She was a junkie anyway."* That one hit the hardest.

Flagging the few emails that seemed promising, I decided the next step is to call the local police department to see if they have *anything* on file. Even if they've long stopped looking; surely, they kept records from when they were. I get patched through to the front desk, and after a long hold, the sound of a phone being fumbled, a gruff voice finally picks up.

"Summit Grove PD."

"Hi, my name is Sloan Mercer. I'm looking to speak with the officer who handled Scarlett Mercer's disappearance. If they're retired, I'd like to speak with whoever took over the case. I just want to review the file." There's a pause. Long enough I start wondering if the call dropped.

"You know it's been over twenty years, right?" the man finally says, his voice crackling through the line. I pull the phone away from my ear and blink at it. *Seriously?*

"Yes. I'm aware," I say, trying to keep my tone level.

"Miss... can I ask why you're just now calling about Scarlett Mercer's disappearance —years later? We've never had a single inquiry from you before." I roll my eyes.

"Oh, I don't know," I snapped. "Maybe because I was a child when she vanished?"

He scoffs. Actually *scoffs*. "Look, Miss. We're a small department with limited resources. We can't keep everything forever. After 2007, everything went digital. Anything before that? It's been disposed of."

My jaw tightens. *Disposed of.* "Oh, well. Sorry she didn't schedule her disappearance more conveniently. Should've waited for the digital age, huh?"

"You don't need to be facetious," he says, tone clipped.

I take a breath, try to count to three, and fail. "Listen... Officer—Detective—Whoever—you are. I just moved back from New York. I still have contacts at several reputable news outlets. So, unless you want a headline that reads 'Small-Town

PD Tosses Missing Person Files in the Trash,' I suggest you find Scarlett's file."

There's a pause on the other end. A stutter. I've hit a nerve.

"I think you need to calm down," he says, voice tight. "You're sounding a little... hysterical."

That's it. "No. You don't want me to be calm," I say, my voice no longer sweet. "Calm me writes articles. Calm me makes phone calls. Calm me ruins reputations. So, find. The. File."

I hung up. I felt the heat creep in and pounding in my ears.

I was so keyed up I couldn't sit still. I paced my room, fists clenched, jaw tight, wanting to scream—*something, anything*—just to let it out. The pressure building in me since the day I got back had finally boiled over. Without thinking, I stormed out of my room and straight into Nathan's room without knocking. He looked up from his bed, startled, a book still open in his hands.

"Sloan?" he said, concern flashing across his face. I didn't answer. I started pacing again, right there in his room.

"This town," I spat, "is *toxic.* Do you know how many emails I just read? People saying I'm awful, that I think I'm better than everyone, that Scarlett was just some junkie who doesn't deserve to be found."

Nate sat up straighter, his brows knitting together.

"Then," I continued, my voice rising, "I called the police department. Guess what? Supposedly her file is just... gone. *Gone.* Like she never went missing."

"Sloan, whoa—calm down. Slow down a second—"

"I *can't*," I snapped, the words tumbling out faster now. "How does one person just vanish, and no one gives a damn? My grandmother is heartbroken. She's been heartbroken for *years*, and I'm the only one who seems to want to do anything about it."

My breathing hitched, but I kept going. "She's a ticking clock, and I'm running out of time to give her something. *Anything*. Instead, I'm getting nowhere. I'm failing her."

The tears came fast and hot, blurring my vision. I gasped, chest tightening, unable to stop the storm inside me. I was unraveling, hyperventilating now, my whole body shaking. He jumped up, crossing the room in two quick strides and wrapping his arms around me. I didn't fight it. The moment he holds me, my body starts to calm, like he's flipping a switch I didn't know I needed. I hate that this man who once broke me is currently piecing me back together.

His voice is soft against my ear. "Sloan, it doesn't matter what they say. It matters what *you* believe. What *you* want. And you're wrong, you're not the only one who cares. I care too. I said I'd help you, remember?"

I nod against his chest, my breath evening out. His hand rubs slow circles on my back.

"If you want," he continues, "I'll go with you....wherever Kent's living. It's not much, but I still have some of my mom's old stuff in the shed. Photos and notes. Her and Scarlett were close back then. Maybe there's something in there."

I nod again, not trusting my voice just yet. The air in the room shifts; the panic that was clawing at my chest finally lets go. I pull back, brushing the tears from my cheeks, embarrassed that he's seen me fall apart, *again*.

"Sorry," I mutter, glancing away.

"Don't be," he says gently.

I glance around, needing something else to focus on, when my eyes land on the book he was reading before I barged in. It's a thick textbook, pages dog-eared and worn. I frown. "Nathan... are you in school?"

He looks caught, grabbing the book and tossing it onto the floor like it offended him. "Yeah… but it's nothing. Just a couple classes online. Here and there in between my landscaping."

My heart tugs unexpectedly. "Why didn't you tell me?"

He shrugs. "I didn't think it mattered." I studied him for a long second, seeing him, *really* seeing him.

Before I can stop myself, I'm leaning in, kissing him.

He responds immediately, his hands on my hips, pulling me closer. My fingers find his hair, and we're moving, breathing into each other, like no time has passed. We ease down onto the bed, the kiss deepening, and for the first time in so long, I let myself want. All too soon he pulls away. I blink, lips parted, confused. Of all people, I didn't expect him to stop. He says nothing. Just looks at me with something unreadable in his eyes.

"Okay," I whisper, swallowing the sting. I sit up, brushing my hair behind my ears, pretending my heart isn't thudding with hurt and confusion. The feeling of humiliation follows as I slip out of his room, feeling foolish. It's been three years of carrying this ache, like a second skin. Heartbreakingly reminded of why it ended three years ago. He didn't just hurt me, *he wrecked me.*

Chapter 18

Three years ago

I spend the entire week crying over Nate and applying for jobs, each one farther from Summit Grove than the last. I would've stayed for him. I *was* going to stay for him. He didn't even ask. He moved on so quickly. That's the part that keeps clawing at me, how fast he seemed to let me go.

Two weeks later, the email came in. *Ink Ever After.* A job I should be celebrating. Something people dream of and all I feel is numb.

Then comes the argument with my grandmother. The one we don't speak about anymore. I tell her everything—about Nate, about the motel, about *her.* She listens quietly, then says something that pisses me off more than anything else.

"Try and talk to him," she says. "You two have been through a lot. People make mistakes, Sloan."

I laugh, sharp and bitter. "He didn't forget my birthday, Grandma. He *cheated.* That's not a mistake, it's a decision. To make matters worse he's been silent through all of it. No call. No text. Not even a knock on the door. He just disappeared."

No matter how many times I explained this to her she didn't get it.

By the last week of the month, my boxes are packed, and my mind is made up. Leaving feels like the only thing I still have control over. Every day that passes only makes me more certain Summit Grove doesn't want me, and I sure as hell don't want it either.

The day before I leave, my grandmother calls up the stairs. "Sloan? Someone's at the door for you." I'm confused. No one comes to see me. My social circle consists of exactly one grandmother, one laptop, and a whole lot of spite. I already know who it is. I *feel* it before I even open the door.

Nate.

He's standing there with flowers, like this is some kind of movie moment and not the wreckage of everything we built.

"Hey," he says, unsure.

"Hey," I answered flatly, arms crossed, heart clenched. We live on the same street, and it took him *this* long to show up?

"I wanted to come over and talk—"

I cut him off. I can't let him speak. I don't want to hear it. Not the explanations, not the regret, not the whatever-this-is.

"I'm leaving," I say. "Tomorrow, and I think we should just save each other from the pain and end it now."

He blinks, like I've slapped him. I see the hurt flash across his face. For a split second, it satisfies something in me. The twisted truth is... I want him to hurt. Because if he's hurting, maybe it means I mattered. Maybe it means I wasn't the only one who lost something. He's stuttering, trying to find his bearings, and I don't give him the chance.

"I don't want to live here," I say, my voice stronger than I feel. "This town's too small for me. For what I want to do. It's holding me back."

"Sloan…" He takes a half-step forward, eyes pleading. "If we could just—"

"No, Nate," I cut him off, lacing the word with the kind of finality I had to dig deep for. My stomach twists, but I don't flinch. He looks at me—*really* looks at me—and for a second, I see the flicker of hope. It makes me ache.

"I can go with you, Sloan," he says. "Or if you just give me time I can figure out a way to go back and forth—"

"No," I say, firmer now. "I don't *want* you to."

That lands like a slap. I see it in his eyes, the way he stiffens, the way his breath catches in his chest. "I don't want to be with you, Nathan. I don't want you to come. I don't want any of this."

I see it happening in real time, the exact moment his heart broke. I'm doing to him what he did to me. Maybe that should make me feel something—relief, power, closure. But all I feel is tired.

"You'll just hold me back," I say.

The words taste like ash, but I don't take them back. I turn, hand on the screen door, bracing myself. This is it, the final cut that makes our relationship bleed out. There's no reviving it now. Before stepping inside, I glance back. His face is blank, scrubbed clean. But his eyes betray him, a glisten there he can't hide.

"Bye, Nathan," I say, using his full name like punctuation. A final period on a chapter I'm done writing.

Chapter 19

I gulp down what little dignity I have left and knock on Nathan's door just after sunrise. He answers groggily, rubbing sleep from his eyes, looking at me like I've grown a second head.

"Can we go through your mom's stuff today?" I ask, trying to sound casual even though my voice is tight with nerves.

He blinks, clearly still half-asleep. "Uh... yeah, sure. Just let me get dressed."

Only then do I realize he's standing there in nothing but gray sweatpants—no shirt, bedhead in full force. My eyes flicker up and down against my will and, of course, my face betrays me by turning scarlet. I glance away quickly, pretending to be *very* interested in the floorboards.

"I'll, um... be outside," I mumble, backing away.

I throw on leggings and a sports bra, knowing those sheds are always about five degrees hotter than the surface of the sun. When I get outside, Nathan's already at the shed, messing with the rusty lock. He turns as I approach, and for a second, his eyes trail over me. He doesn't say anything, but he doesn't *have* to. I feel a flicker of smug satisfaction bubble up. I mentally slap myself. *Sloan. Focus. We're here for Scarlett, not to flirt in front of a moldy shed.* I clear my throat and walk past him, pointedly ignoring the heat crawling up my neck.

"So, where do we start?" I ask, all business. Nathan points me toward a stack of old plastic totes, most of them labeled in fading Sharpie. One simply reads *Pictures.*

I lift the lid and start sorting through them. Inside, I find photo after photo of Scarlett, Karrie, and Tammy, spanning childhood to adulthood. There they are in grade school with crooked ponytails and scraped knees. Then high school, dressed in full glam, laughing at someone behind the camera. Later, at parties, with red solo cups and smudged eyeliner.

I can practically feel the years pass with each snapshot; the toll life started to take. You can see it in their eyes, how addiction doesn't just change your life, it etches itself into your features, frame by frame. I set a few aside, where Scarlett looked her happiest.

I lift the lid on the next tote, expecting more old clothes or forgotten odds and ends—but instead, I gasp. Lying right on top is a black jacket. *Not just any jacket.* My heart skips. I reach for it slowly, like it might vanish if I move too fast. The fabric is worn and soft in places. I can't speak. I just hold it in my hands, stunned. Nathan notices I've stopped sorting. He glances over, his brow furrowing.

"What's wrong?" he asks, moving closer. I finally find my voice, barely above a whisper.

"This jacket," I say, "this is the one. The one she was supposed to be wearing that night."

His face goes pale. For a second, neither of us moves. The shed is silent except for our breath and the distant creak of wood settling. *The jacket* sits in my hands like it's been waiting. I look at him, my grip tightening around the jacket.

"What would *this* be doing in your mom's stuff?"

He shrugs, too casually for the way my stomach is twisting. "I don't know. Are you sure that's it? Maybe it was my mom's jacket?"

I shake my head immediately. "Unless they were wardrobe twins, this is *Scarlett's* jacket. I'd know it anywhere."

He opens his mouth like he wants to argue, but nothing comes out. The air between us thickens. I turn it over, my fingers trembling as I flip the sleeves, and that's when I see it. A dark, crusted residue near the cuff. Subtle, but there. I squint, heart hammering. It's not dirt. It's not old makeup or spilled wine. It's something *else.* My breath catches.

"Do you think... do you think that's *blood*?" Nathan stands up quickly, putting space between himself and the jacket like it might bite.

"Sloan, I had no idea this was in here. I swear. I packed up my mom's things—I don't remember this."

I stare down at the jacket, my mind spinning.

"Karrie must've seen my mom after the bonfire," I murmur, more to myself than to him. "She never said anything."

"We should take it to the police," Nathan says, already reaching for his phone.

"No," I say quickly. He stops and looks at me, confused, maybe even a little alarmed.

"Sloan... what are we doing here then?" I shake my head, clutching the jacket tighter.

"The police can't even find her *file,* Nathan. What do you think they'll do with this jacket?" I meet his eyes, my voice low and steady. "I don't trust them."

He nods slowly, but I can see it in his eyes, he's unsure, maybe even a little unsettled.

"Look," I say gently, "I'll keep it sealed in a bag. If we can't come up with anything, we'll take it to them. I promise. But for now... we hold onto it."

He hesitates for a beat, then finally agrees with a quiet, "Okay." Neither of us says much after that. We lock up the shed, the weight of what we found pressing down on both of us. I slip into the house quietly, heading straight for my room. My heart pounds as I tuck the jacket into a plastic bag and hide it deep in the back of my closet.

I walk upstairs to check on my grandmother and find her sitting on the back porch, the Sunday paper crumpled in her lap like it betrayed her. Her glasses are off, but I can tell she's read every word. I hesitate before stepping out, like I'm walking into a trap. I slide into the chair next to her.

"How are you feeling?" She doesn't respond. Just stares out at the pond, lips pressed into a hard line. Her silence is louder than any answer.

"What's wrong?" I ask softly, though I already know. She slowly lifts the paper from her lap and taps the front page with a trembling hand.

"This," she says. "This is what's wrong."

I glance down and see the headline: '**What Happened to Scarlett Mercer?**' My words, staring back at me in black and white.

"I know I should've told you," I say, my voice quiet. "I just didn't know how."

"You didn't know how?" she repeats, voice sharp now, slicing through the humid air. "You knew how to write about your mother for the whole town to read, but you couldn't sit down and speak to me?"

"I thought—" I start, but she cuts me off with a wave of her hand.

"No, you didn't think; that's the problem." The sliding door opens behind us. I don't need to look to know it's Nathan. He settles into a chair nearby but doesn't speak. Even he can feel the tension vibrating through the air.

"She is *my* daughter, Sloan," Grandma says, her voice cracking. "I gave birth to her. I raised her. I lost her, and now you're digging her up and spreading her story like gossip."

"It's not gossip," I whisper, trying to keep my voice from shaking. "It's a plea. For help. For someone to come forward."

She finally looks at me and her eyes are red around the edges.

"Do you think I haven't spent years begging for help? I went to that police department every week for *months.* I called every friend she ever had. I prayed. I grieved. I *waited.*" Her voice breaks and she turns away again, wiping at her eyes angrily like she resents the tears. "After all this time, you think the answer is to throw it back in everyone's face like they forgot on purpose."

I sit frozen, ashamed and defensive at the same time. "They *did* forget, Grandma."

"Maybe," she says bitterly. "But you didn't have to remind me how little this town thinks of her. You didn't have to read their judgmental letters or field their nasty stares. I did that already. Now you've dragged it all back." Her voice softens slightly, but it's no less painful. "I wanted to protect you from that. Not because I don't want her found, Sloan, but because reopening this wound could tear you apart."

I open my mouth, but nothing comes out. She sighs and looks at me again, exhausted. "You should've come to me first. I would've helped. We could've done this together." I nod, the guilt sitting heavy on my chest.

"I'm sorry," I say, and I mean it. She doesn't respond right away. Just sits there, staring out at the pond. The silence between us isn't angry anymore, it's just... tired.

"I'm going to take a nap," she says flatly, tossing the crumpled paper back onto the table like it burned her fingers. "No one follow me, please."

She doesn't wait for a response, she just stands and walks back into the house, her shoulders set with the kind of exhaustion that doesn't come from physical pain but from heartbreak. The screen door groans shut behind her, and the silence she leaves behind hangs heavy between me and Nathan.

I drop my head into my hands, feeling like this is just my permanent position, forehead pressed to palms, trying to keep everything from spilling out. I bite the inside of my cheek, telling myself not to cry. Not again. Not in front of Nathan. God, how many times does this man have to see me fall apart?

I can feel his eyes on me, the silence between us stretching thin. I don't want comfort. I don't want a lecture. I just want... one thing to not blow up in my face. He doesn't say anything, just places his hand gently on my knee. It's nothing dramatic, no grand gesture. But Lord, forgive me, because the second he touches me, all I can think about is jumping his bones right here on this porch. If that doesn't scream 'something is morally wrong with me,' I don't know what does.

"I better go work," I say, standing up.

"Wait—you're still going to write the weekly articles?" He looks at me slightly puzzled.

"Well, I still have to do obits," I shrug. "And yeah, I am. She'll get over it. She *has* to. Because deep down, I know she needs to know what happened to Scarlett. Before it's too late. Before her time runs out."

"What's your plan today?" I ask.

"Oh, a few lawns to mow and some homework, but that's it," he says casually. I still can't believe he's in school.

I take a deep breath and ask, "Do you... want to hang out later? Maybe a movie or something?" I keep the 'something' vague, soft enough to be casual, open enough to mean more.

"Sure," he says, "we can watch one in the living room, maybe even invite your grandmother to join us."

My insides deflate. It's a sweet thing to say but all I hear is, he doesn't want to be alone with me. Not like before. Somehow, that stings more than if he'd said no. I force a smile, nodding like it doesn't bother me. Like my heart didn't just roll over and sigh with indignation.

Chapter 20

My grandmother is still a little mad at me, but she reluctantly agrees to join us for a movie. It feels like a small win, so I run with it. We go all out with a huge bowl of popcorn, cozy blankets draped over the couch, fresh Cokes from the fridge, and the soft hum of a Saturday night in the background.

"Since this whole night was my idea," I declare with mock authority, "I get to pick the movie."

Nathan groans playfully and rolls his eyes. "Of course you do."

I grin, scrolling through the options before landing on *Catching Fire*, my favorite in *The Hunger Games* series.

"Prepare to be emotionally wrecked," I say, pressing play with a little too much pride.

"We can't even start with the first one?" Nathan groans, playfully annoyed. I grin and nudge his leg with my foot.

"Nope. This is the best one and I will not be taking questions at this time." He sighs dramatically, but he's smiling too. I catch my grandmother watching us from her recliner, a knowing twinkle in her eye that I recognize all too well. I clear my throat and casually shift a few inches farther to my side of the couch. No need to give her any ideas about me and Nathan.

The movie starts, and as always, I'm completely pulled in. I've seen *Catching Fire* at least twenty times, and somehow it never gets old. About halfway through, I glance over to check on my grandmother. She's already nodding off, her chin resting gently on her chest. A knot tightens in my stomach. We can't even make it through a movie together anymore. This is the same woman who used to be bursting with life, who worked full-time driving a school bus, who took me on weekend 'field trips' to random roadside attractions just because she thought I should see something weird and wonderful. Now, a cozy night in is too much.

From the corner of my eye, I catch Nathan watching me instead of the screen. I pretend not to notice, eyes glued to the TV even though I haven't registered a single scene in the last five minutes. I look away, not wanting him to catch me staring. I try to refocus, to lose myself in the movie like I usually do, but it's no use. My thoughts are too loud, my chest too tight. So instead, I settle for mindlessly eating my body weight in popcorn, one kernel at a time, hoping it might fill whatever's hollowing me out.

We get to the part where Jennifer Lawrence's dress bursts into flames, one of my absolute favorite scenes. I sit up a little straighter, eyes glued to the screen, completely transfixed. Even though I've seen it so many times, it still gives me chills. The music swells, the flames dance, and for a moment I forget everything else—the tension, the silence between me and Nathan, the weight of my grandmother dozing behind us. It's just Katniss twirling, burning beautifully, reminding me what it's like to feel powerful.

"She's funny," Nathan says, breaking my attention from the screen.

I nod, still half-caught in the glow of the scene. "Yeah. I mean, not in this movie—but in others, *definitely*."

He shifts beside me, a little awkward. "Yeah, yeah, that's what I meant. Like... in interviews and stuff. She's got good timing. Not that it matters, I guess. I just—"

I glance over, raising a brow. "Are you nervous-talking through *Catching Fire* right now?"

He laughs under his breath, rubbing the back of his neck. "Maybe. Sue me."

I nod, indulging him. "Yeah, she is funny, *especially* in interviews. There was this one red carpet bit where she was mid-conversation with someone, and suddenly goes, *'Oh my god, this dress has pockets!'* Like, completely derailed the moment. I think about that once a week."

Nathan laughs, the kind of laugh that bubbles up and fills the room, warm and familiar. It hits me in the chest. I haven't heard that laugh in three years, and God, I didn't realize how much I missed it until now.

"So let me get this straight. Of all the red carpet moments in history, the one that lives rent-free in your head is Jennifer Lawrence discovering her dress had pockets mid-interview?"

I grin, already feeling the heat of his amusement. "Absolutely. You don't understand. Functional pockets in women's clothing are rarer than a decent man in this town."

He raises an eyebrow. "Hey now."

I smirk. "I said *decent*, not *hot and confusing*."

The second it's out of my mouth, I freeze, my eyes widening just a little as I realize what I've said. God. *Seriously, Sloan?* I look away quickly, suddenly finding the popcorn in my lap extremely interesting.

Nathan glances over, clearly amused, but thankfully doesn't say anything right away. The silence stretches just long enough for me to want to dig a hole and climb into it.

"Hot and confusing, huh?" he finally says, his voice teasing but soft.

"I didn't mean—" I start, then stop, fumbling for some kind of save. "I just meant... your whole personality is... a lot."

He laughs under his breath, leaning back against the couch, clearly enjoying this. He laughs again, leaning in a little. "You really measure quality by pocket depth?"

I inwardly sigh that he let me off the hook for the comment. I lean closer too, playful. "Well, if I can't fit snacks or secrets in them, what's the point?"

He chuckles, eyes lingering on me just a beat longer than they should. He opens his mouth to reply but thinks better of it, only smiling instead and the air between us feels warmer than the popcorn bowl on my lap.

Suddenly, it hits me like a freight train. I jolt upright, popcorn flying everywhere like confetti. "Pockets!" I blurt out, breathless with realization.

Nathan startles, nearly spilling his drink, then stares at me like I've completely lost it.

"Okay... officially concerned for your sanity," he says slowly.

"We didn't check the pockets," I say, already stepping off the couch and pointing toward the stairs like the jacket is just going to be waiting at the bottom to explain everything. He blinks at me.

"Sloan," he says with a smirk and way too much patience, "one of your absolute worst habits—besides pretending you didn't eat most of the popcorn—is starting a sentence halfway through your brain. Please, elaborate."

I'm already halfway to the basement. "The jacket! The one we found in your mom's stuff—we never checked the *pockets*! There could be something in there. A note, a receipt, *something!*"

He stands, the teasing edge leaving his voice. "Okay... actually, that's not a bad idea."

"Not a bad idea?" I toss a grin over my shoulder, adrenaline buzzing through my fingertips. "This could be *huge.*"

"Yeah," he says, trailing behind me, "but I'm not cleaning up that popcorn."

I glance over my shoulder, already bounding down the stairs. "That feels like a future Sloan problem."

He huffed a laugh. "One day future Sloan's gonna sue you for emotional distress."

"Future Sloan's too tired to press charges," I call back, flipping on my bedroom light and heading for the hidden jacket like it's a buried treasure.

"Wait," Nathan says, quickly jogging back upstairs.

I pause at the bottom step, hands on my hips. "And *you* say *I* don't explain things!"

A beat later, he's jogging back down, a pair of gloves in his hands. "I know it's been in that tote for who knows how long, and we already touched it, but... we should still try to preserve something. Just in case."

I blink at him, genuinely impressed. That thought hadn't even crossed my mind.

"Good thinking," I say, sincerity bleeding into every word.

I pull on the gloves, and reach into the front pockets, pulling out nothing but an old cigarette and some dirt. I deflate, my hope sinking, I really thought there'd be something here. I sink down to the floor, clutching the jacket a little too hard, feeling defeated. Nathan puts his hand gently on my shoulder, and I look up at him.

"It's fine," I say softly, "I just thought there'd be something…"

I start to put the jacket back in the bag when something catches my eye—*the inside has pockets.* I gasp, heart pounding with a flicker of hope. I pull out an old receipt and a folded piece of paper from the jacket pocket, my hands trembling as I fumble, trying not to hyperventilate.

I open the receipt first, careful not to tear it. It's faded, but I can make out that it's for five dollars in gas from the 24/7 Crazy 8s gas station, near the motel, and it's dated June 17th around 1:30 am. I gasp. She was at the gas station after she'd been in a car. Everyone always said she left on foot, but this receipt tells a different story. Someone she knew must have picked her up that night.

My heart races, this is the first solid piece of new information in over twenty years. I place the receipt gingerly on the ground, careful not to damage it any further. Taking a deep breath, I unfold the crumpled piece of paper. Immediately, confusion knots my stomach. It's a list of names and amounts scribbled in hurried handwriting. Some names I recognized right away, but others were smudged beyond recognition.

I look up at Nathan, uncertainty written on both of our faces. What did we just find?

CHAPTER 21

I wake up in a haze the next morning, the weight of the scribbled note and crumpled receipt still heavy on my mind. They kept me up late into the night, thoughts looping endlessly, chasing meaning in smudged ink. As I sit up my eyes land on the floor where I see Nathan, sleeping soundly. For a moment, I'm confused, but then I remember: we stayed up together, pouring over the smudged note until we couldn't keep our eyes open, trying to make sense of names blurred by time.

I grab the pillow behind my head and toss it at Nathan. "Ow," he says flatly, not even moving.

"Why are you on the floor?" I mumble, still half-asleep.

"Just where I landed," he mutters, covering his face with one hand.

"Well, one, your room is literally next door. Two, if you were that tired, you could've at least laid up here."

"It didn't seem like a good idea," he says, sitting up slowly with a groan. "Besides... you snore."

I sit up straight, scandalized, and launch another pillow at him. "I do not snore."

He laughs, dodging it. "You do, and you talk, too."

My face burns. "I—what? What did I say?"

He stretches, wincing. "Nothing too bad. Just... a lot of muttering. Something about pockets and vengeance?"

I groan, flopping back on the bed. "Great. I'm an unconscious weirdo."

"I'll take your grandma to the doctor today," Nathan says, stretching like it's nothing. "You need to get some work done. I haven't seen you do any in the last few days."

I roll my eyes. "I *can* do it," I argue.

He gives me a pointed look. I squint at him playfully. "Are you just eager to see Miss Front Desk Highlights again?"

He doesn't smile. In fact, he looks down, suddenly serious. My teasing fades, and I'm confused by his change in demeanor. "It's not her. It's that stupid doctor."

I blink. "The doctor?"

"Yeah," he mutters, eyes still on the floor. "He couldn't stop staring at you last time. It was so... unprofessional. He needs to focus on your grandmother, not... you."

My eyebrows lift as I fight a smile. Was he... jealous?

"Well," I say slowly, trying to sound casual, "I guess I'll stay and work... if you're that worried about attention being taken away from her." I glance up at him, eyes narrowing just a little. "That's all you're worried about... right?"

He dodged my question as his eyes flicked to the clock. "I better go get ready so I can get her there on time," he says, already moving toward the door. I don't call him out on it, but the way he avoids answering only makes the question hang heavier in the room.

I help them load into the car, making sure my grandmother's settled and Nathan has everything he needs, then head back inside to finally tackle the mountain of work I've been avoiding. My *actual* job, not the one I've taken on for free. Hours pass in a blur of obituaries and half-cold coffee. By the time I finally close my laptop, I've caught up as much as humanly possible.

With a deep breath, I shift gears and slide the old receipt and crumpled note back in front of me, inspecting them like they might have changed in the last few hours. Like maybe if I look hard enough, some secret will finally reveal itself.

I can't think of many people who would've picked Scarlett up that night, but I know one person who always chased after her no matter how bad things got between them. Kent. Their relationship was toxic in every sense of the word. Even as a kid, I knew something was off. There were slammed doors, shouting matches that echoed down the block, the sound of fists hitting walls and the sting of tears that came after. They were the kind of couple people whispered about behind closed doors, too volatile to survive, too tangled to walk away.

There's always a Kent on every corner. The kind of guy who tears someone down just to feel bigger. Scarlett wasn't perfect, not by a long shot, but she was *too* good for Kent by a mile. Maybe, just maybe, she finally realized that the night she disappeared. Or maybe... he made sure she never got the chance.

I search for Kent's address and balk when I find it. I can't believe that's where he's staying. Why didn't Nathan tell me? I pace, heart racing, unsure what I should do next. Should I just go over there? Nathan asked me to wait, sure, but he didn't say why. He sure as hell didn't mention *this*.

I hear a car door slam and the sound of shuffling feet entering the house. My grandmother's tired voice floats down the stairs as I move. I grab my coat, mutter that I'm heading out—no keys, no bag—and bolt out the door. Nathan stands there, confused, as I pass. "I'll be right back," I hear him say to my grandmother as I stride down the acreage.

"Sloan!" he calls after me and I don't stop. "Sloan!" He's louder now, closing the distance. "Sloan, where are you going?" His voice is exasperated as he matches my pace.

"To Kent's," I snapped, throwing him a glare. I'm mad. He stays silent, and I look away.

"Wait—Sloan, stop." He grabs my shoulder, halting me. I cross my arms, eyes locked on him.

"Nathan, do you recall saying you'd help me? Do you remember looking me in the eye and promising that?" My voice trembles, not with sadness, but with fury. "Hell, I even gave you an out. You said you still wanted to help."

I blink hard. I *will not* cry angry tears. Not now.

"Sloan-" I cut him off.

"Yet you failed to tell me that Kent—the guy you acted like you had no clue about, no idea of his whereabouts—*lives in your mother's old house*." He opens his mouth like he's about to speak, but I laugh sharp and humorless.

"Huh. So weird," I say, like I'm thinking it through out loud. "Because Kent? He's never had anything to his name. Not once, and I could *never* see him buying a house. Especially *that* house, a house that I was told was foreclosed on."

I let the words hang there, cold and heavy.

"So," I say, stepping back, voice bitter but calm, too calm, even to my own ears. "I looked into it a little more. Silly me..." I give a hollow laugh. "I must've forgotten to send your mom a *wedding gift*." I stare him down. "Because apparently those two got married not long after I left."

Nathan looks at me, and I'm shocked by the emotion in his eyes.

"Sloan... I didn't know how to tell you," he says quietly. "Yeah, they did get married not long after you left. But what was I supposed to do? Call you? Say, *'Hey, by the way, Kent married my mom'?'*"

He runs a hand through his hair, frustrated. "That house, it's been in my family for three generations. I was supposed to be the fourth. It was supposed to be *mine*. But Kent, being her husband, and my mom having no will... he got everything. I was lucky to walk away with those old totes from the shed."

He looks down for a second, then back at me. His voice cracks slightly. "As soon as she was gone, he threw me out. Just like that. Even though I'd been the one paying most of the bills. Your grandmother took me in. That's it." He sighs. "Yes... maybe I withheld that part after I agreed to help. Because I didn't want you to know he was that close. I know what kind of guy Kent is, *just like you do*. He wasn't nice to my mom either."

"I'm still not fully convinced he didn't do something to her," Nathan mutters. I stop. My chest tightens.

"Wait — Nathan..." I say softly, trying to keep my voice steady. "How did your mom... how did she die?"

He looks away, his jaw tightening. "She was high. As always. They think she fell down the porch steps when no one was around. Hit her head." His voice goes hollow. "I wasn't home that night. I came back and..." He pauses, swallowing hard. "I'm the one who found her." My heart breaks for him, because even when your mother wasn't the greatest, losing her still hurts.

"Look, we *can* go see him," Nathan says gently, "but let's do it right. Let's get your grandmother situated. Maybe even talk it through another night before we go."

I shake my head. "No, Nathan. I'm not waiting."

He sighs, frustrated. "Sloan, come on work with me here."

I cross my arms, eyes narrowing. "What did the doctor say today?"

He freezes. The look on his face tells me everything I need to know.

"Yeah. That's what I thought," I say, my voice low, trembling but steady. "I'm *running out of time*, Nathan. Running out of time to give her answers. I don't even have enough to write another article." I can see it in his face, he knows I'm right.

"Fine," he says, exhaling. "But can we give it *one hour*? Just enough time to get her dinner, settle her into her chair for the night."

I nod. "One hour," I agree, as we start walking back up toward the house. "But in one hour, if you're not ready, I'm going. *With or without you.*"

CHAPTER 22

To Nathan's credit, he rushed around for the next hour and managed to be ready exactly on time. He knows me well enough to understand I wasn't joking; I would've absolutely gone without him. I told him we should walk, like I originally planned, but he was firm about us driving the three houses down.

"Better someone sees a car outside his place," he said. "So someone knows we're there."

I scoffed. Did Nathan really think he'd try something with both of us there?

As we pulled up, I finally understood why Nathan had looked so upset. The house was a shadow of what it once was. The yard was littered with junk and trash, the lawn—once kept tidy by Nathan since he was ten—was overgrown and wild, and the gutters hung like loose threads from the roof. I hadn't even noticed it had gotten this bad when I got back. I hadn't looked. The realization stung. I was reminded of how wrapped up in myself I can get, and I silently vowed to do better.

As we approached the door, I could feel the tension in Nathan's shoulders. I wanted to tell him we could leave, but the selfish part of me screamed *no*. Nathan steps onto the porch, which now looks like it might collapse beneath him at any moment. The screen door hangs crookedly, barely attached, swaying slightly in the breeze.

He raises his hand to knock on the door, but before he can, we hear angry grumbling from the other side. "Who is it?" Nathan sighs.

"Nate," he says, voice low. I worry that won't be enough to get the door open.

"And Sloan!" I call out before I can stop myself. Nathan shoots me a sharp look, but it's too late. The door flies open.

"What do you want?" he says, glaring at Nathan.

"Nice to see you too," Nathan replies, sarcasm dripping from every word. I step in before things can go any further. As much as I despise this man, we're here for answers, and we need to get them before he slams the door in our faces.

"I'm Sloan Mercer," I say, stepping forward. "My mother was Scarlett."

At the mention of her name, Kent shifts his gaze to me. A sly smile creeps across his face. "Well, well. Scarlett's daughter, huh? You turned out to be quite a looker."

The words make my skin crawl. I feel dirty just standing there. Beside me, I see Nathan tense, his jaw clenching, and I know he's about to lose it. I grab his arm to keep him grounded.

"I just have a few questions," I say quickly. "If we could come in?"

Kent squints at me. "Questions about what?"

His hand tightens on the door, ready to slam it shut. I inwardly start to panic but hold it together and decide to bluff. It's the only card I have to play.

"I just have questions about the last night you saw Scarlett," I continue. "When you picked her up on the side of the road."

His expression doesn't change much, but something flickers in his eyes, recognition.

"Come in," he says, opening the door. As we step inside, I have to force myself not to gasp. The inside is somehow worse than the outside. The air hits me like a wall—thick, foul, and suffocating, a stench that can only be compared to the inside of a sewer. The walls are stained and grimy, with dark smudges and random holes scattered throughout like the aftermath of years of neglect and rage. I glance at Nathan, he looks physically pained now, jaw tight, eyes hard, as if each step further inside is a personal betrayal.

I stay standing, the couch looks like a dog gave birth to a litter of puppies on it and no one ever cleaned it. The room is dim, but I still catch a bug skittering across the floor, and I have to remind myself: *I'm here for my grandmother.*

"So," Kent says, throwing himself into an old chair, one I recognize from childhood visits to Nathan's house. "How do you know I picked up Scarlett?" His eyes narrow, bouncing between us.

"The cops didn't even ask me anything. Only one other person knew that, and she's dead now," he adds, looking hard at Nathan. "Did Karrie tell you or something?"

I freeze. I don't want to admit to the receipt and the list we found in the jacket pocket, and I *definitely* don't want to admit we found the jacket at all.

"Yep," Nathan says smoothly, lying without hesitation. I'm instantly, eternally grateful.

Kent scoffs. "Stupid bitch never knew when to keep her mouth shut."

I see Nathan's hands curl into fists at the sound of Kent mentioning his mother. His jaw tightens, his whole body bristling. I need to move this along *fast*. I have no idea how long I can keep Nathan from losing it on this man.

"But that's all she told him," I said quickly. "So, I was hoping you could tell us what happened after that. I'm just trying to retrace her steps. I'm trying to find her."

Kent scoffs, shaking his head like I've said something stupid. "You and I both. That bitch owes me money, just like Karrie did. At least Karrie died and I got the house. But Scarlett?" He lets out a humorless laugh. "She disappeared without coughing it up." He grabs an open beer from the side table and slurps it down, making a god-awful sound that turns my stomach.

"Well, how much did she owe you?" I ask, trying to keep my voice even, hoping to draw something useful out of him. Nathan shoots me a look, sharp and incredulous. *There's no way we're giving this man money*, the look says.

"Hundred-fifty," Kent says quickly. "Since it's been years, call it two-fifty with interest."

I curse myself for not bringing my purse. Nathan sighs and pulls out his wallet. I glance at him, surprised, and shoot him a grateful look.

"I've got two hundred," he tells Kent. "It's yours—*if* you answer Sloan's questions." He glares at Nathan for a long moment, but then his eyes shift to me.

"What do you wanna know?"

"Where did you go after you picked her up?"

"Well," he starts, leaning back with a grunt, "I made her give me the last of what she had in her wallet for gas. Like I said—she owed me money."

"Wait," I cut in, frowning. "What did she owe you money for?" He rolls his eyes, clearly annoyed I interrupted him.

"For ice," he says flatly. "I fronted her back then. I was nice enough to let my close friends pay me back when they needed a fix."

I want to scream at him. The *audacity* of this man thinking he was doing anyone a favor by selling them one of the most addictive substances, like handing out poison with a smile. As if that made him generous. But I swallow the rage, choke it down. We need answers more than I need to tell this man exactly what I think of him.

I only nod, not trusting myself to speak. "Then we came here," Kent continues. Nathan squints, clearly surprised. He didn't know that, but how could he? It was late at night, he was just a kid, and asleep.

"Why here?" I ask, voice steady despite the rage burning inside of me.

"Well, Karrie owed me money," Kent says, his voice low and hard. "And Scarlett was working off part of *her* debt by tracking down other people who owed me to make sure they paid up." *The list* I think that's what it was, it had to be.

"So, we get here," Kent says, "and Scarlett tries to make Karrie cough up the money. But Karrie's pissed. They get into it, throw a few blows. Then it really gets ugly." His voice drops, heavy with bitterness. "Karrie tells her we'd been sleeping together behind her back for months."

I try to picture if this man was ever a prize, someone worth two women fighting over. But no. He never was. Addiction is a hell of a disease; it makes people believe someone like him was worth the fight. When two best friends let someone like this grotesque excuse of a man come between them, it's heartbreaking.

"I let them have it out for a while, but I got bored and it didn't seem like I was getting any money that way, so I pulled them apart and Scarlett left. I stayed the night with Karrie. She paid off her debt in *other* ways." Kent turns to Nathan, a wicked grin spreading across his face.

"Okay, we're leaving," I say. Nathan reaches to hand him the money but drops it on the floor instead of handing it to him.

"Little shit," Kent mutters under his breath. We make it to the door, but I stop and turn back.

"One more question," I say. "When Karrie and Scarlett got into it, did they draw blood at all?"

Kent scoffs like I just asked the dumbest thing in the world. "Well, yeah," he says. "They were really going at it. Both of them looked pretty rough afterward."

I walked out the door wordlessly, careful not to step through the missing slats of the porch. I feel Nathan close behind me. We have to get out of here before we both lose it. That man was vile, but I don't think he did anything to Scarlett.

As we start toward the car, Kent yells after us, "If you ever want a real man, Sloan, come pay me a visit." I spin around and grab Nathan's arm, knowing if I didn't, he'd be back at that door in a heartbeat.

"He's not worth it," I say quietly. "Let's leave, please. I feel like I need a tetanus shot just from being in that house." Nathan nods wordlessly, and we pile into the car.

"That man..." he says once we're inside, staring ahead like he can't believe what just happened. "I don't know what they saw in him." He's echoing my exact thoughts.

I glance at him. "Rest assured, they didn't *see* anything in him. Addiction made them blind to what absolute garbage he is." I place my hand on his shoulder, and I feel him flinch.

"Let's go home." Nate whispers.

CHAPTER 23

The sun had set by the time we pulled into the driveway. I'm still trying to talk to Nate about everything we just learned, still trying to make sense of it all, but he cuts me off.

"Not now, Sloan," he says, voice tight and pained. I didn't expect being back at his old house to hit him this hard. I didn't think talking to Kent would drain him like this. I reach for his hand, resting on his lap but he moves it, placing it on the steering wheel instead. I flinch, the gesture sharper than words. Did that really just happen? The space between us suddenly feels wide and cold. I lean back in my seat, trying to swallow the sting.

"I told you," I said quietly. "I would've gone on my own." I blow out a breath, voice even lower now. "I *should* have gone on my own. This is my thing."

"Yeah, maybe you *should* have," he mutters. He's clearly mad.

"I know it's hard to hear all of those things, Nathan, but he was talking about *both* of our mothers, not just yours."

He scoffs, and I rear back, insulted. "What's that supposed to mean?" I snap, mocking his scoff.

"You know what it means."

"No, Nate, I *don't* know what it means please, enlighten me."

"It means your mom could be anywhere. She could've left, could be living another life who-knows-where. She could've lost her memory and she's wandering around, not even knowing who she is. She could've joined a cult that doesn't allow outside contact. But *my* mother? She's *gone*. She's *dead*. That house was the only thing I had left of her. Now I don't even have *that*. You still have your grandmother. She's been more of a mother to you than Scarlett ever was. She's done everything for you. Instead of letting this go like she asked, you're digging even deeper. We both know you're not going to let this go... but ask yourself, are you doing this for *you* or for your grandmother? Really think about that."

He gets out of the car and heads inside, leaving me speechless. He's wrong. My grandmother *does* want to know what happened to her daughter. She's been carrying that constant pain for years. And there's no way I'm going to let her die without at least *trying* to find out the truth for her.

I check on my grandmother. She's in her chair again, looking pale. Too pale. I step closer and feel the heat before I see it—she's drenched in sweat. My heart quickens. I place a hand on her forehead. She doesn't even flinch. I tap her shoulder. Once. Twice. Nothing. Panic grips me. I reach for her wrist and feel her pulse—it's there, but it's all wrong.

"Nathan!" I scream his name at the top of my lungs, my voice cracking. I'm losing it fast. I hear him bounding up the stairs.

"What's wrong—" But the moment he hits the doorway, he sees her. He doesn't need any explanation. "I'll call 911!" he shouts, disappearing in a flash to grab a phone.

I sink to my knees. I'm unintelligible now, crying, screaming, and shaking. A complete and utter mess.

"Please don't leave me," I whisper, clutching her hand tightly. She doesn't squeeze back. "I'm sorry for going to New York. I'm sorry you didn't think you could tell me you were sick until it was too late. I'm sorry for that time we were back-to-school shopping at Kmart, and you said I couldn't get that shirt I wanted, and I threw a fit, so you bought it for me anyway. I'm sorry for every time I said I'd hang out with you and didn't. I'm sorry Scarlett's not here. I'm sorry that, out of all people, *I'm* the one you got stuck with, because I am absolutely the worst. I'm sorry for every bad thing I've ever done. So please... Please don't leave me."

Nathan has to physically pull me back as the ambulance pulls up, and I only cry harder. My chest tightens in panic as they lift her onto the gurney. "Be careful with her!" I scream, trying to follow, but Nathan turns me around, blocking my path.

"Sloan, you have to let them do their jobs."

"She's *all* I have, Nate," I say, looking at him through blurry eyes. He pulls me into a hug, and for a moment, I can't tell if he's comforting me or holding me in place, so I don't interfere with the paramedics. Maybe it's both. They start to wheel her out, and I move forward again. "I want to ride with her," I plead, desperate. A paramedic glances at me.

"I don't think that's a good idea," she says gently. "We need to be able to focus on her. I'm sorry, ma'am you might interfere with that." I want to argue, but I know she's right. I'm a mess.

"Okay... I'll follow you," I manage to say.

"We're going to Capitol Hill General. It's the closest hospital." I nod, fumbling for the keys, but Nathan grabs my wrist.

"Sloan, you're not driving. I'll drive." I drop the keys into his hand without argument.

"Fine. Let's go. I don't want to be too far behind them."

Nathan stays a safe distance behind the ambulance while I collapse into the passenger seat, tears streaming down my face. *This cannot be happening.* I thought we had more time. The ambulance rushes into the hospital parking lot, and we follow quickly, racing to the entrance. I try to tell the front desk who we're here for, but everything I say comes out unintelligible, broken by sobs. Nathan gently moves me aside.

"We're looking for Marilyn Mercer. She just came in," he says firmly.

The receptionist nods politely. "Please have a seat. As soon as we know anything, someone will come find you."

I sit down but can't stop crying for what feels like twenty minutes. I can feel the few people in the waiting room staring at me, some with sympathy, others starting to look uncomfortable. Unable to bear it anymore, I stand and walk outside, desperate for some cool air or just to give those people five minutes without the sound of me falling apart.

The cool night air hits my face, and for a moment, I feel a small sense of relief in the open space. I hear Nathan's footsteps behind me and spin around, panic rising.

"Nate, what are you doing?" I say, voice shaky. "What if someone comes out to get us?"

He places a steady hand on my shoulder. "Don't worry. I told her we were right out here, just in case."

I exhale, letting some tension go. We stand together in the night air for a while, and I feel him looking at me. "Sloan, I'm sorry."

I look down, swallowing the lump in my throat. "Nate, you don't have to—"

"Yes, I do," he cuts me off. "What I said was shitty. I shouldn't have unloaded on you like that. None of it is true."

I sniffle. "Some of it is." The tears are back, stinging my eyes. "Since the day she went missing, all I could think was: what did I do wrong? Why didn't she want to stay? I used to stare at the sky at night, wondering if she was looking at the same sky in her new better life, without me. I know how ridiculous that sounds because I was just a kid, and I know logically I couldn't have done anything to make her leave. If she really did leave, it wasn't because of anything I did. It's because... *I wasn't enough to make her want to stay.*"

I watch as my tears hit the pavement, and I feel Nate's hand wrap around mine. It's more than I deserve.

"You're right," I say quietly. "The article... it *is* partly for me. I want to find her because if she's alive, I want to ask her *why.*" I stare at the ground, my voice barely holding together. "I've imagined it in my head so many times, what I'd say, what I'd do. It's all so selfish. Because while I'm out here writing these pointless articles, she's fading. I'm wasting time I could've had with her."

A fresh wave of guilt crashes over me. "I should've been with her tonight. Instead of dragging you to Kent's... instead of making you sit through that awful conversation." I feel Nate squeeze my hand.

"She's not all you have, you know," he says, still looking up at the sky. "You have me too." I squeeze his hand back a silent *thank you* spoken through touch alone.

"I don't think you should stop," he adds. I turn to look at him, surprised. "If it were me... I don't think I could stop either."

He exhales softly. "Your grandmother *does* miss her. I've heard her say Scarlett's name in her sleep more times than I can count. I see her flinch every time the house phone rings, like maybe this time it's Scarlett on the other end. The way she looks at those photos of Scarlett on the wall... I see the devastation in her eyes."

He looks at me now, steady and sincere. "I don't think you should stop, Sloan."

Chapter 24

It felt like hours before someone finally came to get us. The nurse appeared at the end of the hall, her expression calm but unreadable, and beckoned us to follow. We walked behind her in silence, the echo of our footsteps loud in the still corridor. Just outside the room, she turned to us, her voice low and careful.

"She's not awake just yet, but she's stable for now," she said. "The doctor will be in shortly to explain some things."

With that, she pushed the door open, and we stepped inside. I had to stop myself from gasping. She looked so pale, drained of color, like all life had been siphoned out of her. She looked like a shell of herself, like someone who had walked through something unimaginable. I moved to the chair beside her bed and sat down, reaching for her hand with trembling fingers. I held it gingerly, afraid I might hurt her even with the slightest touch. The tears came quietly, sliding down my cheeks as I whispered over and over how sorry I was.

"I'm so sorry," I told her, voice cracking. "I'm so sorry."

I felt Nate's hand on my shoulder. "Sloan, this is not your fault. She's sick. Stuff like this is going to happen."

I don't respond. If I'd been paying more attention to her, maybe it wouldn't have gotten this bad. Maybe I could've done something. We stay like that in silence until the doctor finally walks in. I try to focus, because I *need* to pay attention, I need to understand what's happening to her. But it's so hard. Everything feels distant, like I'm watching the moment unfold through glass.

"She will need to stop treatment at this point," the doctor says, voice careful, clinical. "I would highly recommend palliative care and hospice to make everything easier on her. This is something you'll need to discuss with her regular doctor, though."

I stare blankly. I can't speak. The words feel foreign, like they don't belong in the same world I was living in just yesterday.

"Wait," I manage, my voice cracking. "What do you mean *stop* treatment?"

The doctor looks at me, a flicker of confusion crossing his face, like he doesn't understand why I don't understand.

"Well," he begins carefully, "she can't keep taking treatment. At this point, it's more like physical torture. Her body can't handle it anymore. It's doing more harm than good." He pauses, like he's giving me time to absorb it, but it only makes the silence feel heavier.

"It's best to let her live out the rest of her time as comfortably as possible." I just stare at him, words caught in my throat. *Comfortable. Rest of her time.* Those phrases clang around in my head like they don't belong to her. Like they belong in someone else's story. Not hers. Not ours.

"This can't be a shock, she has stage four pancreatic cancer. Her odds were never good," he says, not unkindly, but with a clinical bluntness that makes me want to scream.

"I just thought…" I trail off, unable to finish the sentence. *What did I think?* That because she was *my* grandmother, she'd somehow be the exception? That love could outweigh diagnosis? I remember the doctor's voice from that first appointment, calm but unflinching. *Her time is limited.* I heard it. I nodded like I understood. But *this* limited?

I look at her, so still, so small in that bed. The room feels too quiet, like the air itself is bracing for goodbye. I was back to feeling like I couldn't breathe. The weight of it all felt like it was wrapped around my neck, strangling me. Every word the doctor said echoed in my skull, too loud and too far away at the same time. I heard Nate clear his throat beside me.

"Thank you," he said, his voice strained, barely more than a whisper. The doctor gave a small nod.

"I'll leave a list of recommended hospice agencies. She'll need to stay another 24 hours, so I suggest making a few calls while she's here to help make the transition home easier."

Transition home. The words felt cruel, like the final line in a book I wasn't ready to read. I held her hand, refusing to let go. Her skin felt cool, fragile, like if I let go, she might slip away entirely. I heard Nathan saying my name softly, trying to pull me back to reality.

"Sloan… we need to go home. It's the middle of the night. She's asleep, and this hospital isn't far. We'll be back." I didn't move. Couldn't. My body was still, but inside, everything was screaming. Leaving felt like abandonment. Like I was walking away from time that I could never get back.

"What if she wakes up and I'm not here?" I whispered, my voice cracking. "She'd think I abandoned her again."

"Sloan," Nathan said, more firmly this time, his hand on my shoulder. "She wouldn't think that," he added, softer now. "She knows you're here. She knows you haven't left her."

But he didn't understand. Her husband died young, Scarlett went missing and I left her for New York. It felt like all she's ever done is give, and everyone else just took. Piece by piece, life pulled everything from her. And yet she still showed up, with warmth, with love, and with grace that most people didn't deserve.

"Sloan, we need to go," Nathan said gently but firmly. "Get some rest. Call her doctors, call these agencies, get everything set up at the house. That's what she needs from us right now." His words settled over me like a lifeline, pulling me back from the edge.

"Nate…" I said, my voice barely above a whisper, trailing off as I stared at the floor. I couldn't bring myself to look at him. "I don't know if I can do all of that. Just the thought of it…"

My throat tightened. "I just…" I didn't finish the sentence. I couldn't. The weight of what was coming, of what had already happened it felt too big, too heavy to hold.

"I'll help," he said softly, "but we have to leave. We both need rest."

I nodded, barely, and stood slowly. My limbs feel heavy, like they are moving through cement. I gave her one last look before we walked out of the room. Walking out of that hospital was one of the hardest things I've ever done. Every step felt like betrayal. In the car I pressed my forehead against the cool glass of the windshield letting it ground me.

When we finally got home, I went straight to my room. Exhausted. Hollow. Still… I couldn't sleep. I sat at my desk, furious at the world. Email after email. More cruel speculation. More strangers saying awful things about Scarlett, like her pain, her disappearance, her life was some kind of punchline.

I clenched my jaw so tight it hurt, fingers trembling above the keyboard. Before I even realized it, I was typing. Fast. Furious. The keys felt like they were on fire beneath my fingertips, like every word pouring out of me was a spark, and I was finally striking the match.

Happy Sunday, Summit Grove.

Turns out Summit Grove isn't as warm and wholesome as we like to pretend. Since publishing my first article asking for any information about Scarlett Mercer, my inbox has been flooded. Let me be clear, most of those messages weren't helpful. They were cruel, dismissive and dehumanizing. I guess I expected more from this town. That was my mistake. I reached out to the local police. Do you know what I got? Nothing. Not even a properly filed missing persons report. No paper trail. No evidence that anyone ever truly cared that a young woman vanished. That kind of silence should make all of us uneasy. Because if that's how they handled her case, how will they handle yours? We like to brand ourselves as a small, sweet, simple town but that's a lie. The truth? We have a dark side. This town has a drug problem, and we've had one for years. It's been slowly creeping through the cracks of this town while we looked the other way. While we hosted bake sales and took Christmas card photos on Main Street, people were falling apart—people like Scarlett. Shame on this town for the way you've talked about someone's mother. Someone's daughter. Shame on you for forgetting that she was a person—not a rumor, not a cautionary tale, not a mistake whispered about over coffee. Shame on every single one of you who didn't even try. You could've looked. You could've asked questions. You could've cared. But you didn't. I only hope that if this ever happens to someone you care about, the outcome is different. But if history's any indication... probably not. Have fun at Sunday service today—and don't forget to dress your best. Appearances matter more than truth here, right?

Before I could second-guess myself, I hit submit—sending the post and my other work off for the Sunday paper. I exhaled a long breath I didn't realize I was holding. It felt like a weight lifting, like maybe this was exactly what I needed. For the first time in days, I thought I might finally be able to sleep. But as I lay down, the room felt suddenly cold and empty—like a place no longer meant for me. Not habitable.

I stood at Nate's door, torn between knocking and leaving him be. Slowly, I lowered my hand. This man deserved some peace. Just as I turned to walk away, the door swung open, and I was suddenly at a loss for words.

"I... um... can't sleep," I muttered, embarrassed and unsure of what else to say. Without a word, he held the door open wider, motioning for me to come in.

"I can sleep on the floor," I said softly. "I just didn't want to be alone." I felt stupid saying it, he was literally just a door away.

"No, no," he said quickly. "I'll take the floor. You take the bed." I hesitated, glancing at the bed, both of us clearly exhausted.

"Actually... how about we share it?" I suggested, heart pounding. "It's big enough. Nothing weird. Just... to keep each other company."

Nate looked momentarily shocked. "Sure," he said quietly.

"Just don't hog the covers," I teased. He snorted softly.

"Just don't snore," he shot back.

"Hey, I don't snore," I said, laughing a little before it turned into a yawn. Nate chuckled quietly beside me as the room grew still and calm. In the quiet stillness, I felt myself slowly drift toward sleep. A blanket was gently tucked around me—soft, careful, like a promise. I wasn't sure if I was dreaming or awake when strong, steady arms wrapped around me, holding me close. For the first time in what felt like forever, I finally let myself fall into a deep, peaceful sleep.

CHAPTER 25

I woke up alone in Nate's bed, the sharp ringing pulling me from sleep. I sat up slowly, trying to pinpoint where the noise was coming from. Light streamed through the windows, casting soft patterns across the room, but I still felt disoriented, like I was waking from a long heavy dream. I looked around, but Nate was nowhere to be seen. The ringing abruptly stopped, leaving an unsettling silence in its wake. Then, from above me, I heard footsteps, slow and deliberate, coming closer. I moved slowly, trying to sit up and steady myself.

Nate startled me as he appeared in the doorway, and for some reason, I felt embarrassed lying in his bed like this. He held out a mug to me, and I was surprised to see he'd brought me coffee. He handed me the mug, and I took a sip, it was exactly how I liked it.

Damn, I thought. *This man doesn't forget anything.*

"What time is it?" I asked casually, taking another sip.

"Noon," he replied. I nearly spit out my coffee.

"Noon?" I practically yelled, scrambling upright. "You let me sleep until *noon?*"

Nate raised an eyebrow, calm as ever. "Nate, there's so much to do! I need to call her doctors, the agencies, the hospital—"

"It's done," he said calmly. I froze. "What do you mean, *it's done*?"

"I did it all," he said, like it was no big deal. "I woke up early, weedeated around the pond, took a shower, called all the important places. I even have a hospital bed on the way and took apart her old bed, so it'll fit in her room." I stared at him, completely speechless.

"You're joking," I said, blinking at him. "How long have you been up to do *all* of that?"

"Just since 5:30," he replied casually, like it was nothing.

"Nate, we went to bed around two. That's, like... no sleep."

He chuckled, shrugging. "I'm fine. I'm used to it. Don't worry."

I crossed my arms at him. "You could've woken me. I could've helped."

"Sloan," he said gently, "it's fine."

"I *wanted* to help," I insisted.

He gave a small smile, calm and steady as always. "I like helping you, and your grandmother. It's not a big deal." He smiles at me, and my heart betrays me by melting instantly. *Stop it,* I tell myself. *You should know better by now.*

"What did the hospital say? When can we go pick her up?" I asked, watching as Nate started making the bed. I felt dumb just standing there, so I moved to help with my side.

"They said she's still stable," he said, smoothing the sheets as he talked. "They want to keep her a little longer, until tomorrow. The hospital bed's supposed to be delivered today, so... good timing, I guess."

My heart sank. I knew waiting one more day made sense but the thought of her spending another night there instead of home made my chest ache.

"I'm going to clean up before she gets home," I said. "I finished my work last night, so I have time."

He nodded. "Sounds good. I've got more yard work to do and a few lawns in town to mow, so I'll be out, but call me if you need anything."

"Okay," I said, watching him grab his keys and head out.

I scrubbed, dusted, and organized. Wiped down surfaces that didn't need wiping. Rearranged things that were already fine. I kept going until there was nothing left to clean.

I stepped into my grandmother's room, and the sight of it without her bed caught me off guard, an empty space that felt too quiet, too still. I moved to dust her blinds, then the filing cabinet, something I'd never really thought much about before. But now, with her condition worsening, maybe I should.

I opened the top drawer. The usual: deeds to the house, birth certificates, Social Security cards, passports all neatly organized. The second drawer was filled with a jumble of old receipts. I shut it quickly before the urge to sort through them overwhelmed me. Then I reached for the third drawer, and it was locked, catching me off guard. The drawer with birth certificates and Social Security cards wasn't locked, so why was this one?

My curiosity flared. I had to know what was inside. I thought hard about where my grandmother would hide the key, not on the keyring, that would be too obvious. If I knew her at all, she wouldn't dare do that. I checked her nightstand. Nothing. Then, crouching down, I reached under her bed and found her old sewing tin. I opened it carefully and sure enough, nestled inside was a small worn key.

Without hesitation, I slid the key into the lock and turned it. I opened the drawer and pulled out the first file. As I unfolded the papers, my eyes filled with tears. They were articles from *Ink Ever After*, the ones I had written. I realized she had kept every single one, quietly holding onto them for three years. Every article. Every mention of me. I pulled out the next file. Inside were every English paper I'd written in high school, carefully preserved the edges worn from being read and reread countless times. It was clear she had treasured them, holding on to each word like they meant the world to her.

Every file I pulled out held something from my past, work I had done over the years, all the way back to kindergarten. It was like she'd been quietly collecting pieces of me, preserving my story. I silently cried, the weight of it all settling in my chest. I'd spent so much time feeling distant, guilty, and selfish. But here she was, my biggest fan. She hated the internet, barely trusted it enough to check the weather. But somehow, she'd gone online just to print out every article I ever wrote.

Almost to the back, I grab the next file and several envelopes fall out. They were addressed to me. I opened one reading it slowly, realizing they were from Scarlett.

Hello, baby girl,

I hope you're having lots of fun with your grandmother. I know you're being on your best behavior, because you always are. I miss you so much. I'm sorry I had to leave for a while. I made some bad choices, and now I have to face the consequences. While I'm here, I'm taking time to really think, to reflect on the things I've done and make sure nothing like this ever happens again. I never want to be away from you again. I know this is hard on you and your grandmother. It's important that I say I'm sorry—really, truly sorry. I never meant to hurt you, but I know I have. I've made stupid decisions. I've made mistakes. But I promise, I'm going to do everything I can to come back to you. Things will be better. Things will be different. I drew you a picture, something you can color. Keep it safe for me, okay? I want to see it when I get back. I love you more than words can ever say.

Love, Mom

I looked down, reading through the others, tears falling freely now. Each letter came with a coloring page, carefully folded, lovingly kept. All of them had been colored by a younger me, then tucked neatly back into the envelopes. I didn't remember these letters. I must've been too young. But I remembered learning that Scarlett had been to jail a few times. I'd known that much. What I hadn't known, what I'd never seen until now—was this: She *tried.* She wrote. She sent love. She held on the only way she knew how.

Even more heartbreaking, my grandmother kept them. The envelopes were worn, the pages soft at the edges from being handled so many times. Some of them had faint, discolored spots—tiny watermarks where tears had clearly fallen. Not mine. *Hers.*

I cried harder, the ache settling deep in my chest at the thought of her sitting alone, reading these over and over. Holding onto every word. Every broken promise. She never stopped hoping—for Scarlett, or for me.

I decided that was enough. Going through the filing cabinet had already hurt more than I expected. I gently placed everything back where it belonged, except the letters. Those, I kept. My grandmother had held onto them all this time, and now it was my turn.

I put the key back in the sewing tin and took a moment to clean myself up, wiping my face and trying to look less like an emotional train wreck. I decided I was going to make Nate dinner. He's done so much, more than I have, and with everything happening, I couldn't remember the last time we shared a real, sit-down meal. Just something simple. Something normal.

I pulled out a couple of defrosted steaks from the fridge and set them on the counter. Then I grabbed the potatoes and started peeling, letting the steady, familiar rhythm quiet my thoughts. This wasn't just about food. It was a thank you. A moment of peace. Maybe even a small way to say *I see you. I appreciate you.*

I cut the steak into bite-sized pieces and did the same with the potatoes, tossing them into a skillet with garlic and herbs. The smell of searing meat and roasting garlic filled the kitchen as I finished it off with a generous drizzle of melted butter. Just as the old oven gave its faint *ding*, I heard the front door creak open.

"What is *that* smell?" Nate's voice rang out, loud and dramatic, like he'd never smelled dinner in his life. I roll my eyes but smile anyway. As he walks into the kitchen, I notice his shirt is soaked with sweat, clinging to his arms in all the right places. I can't help but admire the way it fits him so effortlessly. He catches me staring and raises an eyebrow, clearly guessing what I'm really looking at.

"Sorry," he says with a sheepish grin. "I tried to knock off a lot of this grass outside, but you can never really get it all off."

"It's fine," I say quickly, not wanting to admit that wasn't what had my attention. I grab the rolls fresh from the oven.

"Hungry?" I ask, setting the table like it's no big deal, like I'm not making this dinner just for him.

"Of course this smells amazing," he says, sniffing the air like he hasn't eaten in days. "But maybe I should take a quick shower first. Looks like you cleaned up the house. I don't want to undo your hard work." His eyes flicker back to the food longingly.

"No, don't be silly," I say, smiling. "Eat this fresh, then take a shower."

He smiles, shaking his head. "Well, if you insist." I set a full plate in front of him, watching as he takes a bite. The man literally moans. My cheeks flush, and I push down the racing thoughts swirling in my mind. I catch myself stealing glances, pushing those tempting thoughts away, trying to stop the slow-burning flame. *Focus, Sloan. This is dinner, not foreplay.*

"Sloan, this is amazing." I smile, chewing slowly. I knew it was good.

"Learned from the best," I say, thinking of how my grandmother has always been a magician in the kitchen.

"Well, no offense," he says, "but I've lived with your grandmother for over a year and eaten here plenty of times before that, and she's never made me a dish like this."

I smile to myself, a little sheepish. "Well, you know... New York's cost of living is brutal. Eating out every night? Not really an option. So, I got into the habit of playing chef. I cooked for myself almost every night and leftovers were my best friend." I give him a sideways glance, feeling a little proud of my solo kitchen adventures. "I used a lot of what my grandma taught me and put my own spin on some things. Definitely a good cook, thanks to her."

I catch his eye and add with a teasing smile, "This is my favorite meal to cook, one of the first dishes I made for myself when I moved to New York. I'll admit, I bought the cheapest cut of steak back then, but somehow it still turned out damn good."

He's watching me now, a look of amusement on his face while he chews. His eyes lock onto mine, smirking slightly.

"So... in New York, you cooked *just* for one the whole three years you were there?" I cleared my throat, unsure if he's really asking what I think he's asking.

"Yep," I admit, taking a long sip of water and looking away, feeling a little embarrassed. I didn't want him to think I'd been pining over him for three years, that I never got over what we had, not even once while I was states away.

The truth is, I wasn't pining... but I wasn't over him either. No matter what I saw between him and Taylor that night, no matter the hurt and pain it caused me, you don't just get over a love like that. At least, I don't. Maybe he did. For all I know, he dated Taylor for a while after I left. Hell, he could be with someone now and hasn't said a word.

I flush, thinking about the times I've kissed him since I've been back. I clear my throat. "What about you?" I immediately cursed myself, that was *way* too obvious.

"Nope," he says, and I'm annoyed by the short response. I wanted him to say something more. I wanted him to look at me and admit he couldn't get over a love like ours no matter how hard he tried. But I guess the same could be said for me.

I glance out the window, trying not to sound pathetic. "I mean, I got asked out a few times. I went on one date but it didn't go anywhere. Cancelled a couple more. Just... really busy, you know?"

I'm hoping this makes me sound less like I spent three years hung up on him.

He nods, then says, "Well, I didn't see anyone or go on any dates." His voice sounds a little tight, like I said something wrong. I don't know what I could have said wrong, we weren't together then, and we're not together now.

I tell myself to leave it alone, but I stupidly ask anyway. "What's wrong?" I say, my voice softer than I intended.

"Nothing," he mutters, and my annoyance peaks—I mean, what did I even do wrong? I cooked him dinner, for God's sake.

"Nate come on, if you have something to say, just say it."

He puts his fork down and locks eyes with me and those green eyes stop me cold. Did they get more intense while I was away? Or is that just a special trick he pulls on me when he's serious?

"I just thought..." he trails off, eyes fixed on his now-empty plate like it was suddenly the most fascinating thing in the world.

"Spit it out," I say, impatience creeping into my voice.

He finally meets my gaze, voice low and hesitant. "You started calling me Nate again... and I thought I felt something. Like old times." My heart skips. The weight of those words hangs between us, thick and electric.

"Nate, I don't think it can ever be like old times... and I think you know that." I meet his eyes, even though it hurts, because I can see that what I said has hurt him.

"Right," he says, grabbing his plate to clear the table.

I say quietly, "I'll clean up. You go take a shower."

He walks away, and I cringe as the bathroom door slams shut a little harder than necessary. The house suddenly feels suffocating, the walls felt like they were closing in on me. I get up, trying to clear my head, willing my racing thoughts to slow down but nothing works. Frustrated, I decide I need to get out. Grabbing the keys, I leave a note for Nate on the counter and head out for a drive.

I start driving, not really sure where I'm headed. Since I've been back, I haven't been out much, and almost everywhere I've gone has been with Nate. I lived in this town my whole life before I left. I tell myself I'll be fine.

The sun slowly sets as I drive, and I lose track of time. Passing Crazy 8's gas station, an idea strikes me: What if I went to the bonfire? It's Saturday night, I'm sure there's one happening behind the motel right now. These things are always the same. Hell, sometimes even the same people.

I pull up and stare at room 13, cringing as I try not to think about Nate. Walking behind the motel, I found the bonfire just like I thought, people were scattered around, drinking and talking loudly. I never understood how this was fun, but so many in town seemed to. Scanning the crowd for anyone familiar, I spot several coolers, the usual scene.

"Hey, you!"

A woman stumbles toward me, maybe Scarlett's age. Her face feels familiar, but I can't place her. She's clearly drunk, maybe high, or both.

"You work with my mother," she slurs, squinting at me.

"Hey," I say cautiously. "Emily, right?"

She scoffs, like her name's an insult. Her shirt's lopsided, hair wild in the wind.

"Yeah, you're Scarlett's daughter, aren't you? The one who wrote that snotty article," she spits out. I tell myself not to argue, she's clearly wasted.

"Yeah, but if you'll excuse me—"

"You know you got my mother in trouble for publishing that," she interrupts, slurring the words. I pause, unsure if it's true coming from her.

"She hasn't said anything," I mumble, glancing around, hoping to spot someone I know so I can bail.

"Well, she wouldn't because she feels bad for you and your grandmother... and your whore of a mother who went missing," she snaps sharply. Her words hit hard. I glare at her, but her expression doesn't change. "You know, I was dating Kent back then and she had the nerve to try and collect money I owed to Kent, like we didn't already have something worked out."

Another person who was on the list.

"Did you see her that night?" I ask, suddenly not caring about escaping this conversation anymore.

"Yeah, she tried to shake me down," Emily admits, voice slurring a bit. "I wouldn't give her anything. Told me I had a week to pay up." She scoffs, rolling her eyes like it's some joke.

"You know, Kent was dating you, her, and Karrie," I say bitterly. She ignores me, looking away and scanning the bonfire for someone else to bother. Stumbling, she heads toward someone sitting on a cooler. Squinting through the flickering firelight, I realize it's Kent. I follow behind her, anger bubbling up inside me. Kent's presence here, probably selling his supply to vulnerable people, spreading his poison through the town, it infuriates me. He won't stop until everyone is as miserable as he is.

Halfway there, I pause to grab a wine cooler from an ice chest. As I twist off the cap, a sharp flashback hits me—the night I saw Nate and Taylor together. The memory stings as much as the bitterness I feel right now. Taking a long drink, I steel myself and walk up to Kent just as I hear Emily laying into him.

"I mean, how many people *were* you dating besides me? How many people are you dating *now* besides me?" Her voice rises, shaky but fierce. Kent squints at me over her shoulder, the silent accusation clear—he knows I'm the one stirring this mess.

I smile at him sweetly, just enough to let him know it was me. He deserves that smile, and so much worse. I take a slow sip of my drink, eyes locked on Kent, one eyebrow raised in silent challenge as he sneers at me like he's the victim here.

Pathetic. I shift my gaze, scanning the other side of the bonfire, and that's when I see her.

Taylor. She's standing there with a red cup in her hand, laughing at something someone just said. With half my drink gone and a mess of emotions tightening in my chest, I start walking toward her. I don't know what I'm going to say—if I'm going to say anything at all—but something in me pulls me toward her anyway.

By the time I reach her, my drink's gone, and a warm buzz settles just beneath my skin. Taylor's eyes widen when she spots me, blinking like she's not sure I'm real.

"Sloan… it's you," she says, clearly surprised.

"Hey, Taylor," I reply, keeping my tone light, casual, like we didn't share a complicated history. Her eyes drop to the empty bottle in my hand and then flick back up.

"You want another drink?" she offers, like it's a peace offering more than anything else. I shake my head, giving a small wave.

"No, thanks." I fell silent. I didn't want another one, I was already feeling light on my feet. In other words, I'm a total lightweight.

A silence settles between us, not hostile, just heavy. The kind that comes when the past presses gently against the present, reminding us it's still here.

I stare at her, trying to see it—whatever *it* was that made Nate throw away *years* of friendship, trust, and love for just one night. What did she have in that moment that made her so irresistible? What made her the choice instead of me? Instead of calling, explaining, holding on to *us*—he chose *her*. My skin prickles, the air between us crackling with static, and I know she feels it too. She shifts, visibly uncomfortable under the weight of my gaze.

"Taylor," I say, my voice bolder now, steadier, like the heat in my chest finally found its voice. "Why Nate?"

She blinks at me, confused. "What?"

"Three years ago," I clarify, my words crisp even if my heart is anything but. "You were with Nate, and we were still together. I just want to know... why him?"

She looks at me like I've lost my mind. "Sloan... are you *seriously* asking me about some hook-up from three years ago?" She lets out a sharp laugh, dry and dismissive. "I mean, come *on*. Does it even matter now?"

The words hit like a slap. Her tone is careless, like the end of my relationship—everything Nate and I were—was barely a blip on her radar. Like it was just another night to her. Nothing. My stomach turns. I feel the heat rise in my chest, my jaw tightening.

"I mean, from what I heard, you were in New York. I'm sure you've dated a ton of people since then. Besides, Nate and I were never a thing after that night—not that I didn't try," she mutters, annoyance dripping from every word.

I don't even know what I'm doing as I reach out and shove her, and whatever's in her red solo cup spills all over her shirt. She stares at me, furious.

"You crazy bitch," she spits.

"Takes one to know one," I sling back like a stubborn kid, even though I know it's childish. I want to blame the drink, but it's more than that. I'm just so damn angry, angry my grandmother's sick, angry Nate and I didn't work out, and angry this town is so freaking awful. Maybe I hadn't thought this through. *Wow, you think, Sloan,* I chastise myself.

Then Taylor suddenly shoves me hard, and I stumble backward, hitting the ground with a thud. Panic claws at me from the inside. Everyone here's probably mad at me for one thing or another, and I can already feel the heat of a mob mentality starting to spark around us. This could get ugly—*fast*.

"Sloan!" someone yells, and before I can even process it, an arm yanks me up. I'm blinking, confused as hell, staring right at Nate. Wait, where did *he* come from? Didn't I leave him at home? I took his damn car, didn't I?

"Come on," he grunts, dragging me away from the bonfire like I'm a stubborn puppy on a leash.

"Wait!" I gasp, trying to catch my breath, but he just keeps dragging me along like I'm a stubborn suitcase.

"Nate!" I say again, but he's got that serious look and doesn't even slow down.

"You're hurting my arm," I snap, tugging it free. "I can walk on my own, thanks." He falls into step behind me, making sure I stay in his line of sight.

"Give me the keys," he demands. "You're not driving my car after you've been drinking." I roll my eyes.

"I'm not stupid, Nate. I've had one drink." He scoffs.

"Right," he says with a smirk. "'Cause the Sloan I know goes around pushing people in the woods. Hell, the Sloan I know doesn't even drink."

I toss the keys at him as we reach the car, crossing my arms like a stubborn kid. "Maybe you don't know me at all anymore."

CHAPTER 26

I sit in silence as Nate drives, arms crossed like I'm auditioning for *Grump of the Year*. But curiosity, that nosy little gremlin, eventually wins.

"How'd you get here anyway? Better yet, how'd you know where I was?" I ask, stealing a glance his way. He doesn't answer right away. Finally, he shrugs.

"Well, this is a newer car... it's got a location app."

Turning to the window, I try to imagine already being home, wrapped in a blanket burrito, washing this entire evening off me with a scalding shower.

"I took your grandma's car to come find you," Nate says dryly. "We'll have to swing by the motel in the morning before she gets back."

I sigh, rubbing my temples. Yeah, this night's been one for the books.

"So... why'd you push that girl?" he asks, trying to lighten the mood.

"That girl? You mean Taylor? You know her pretty well," I shoot back, arching an eyebrow. He looks at me like I've lost it.

"What are you talking about?"

"That was Taylor," I say, watching his face but he keeps his eyes on the road. "You knew her pretty well three years ago anyway." We pull up to the house just as the words leave my mouth.

"Sloan, what the hell are you talking about?" Nate asks, his voice sharp. Is he seriously joking? Pretending it didn't happen?

"Nate, no need to hide it," I say firmly. "I know what happened. I've known for three years." He's staring at me, expression blank, like his mind's gone somewhere else entirely. But I keep going, because apparently, he's really going to make me spell it out.

"Three years ago. Right after we fought. You weren't calling me back, you were so mad... I went by your house a dozen times, and you were never there." My voice cracks, but I don't stop. "I ended up at a bonfire, just like tonight. And you were there. With *her*."

That finally gets a reaction. His face shifts and a look of pain flashes across it, sharp and sudden. He remembers. Of course he does.

"I saw you," I say, quieter now. "I saw you go into a room with her. Fairly hot and heavy, from what I could tell." He doesn't speak. Just grips the steering wheel like it's the only thing keeping him grounded.

"Don't worry, Nate. I'm not mad about it anymore," I say, though the words taste like a lie, and if tonight was any indication, I'm definitely still a little mad.

"Mad?" he repeats, his voice low, edged like a blade. "Why would you be mad, Sloan? Why would you even *have the right* to be mad?"

I stare at him, stunned. It's like the air's been sucked out of the car. My chest tightens. I can't tell if I'm more shocked or hurt.

"Are you serious right now?" I ask, my voice thin, brittle with disbelief. He gets out of the car without another word, and I scramble to keep up as he storms into the house. The second the door shuts behind us, he whirls around, face-to-face with me, anger simmering in his eyes.

"You've got some nerve, Sloan. First you blindside me by applying to a job in New York without saying a word. Then, after one fight—*one*—you tell my *mother*, of all people, that you're taking the job and to pass the message on to me? That you're just… leaving?"

I stare at him, completely confused, like I've stepped into a fever dream. Did I drink more than I thought?

"What the hell are you even talking about?" I shout, matching his volume now. If he's going to yell, then so am I.

"So, I make out with someone after *you* leave me, and *you're* mad?" He throws his hands up, incredulous. "I forgave you for everything, Sloan. I'm here, helping you—*willingly*—and you're seriously trying to tell me you're mad about something that happened when we weren't even together?"

I'm trying to shake off what I'm hearing, like somehow I've misheard him, misunderstood all of it.

"Nate, what are you even talking about?" My voice rises with each word. "I didn't break up with you. Not until *you* showed up at my door with flowers. We were *not* broken up when I saw you making out with Taylor at that bonfire." I'm following him downstairs now, breath catching in my throat. "And don't even try to deny it. You went into a room with her that night, you clearly slept with her. Why else would you go in there with her?"

He stops short and turns around, eyes sharp. "Do you have X-ray vision, Sloan?" he snaps, turning to face me again. I stare at him, stunned. "No, you don't, and if you had stayed a little longer, you'd know I left shortly after that. Even though we were broken up at the time, it still didn't feel right."

He turns back around, heading to his room like he didn't just drop a bomb in the hallway. I stood frozen, the weight of it sinking in. This whole time, I thought he slept with Taylor. I thought he did it to hurt me. Now he's telling me he didn't.

"Nate," I say, grabbing his shoulder to stop him. He doesn't turn, but he doesn't pull away either. "I didn't decide to break up with you until I saw you at that bonfire. I didn't take that job until after I saw you with her." He's frozen in place, listening. "I went by your house every day to talk to you before that. Your mom always said you weren't there. Every time, I asked her to pass on a message. I called you, over and over, and you never called me back." I swallow, the words scraping on their way out.

"The last time I saw your mom, I might've said something about New York. But I never said I was going. And I never said we were over." The silence between us feels deafening. Finally, he speaks, his voice quiet and fragile.

"I ran my cell phone over with a lawnmower," he says. "After we fought, I went to work the next day, and... yeah, I ran over my phone. I told my mom to tell you if you stopped by."

He turns toward me with tears in his eyes.

"Are you seriously telling me my own mother lied to me? That I cheated on you because of her lies? Do you even realize what that means? I lost three years—*three years* of my life with you—because she wanted me to be as miserable as she was. I was stupid enough to believe her, to let her poison my mind, without even having the guts to ask you myself. I trusted her.

She twisted everything, and I believed her." His voice breaks, tears spilling over, and I pull him close, resting his head on my shoulder.

If anyone else had done this, I might have been shocked. But Nate's mom… she made him pay every bill, kept him tethered. She must've been terrified he'd leave if I did. Suddenly, it all made sense, the silence, the distance, the mistrust. It was all so tragic.

I cup his face gently between my hands, searching his eyes. "Nate, for the past three years, I've never stopped loving you. I couldn't even think about anyone else. I love you so much… I was mad at myself because it hurt so damn much." I don't know if it was him or me, or some messy mixture of both, but suddenly our lips crashed into each other, and it was *everything*.

Chapter 27

I'm entranced by his lips, lost in the way they move with mine, feeling soft, certain, and familiar. I'm falling into him fully, completely, without a single care in the world. I'm so close to him, our bodies pressed together, his hands on my back like he's anchoring me, grounding me in the best way. Somehow, it still doesn't feel close enough. Like we're trying to make up for three years in the span of a single breath.

His lips brush my cheek, then my jaw, slow and deliberate now. My heart stutters at the contact, and I can't help the way I lean into him. There's no hesitation, no fear, no anger. Just *us*. Every part of me is humming, not from nerves, but from recognition. This is where I've always belonged. Right here.

My hands slide beneath the hem of his shirt, fingertips brushing the warm skin of his chest. He's definitely filled out over the last three years—stronger, broader— my mind can't help but marvel at the difference. It's familiar and new all at once, and I feel a strange kind of ache in my chest, like I'm touching not just the person in front of me, but the time we lost. He watches me, eyes soft, as if he's memorizing the way I look right now. Like he's marveling at me too.

"I want you," I say, my voice steady and sure, so there's no room for confusion, no chance for another misunderstanding between us. His eyes lock on mine, something raw flickering in them, and for a moment neither of us breathes.

Before I can say anything else, he lifts me effortlessly, and instinct takes over as my legs wrap around him. My body responds before my brain can catch up, every movement between us charged, familiar, and electric. My lips find his again, and before I know it, we're in his room, and he's sitting me down on his bed gingerly. Without any hesitation I pull off my shirt.

He pauses, eyes locked on me, and the look on his face is nothing short of awe. He traced a finger down my collarbone, his touch leaving a trail of fire. He continued down, his fingers tracing the edge of my bra. I shuddered as he reached the clasp, undoing it with ease. He pushed the fabric aside, his eyes darkening as he took in the sight of my bare breasts. He cupped them, his thumbs teasing my nipples. I moaned, my head falling back as he leaned down, taking one into his mouth. He sucked and teased, his tongue swirling around the sensitive bud. He moved to the other, giving it the same treatment.

I could feel the heat building between my legs. He continued his exploration, his hands moving down my body, tracing the curve of my waist, the swell of my hips. He hooked his fingers into the waistband of my pants, pulling them down along with my panties. I reached for him, my fingers clumsy with urgency as I tug at his shirt. When it finally slips off, my hands find his skin, and I close my eyes for a second, letting the reality of this moment sink in. The warmth of him, the steady rise and fall of his chest beneath my touch.

"You have no idea how many times I've dreamt of this moment," he said, his voice husky. He knelt before me, his hands on my hips, his breath hot against my inner thighs. He looked up at me, his eyes filled with a hunger that made my whole body shiver.

I gasped as he leaned in, his tongue darting out to taste me. He licked and sucked, his tongue delving into my depths. I tangled my fingers in his hair, holding on as he drove me wild with his mouth. I swear, I could see stars as his fingers entered and moved rhythmically inside me.

"You're driving me crazy, Nate," I whisper. "I need you."

He took his time, lavishing attention on every inch of me, his tongue and fingers working in tandem to bring me to the brink of ecstasy. He moved slowly, deliberately, as if memorizing me all over again. Every touch felt intentional, his hands mapping my skin like he was rediscovering something. The way he looked at me—like I was the only person in the world—made my heart ache in the best possible way. My body arched beneath the overwhelming pleasure, my breath coming in short gasps. I was close, so close, and I wanted him inside me.

"*Please*, Nate," I gasped, my fingers clutching at the sheets as I struggled to stay in control of my own body. He didn't need any more encouragement. He positioned himself at my entrance, his eyes meeting mine. I nodded, my body tensing in anticipation.

He thrust into me, his body claiming mine. I cried out, my body arching beneath him. He moved inside me, his thrusts slow and deep. Our bodies moved together, like a symphony reaching its crescendo. In that moment, nothing else existed—just heartbeats, warmth, and the quiet understanding that this was more than longing. It was love rediscovered, raw and real.

My nails raked down his back, as I writhed beneath him. I could feel the familiar coil of pleasure building inside me as his thrusts became more urgent, his body driving into mine with a desperation that sent me over the edge. My release hit me like a wave, my body convulsing beneath him. Nate's thrusts became more frantic, his body seeking its own release. He groaned, his body shuddering as he found it.

For a moment, time stood still. He leaned in, resting his forehead gently against mine, his beautiful green eyes locking with mine in a gaze that felt endless. In them, I saw everything, his hopes, his fears, the quiet vulnerability he rarely revealed. He was unguarded and completely open. I felt my love for him, it was fierce and endless, the certainty of it settling in my bones. He moved to lie beside me, his eyes locking with mine—and God, I could look at him forever.

"I've missed you, Sloan," he said, his voice thick with emotion. I smiled, reaching out to gently caress his cheek. We were both breathless and spent, but the silence between us felt full in the best way. He rested his forehead against mine, his gaze steady—like he was seeing me for the first time and the thousandth, all at once.

"I love you, Sloan," he said, voice low but sure. Tears pricked at the corners of my eyes, not from sadness, but from the overwhelming joy of finally hearing those words after three long years.

"I love you too," I whispered, pressing a soft kiss to his lips. In that moment, with his arms wrapped around me and our hearts finally beating in sync, I felt like I was finally home.

CHAPTER 28

I woke up the next morning and felt the stillness in the air. For a split second, it was as if no one was sick, I hadn't moved to New York, and Nate and I had never broken up. Just a moment, but then reality hit. All of those things *were* true. I stayed still, not wanting to panic beneath the weight of that false comfort.

Nate's arms were wrapped around me, his breathing slow and steady in sleep. Even in rest, I could feel something different radiating from him, an energy I couldn't ignore. My heart felt heavy. We hadn't thought last night through. It was too impulsive. What the hell were we doing sleeping together when we were supposed to be focused on taking care of my grandmother, and finding Scarlett? Maybe I have an aversion to stability. Or maybe it's something deeper, something in my blood, this need to make wild, reckless mistakes.

I heard my phone vibrating on the floor and tried to get up to answer it without waking Nate, failing to do so. He stirred, grinning at me lopsided and half-asleep, those damn green eyes staring straight into my soul. My heart clenched, and I looked away, scanning the floor for my phone. Diane's name flashed across the screen. Of course she was calling. I mean... the article wasn't exactly nice.

I took a deep breath and answered the phone, summoning the energy I knew this call was going to demand.

"Diane, hello!" I said, sounding absolutely chipper, which was about a million miles from how I actually felt.

"Sloan, I'm going to need you to come see me at the office this morning." I stuttered, caught off guard. I hadn't expected this to be an in-person conversation. If I was going to be chastised, I'd much rather it be over the phone.

"Well, I actually have to pick up my grandmother from the hospital today..." I said, hoping to appeal to Diane's softer side.

"Sloan, this is not up for debate. I need you to come see me as soon as possible. I expect you here within the hour. I'll be waiting." She hung up and I stared at my phone, stunned. I couldn't ever recall hearing her angry. When I looked up, Nate was already watching me, his expression serious.

"I, uh... I have to go see my boss at the paper," I said quietly.

He looked confused. "Why?" I glanced away, avoiding the question. "Sloan. What's going on?"

Still, I didn't answer. He got up, pulling on his shirt, and a wave of last night's memory crashed into me. A spark. A mistake. I hated how easily I let myself get distracted by him. He left the room, heading upstairs, and I wondered if he was mad at me for ignoring his question. But it was much worse when he came back, holding the Sunday paper. I wanted to crawl into a hole. Maybe hide in my room and never come out. He stood there reading it, his face unreadable.

"Sloan..." he whispered, "this is not good." I looked away, unable to face the disappointment in his eyes.

"I may have let my anger at the town seep into the article... a little too much." I say attempting to downplay it.

"Sloan, *a little?*" he snapped. "You called out the police department, and in the same exact article, you called the whole town cruel and conceited!" His voice rose, and I felt my defenses snap into place. My body went rigid, my subconscious slipping straight into the fight-or-flight mode it knew too well. I shot up from the bed.

"So what? They *are* all of those things! They treat people like Scarlett and Karrie like they're nothing but the dirt on the bottom of their shoe. Why should I sit here and pretend otherwise?" My voice shook with fury. "They let people like Kent run around ruining lives and don't even blink." I looked him straight in the eyes. "Do you think I'm wrong?"

He closed his eyes, unable to meet mine. "Sloan, you're not wrong, I'm not saying you are. But this is a small town. This has been going on for years. I live here. I work on a lot of these people's lawns. I rely on that work to get by, especially while I'm saving up and paying for school."

"Nate, *you* didn't write the article. *I* did. I still don't understand what that has to do with you." I watched him, waiting—needing—to hear it. Why my words, my truth, suddenly felt like a threat.

"Sloan, you know why it matters," he said quietly. "Once people know we're together, it won't take long before your words become *mine* in their eyes. That's how it works here." I stared at him. Wasn't that what I wanted him to say? Wasn't that what I'd been waiting to hear?

"Nate... last night was just one night." My voice softened, but my chest ached. "We don't know what this is. We don't know what we're doing. We can't just pick up like the last three years didn't happen." My voice dropped.

"You were out kissing someone else the moment you thought we were over, like we were nothing. Like what we had didn't matter. I can't just forget that." I paused, swallowing the lump rising in my throat. "I waited for you after that night. I waited for you to come and say it didn't mean anything, that it was a mistake. If you had shown up, if you had come to me, I would've taken you back right there and then."

I shook my head, eyes stinging. "But you didn't. You waited *weeks* to come to my door. Weeks where I cried myself to sleep thinking the boy I'd loved since I was thirteen didn't love me the same way. I was broken. Losing you broke me."

My voice cracked. "You broke my heart, Nate. Whether it was a misunderstanding or not, you never came to check on me when I disappeared. You just froze me out. I thought you were my *best friend.* You showed me you couldn't even be that."

His face twisted with pain, and suddenly, I didn't want to have this conversation anymore.

"Listen," I said, pulling myself together, "I have to go talk to Diane. Clearly, she's upset about the article. After that, I need to pick up my grandmother and get her settled."

I felt hot tears sting behind my eyes, fighting to hold them back as I gathered my clothes from the floor. Just as I turned to leave, he reached out and grabbed my arm, gentle but firm.

"Sloan, I..."

I silently begged him not to say any more. This man cannot be my undoing again. Once in a lifetime was more than enough.

"I can take you to get your grandmother's car," he says quietly, pulling my arm free. "I'll pick her up, and you go talk to Diane. Then we can meet back here."

He intertwined his hand with mine. "When you're ready to talk about this, I'll be waiting. Patiently." He looked into my eyes. "But Sloan... don't run. Just... think about giving us a chance."

I don't say anything. I can't. His hand is still warm in mine when I gently pull away. I leave his room without answering, the weight of his words pressing against me. Behind my closed door, I let the tears fall as I silently mourned everything we were, everything we could have been, and the future I'm so afraid of.

CHAPTER 29

My stomach felt like it was doing somersaults as I pulled up to the *Summit Gazette* office. I thought the ride to pick up the car from the motel was awful, but I was sure this would be just as bad. I walked in cautiously, making my way toward Diane, whose face was already wearing a clear expression of agitation.

"Sloan," she says, acknowledging me with a look that scans me up and down. "I've received so many calls today about your article. When I ran your first one, I didn't think much of it. I mean, I've known your grandmother for years, and as a mother myself, I want her to find her daughter. People didn't like it, but it wasn't anything too awful, so I let it go. Unfortunately, I didn't review *this* article. I didn't think you'd talk about the town you were raised in in such a way."

I look down, knowing I didn't regret the words I wrote, I meant every one of them. But maybe... maybe I should've thought twice before pressing send. When my grandmother reads it, she will be livid. If she was upset about the first article, she'd be furious about this one.

"So now," Diane continues, voice sharp, "I've missed church, had a call from the owner of the *Summit Gazette*, the *very* person who keeps the one paper we publish each week afloat. On top of that, I've gotten calls and emails from half the town. They're mad, Sloan. They want you fired."

Of course they do. They didn't like it when the mirror was turned on them, they didn't like being reminded they were just as human as the people they looked down on. They clutched their pearls, convinced there was no way *they* could have flaws of their own.

I sigh, having no idea what to say. She'd been an amazing English teacher back in high school, always praising my work, always pushing me to write with purpose. She gave me this job the moment I asked for it, and I repaid her by jeopardizing her livelihood.

"Diane, I'm sorry. I don't even know how to explain what I carry every day. My whole life, I've heard one thing about Scarlett, just one story repeated over and over. I watched my grandmother carry it, like a weight she never got to put down. Now I carry it too, and I'm *tired*. So damn tired of pretending it didn't happen, or that it didn't matter, or that it doesn't still hurt. Because it does. It *always* hurts. If you need to fire me, I get it. I won't hold it against you. But I'm not sorry for what I wrote. That's how people in this town act, and I know you know that. The same reason I know why you need this job." I look at her, pleading for her to understand.

"Your daughter, Emily... she's an addict, isn't she? Just like Scarlett. You try and try to help her. You ask yourself where you went wrong. You take the late-night calls for money, the calls from jail, the knocks at the door when she needs a place to stay. You do all that and still wonder why it never gets better. You beg her to be better, to get clean. She says she will. But something always throws her off track, and it's always next time. You think this is as bad as it can get? It's not. You could have no idea where your daughter is. You could have no idea if she's coming home. You could live more than twenty years not knowing. Meanwhile, the town talks. They say vile things about her. They don't understand that beneath all the addiction, she's still your daughter. Someone who used to draw you pictures as a kid. Someone who used to give you the best hugs. They don't know the person behind all the bad things they're saying."

Diane sighed and looked at me, tears glistening in her eyes. "You know Emily?" Her pain was so raw, so palpable that it made me ache for her.

"I met her the other night, behind the motel. She was at a bonfire with... um... Kent."

She scoffed in disgust. "That man is a menace to society. Ever since Emily met him, she's been nothing but a mess. It's like he chewed her up and spit her out."

"She thinks she loves him," Diane said bitterly, "she says I don't understand. But I know what he is. He finds vulnerable women and slowly reels them in. Gets them hooked, and from there, it's over."

She looked worn out, unable to argue any further. "Sloan, I don't want to fire you. Trust me, I don't. But you cannot write those articles anymore. I need this job. I can keep you on for obituaries, but that's it."

I nodded, knowing I had no choice. It was either this or no job at all. As I turned to leave, I remembered the list and took a shot in the dark. What did I have to lose?

"Diane, I know this is hard, but do you recall when Scarlett was around, did Emily ever say anything about her collecting drug debts from her?" Diane looked up, surprised.

"How did you know that?"

I kept a straight face, not wanting to know she was the one who had told me.

"I just found some of my mother's old things and was wondering... so it's true?"

Diane sighed and pressed her hands to her head. "Yes. Unfortunately, when I found out, I didn't take it well. I called your grandmother and told her daughter to leave mine alone. She was in the dark about Scarlett collecting drug debts until then, so it caught her off guard. As far as I know, it ended up getting settled. Emily never mentioned it to me again."

I nodded and murmured an apology for asking, but Diane just gave a tired wave of her hand, like she was too worn down to be upset. Even though it was only a small detail, I knew it was another piece of the puzzle, one I didn't have before. Article or no article, I was still going to try my damnedest to find Scarlett.

CHAPTER 30

I let out a frustrated groan as I pulled into the driveway. Nate had beaten me home, which could only mean one thing—my grandmother had too. He met me at the door, his expression carefully neutral.

"I threw away the paper," he said quietly. "She hasn't asked for it. Just said she wanted to lie down for a bit."

I gave him a grateful smile. "Thanks." He looked at me, a question in his eyes.

"I still have a job... for now," I said, trying to sound more okay than I felt. "I just can't write the articles anymore. Just obits."

He stared at me with a look of pity. "Sloan, I'm sorry... I know how much those articles meant to you."

I looked away, swallowing the lump rising in my throat. It wasn't just about the writing. It was about being heard, about telling the truth even when no one wanted to hear it.

"I thought maybe," I said quietly, "if I laid it all out someone would finally listen. Someone would care."

Nate didn't say anything right away. He just stood there, and for a second, I thought he might hug me or say something that would make it worse. But then he nodded, slow and steady.

"I care," he said. "I'm still listening, even if no one else is."

I gave him a tight smile and stepped past him into the house before my emotions could spill over.

"Is she in her room?" I asked, not turning back.

"Yeah," he said softly. I didn't wait for anything else. I headed to her room, the floorboards creaking under my feet.

I peered into her room and saw her lying quietly in the hospital bed Nate had delivered. An oxygen tank stood beside her, its gentle hum the only sound in the room. A chair sat next to the bed, pulled close, angled just right. He'd put it there for me. The afternoon light slipped through the curtains in thin golden lines, casting a soft glow across her face. She looked smaller than I ever remembered.

I stepped inside, careful not to make too much noise. She heard me and turned her head, her face lighting up the moment she saw me. My heart felt instantly lighter. It was like a breath I didn't realize I'd been holding and finally let it go. It felt like weeks since I'd seen her, even though it had only been two days. I had no idea how I went three years without her.

"Hey, Grandma," I said, sitting down in the chair beside her.

"Hey, sweetie. You okay? Nate said you were sleeping in."

Of course he didn't tell her where I really was. He was protecting me, *yet again.*

"Yeah, I was just tired," I said softly. "But I'll sit with you for as long as you want."

Even though I was running out of time to find Scarlett, I was also running out of time to spend with her. I couldn't decide which was worse, but I couldn't be in two places at once either. I sat with her in peaceful silence, watching reruns of *Dateline*, going back and forth about each episode like we used to when I was younger. It never got old.

"That Keith Morrison is a fox, isn't he?" she said, her eyes twinkling. I laughed, the sound surprised even me.

"You've been saying that since I was ten," I said, shaking my head.

She gave a small shrug, a mischievous smile tugging at her lips. "Well, some things never change. He's aged like fine wine, that one."

I leaned back in the chair, the cushion slightly too thin, but I didn't care. It was one of those rare moments that felt untouched by time. For a few minutes, we just sat there. She commented on suspects like she knew them personally and I chimed in with my own theories. It felt like coming home to a version of myself I hadn't seen in years.

She drifted off, her breathing slow and even, and I sat there feeling the sadness settle in, the moment was over. I slowly got up and stepped out into the living room, only to be surprised by the sight of Nate. He was hunched over his textbook and laptop, studying away with quiet focus. It was clear he stayed nearby for my sake, because that couch didn't look like a comfortable place to study at all. I sat down next to him, not saying a word. He looked up at me, his eyes soft but unreadable.

"Thanks for putting the chair in there for me," I said to him quietly.

"What did Diane have to say?" Nate asked, his eyes searching mine. I looked away, taking a slow breath.

"Well, people want me fired, but I'm sure you guessed that. She spared my job, but I didn't leave empty-handed." He furrowed his brow, waiting. "I found out Emily was on that list. Not only that—Diane found out. She even complained to my grandmother about it. She said when she called my grandmother, she had no idea Scarlett was collecting drug debts from people in town."

I looked at Nate, and he was thinking what I was thinking—this was another thing that broke my grandmother's heart. Every time Scarlett did something wrong, I knew my grandmother took it personally, like she hadn't done a good enough job raising her.

When Scarlett stole money from her for the first time—*crack*. When Scarlett tried drugs for the first time—*crack*. When Scarlett went to jail for the first time—*crack*. The first time Scarlett crashed her car, out of her mind high—*crack*. When she pawned her wedding ring, and my grandmother never got it back—*crack*. When she found out Scarlett was collecting drug debts—*crack*. Scarlett goes missing—the final *crack*, and every year after, her heart breaks over and over again. All the while, raising me, a daily reminder of Scarlett.

She went through life raising me as if those cracks weren't there. But I loved her so much, I could feel each one as if it were my own. She stayed in this town just in case Scarlett came back. Year after year, she endured the whispers, the looks, the judgment. All for the chance that one day, the door might open, and Scarlett would walk through it. That kind of hope was brutal.

"I'm still going to try and find Scarlett," I said, my voice barely above a whisper. "Even if I can't write an article about it. Even if no one cares. Even if I don't make it in time..."

I couldn't say the rest. The words stuck in my throat, heavy and sharp. Saying them out loud felt like a curse, like naming something we all knew was inevitable would make it all too real.

"Unfortunately," I say, leaning back against the couch, "the list of suspects is long. Who knows how many names were really on it? The list we found was old and faded. Probably not even complete."

Nate nodded, his brows furrowed. "There's no telling how many more people she crossed that never made it onto paper."

"Exactly," I say. "Which makes this feel impossible some days. Like trying to trace shadows." But even shadows had a source, and I wasn't done chasing them.

Chapter 31

I told Nate I was going to run out and grab some groceries while my grandmother was sleeping. He offered to come with me, already halfway to standing, but I shook my head.

"Someone has to be here with her," I said. "Besides, you really should be studying. I keep interrupting." He looked like he wanted to argue, but instead he gave me a small smile and sat back down.

"You're a welcome interruption," he said, his voice carefully folded in warmth just for me. I didn't know what to say to that, so I just nodded, grabbed my keys, and slipped out the door.

I stuck to the local grocery store, even though part of me considered driving out of town. I didn't have the energy for anything more than familiar. As I pulled into the lot, I silently prayed Taylor didn't work there anymore. The last thing I needed was a confrontation. I grabbed a cart and pushed through the automatic doors, keeping my head down and my thoughts steady. Just groceries. I moved through the aisles, grabbing things that were easy to cook, frozen meals, soups, simple ingredients. It'd mostly be Nate and I eating them anyway. My grandmother's appetite was slowly fading, no matter how hard I tried to tempt her.

In the candy aisle, I paused, scanning for the circus peanuts she used to love. I figured surprising her with them might earn a small smile. That's when I felt it, someone behind me. The kind of presence that crawled up your spine before you even turned around.

"Well, isn't it Scarlett's daughter again," a voice sneered. I didn't have to look. I knew the voice. I knew the stench—sweat, stale cigarettes, and something rotting just beneath the surface.

Kent.

I turned slowly, already bracing myself. He was leering at me, eyes bloodshot, a smug twist to his mouth like he thought he had some kind of power. I turned away, refusing to acknowledge him. Kent thrived on making people squirm and I wasn't about to give him the satisfaction. But he caught up quickly, his cart bumping against mine, loaded with beer and junk food. I kept my eyes forward, jaw set.

"Oh, what—you can't hear me now?" he said, voice edged with annoyance. I didn't answer. He cut me off, shoving his cart sideways into the aisle to block mine, forcing me to stop. He leaned in just enough to make my skin crawl.

"What do you want?" I said through gritted teeth.

"You think you can just go around causing problems for me? Causing problems with Emily the other night at the bonfire? Your little article you wrote?"

I barked out a laugh, truly unfazed by him. "I wasn't aware you could read, Kent."

He stepped closer, his rancid breath hitting my face like a punch. But I forced myself not to flinch, meeting his eyes without backing down.

"I'm not playing with you, Sloan. Stop sticking your nose in things that don't concern you. Stop running your mouth like you know what you're talking about—or I'll put something in it to shut you up." His hand shot out, gripping my forearm and sliding down in a way that made my skin crawl.

"Get the hell off me," I whispered, trying not to cause a scene. Not sure it mattered anyway—the whole town read the article and probably hated me for it. I yanked my cart forward, slamming it hard into his side. "In case you forgot—I'm not Scarlett. You can't bully me or intimidate me like you did her. You're a menace to this town, spreading poison like it's your personal mission to make everyone as miserable as you are."

He laughed, like this was some kind of joke. "Oh, honey, you have no idea how many of these people beg me for their next fix. I've had people offer me their firstborn just for one hit. Women who can't get enough of me in this town."

I scoffed, stepping closer. "They only do that because you're the one holding the next fix. They wouldn't want anything to do with you if it wasn't for that. Face it, you're a one-trick pony. Without that one trick, no one here would be impressed by you. No one would need you. No one would be throwing themselves at you. Hell, they wouldn't even know your name."

I smiled cruelly. His face shifted, *finally*, I'd hit a nerve. I backed away, turning to leave the aisle. I was done with this conversation, done with this waste of space. I was almost out when his voice slithered after me.

"Well, your mother sure loved me. Did any and everything for me. Let me do whatever I wanted to her. The offer still stands, if you ever want to know what a real man is. If you ever get tired of Nate... come see me. I'll show you, just like I showed your mother."

Even with my back turned, I could feel his eyes raking over me. I rushed out of the aisle, straight to the checkout. It took *everything* in me not to turn around and kill him right there in the middle of the store. I shoved the groceries onto the checkout belt, barely remembering what I'd even picked up. I don't even remember walking to the car. Just the cold metal of the handle and the way my hands shook as I opened the door.

Once I was inside, I slammed it shut and sat there, gripping the steering wheel like it was the only thing keeping me upright. My breath came in short bursts, shallow and furious. My jaw ached from how tightly I was clenching it. The things he said about Scarlett. The way he looked at me. I wanted to scream. Hit something. Be violent in a way that would make the world feel even for just a second.

Instead, I sat there, surrounded by bags of groceries and the sound of my own heart pounding. I silently promised myself that I would make Kent pay. Scarlett deserved better. My grandmother deserved better. *I* deserved better. I wasn't sure how yet, but I wasn't going to let Kent rot another woman from the inside out. Not ever again.

Chapter 32

I decided I was going to cook dinner, not just to work out the frustration of the day, but to try and have a real meal with my grandmother. Something small and simple. Chicken noodle soup, made easier with the rotisserie chicken I'd picked up in a haze at the grocery store. I added a side of bread, hoping the comfort of it might coax her into eating even a few bites.

Nate helped her to the table while I set everything out. To her credit, she sipped at the broth, slow and steady, and after a moment, she smiled.

"This is good," she said, her voice thin but warm. "Really good." I smiled back, heart lifting just a little.

"Well, I learned from the best," I said, tipping my glass toward her.

Nate nodded in agreement, tearing into his bread like it was the last carb on earth. My grandmother managed a few more sips before she started pushing the food around her bowl. She didn't say anything, but I knew the signs. She was done eating but didn't say so, probably afraid of hurting my feelings.

"I'm full," I announced, louder than necessary, giving her an easy out. "You want to play some cards, Grandma?" Her face lit up, just a little, but it was enough. A flicker of life.

"Do I ever," she said, setting her spoon down. "I was hoping you'd ask."

Nate cleared the table while I shuffled and dealt out the cards. We decided on gin rummy—her favorite.

"Don't go easy on me," she warned, narrowing her eyes as she adjusted her cards. "I've still got a few tricks left."

"Please," I smirked, "I've seen you bluff Nate out of a full house with a pair of sevens. You're a card shark in a cardigan." She let out a raspy laugh, one of those full-body chuckles that made her shoulders bounce.

We played three hands, full of playful jabs and exaggerated groans every time one of us drew a bad card. Nate narrated like he was a sports commentator until she threatened to throw her slipper at him. But by the third hand, I could see her arm trembled slightly when she lifted her cards, her breathing just a little more labored. I placed my cards down, face-up.

"I'm beat, and I'm tired of you beating me," I said with a tired smile I didn't feel. "You want me to help you get ready for bed before I turn in?"

She looked at me for a moment, her lips curling into a faint, grateful smile. I helped her get ready for bed, her voice soft with embarrassment as she apologized here and there for needing the help at all.

"I'm sorry you have to do this," she murmured as I guided her to sit.

"Grandma," I said gently, brushing a blanket over her lap, "it's my pleasure. There's no place I'd rather be."

I meant it. Not just because she was sick. Not just because the clock was ticking louder every day. I meant it because

I would do anything for her. Once she was settled in bed, I reached for the small bottle in the nightstand and shook out a pill into my palm. But as I handed it to her, she lifted her hand and shook her head.

"I don't want that." I hesitated, confused, she was clearly in pain. Her breaths are shallow, her body taut.

"Grandma, they're for your pain," I said gently, sitting on the edge of the bed. "I *know* you're in pain. There's no reason to suffer when you don't have to."

She looked away, her voice barely above a whisper. "Stuff like that is why Scarlett was taken from me."

I felt one of those all-too-familiar cracks bloom in my chest. I sat next to her, quietly unfolding an extra blanket across my lap. I didn't want to upset her by arguing with her.

"You're not sleeping in that chair all night," she said, narrowing her eyes at me. Concern edging her voice. Of course, that *was* exactly what I had planned to do.

"No, I'm not," I said, flashing a soft grin. "I just wanted to sit with you for a while. Or is that not allowed anymore?"

She gave me a tired, almost amused look. "You always were a smart mouth." I pulled the blanket up and leaned back, letting the quiet settle in between us. "So... what's going on between you and Nate?" I froze, caught completely off guard.

"How did you even—?" I started, eyes wide. She gave me a knowing smile, eyes twinkling despite the weariness.

"Even a sick old woman can tell," she said with a sly smile, her eyes sparkling despite the fatigue. "But to be fair, that boy has loved you forever. It's not hard to see." I hesitated, looking down at my hands.

"It's complicated," I admitted. She reached out, gently squeezing my hand.

"Complicated is how all the good things start."

I smiled at her, unsure where to begin or how to put the jumble of feelings into words. "I don't know... we're not together or anything," I said quietly, "but he made it clear he *wants* to be." I glanced down at my fingernails, wanting to tear at what was left of them.

"So... what's the problem then?" she asked, her voice gentle but firm, like it should be as simple as that—he wants to be, so I should just accept it.

"Part of me wants to say yes," I admitted, surprising even myself by opening up. "But another part is scared to." She watched me closely, waiting for me to say more.

"I'm just ...scared that if I'm with someone—whether it's Nate or someone else—I'll grow complacent. I'll rely on them. I'll love them with my whole heart, my whole soul. They'll leave me, and all the wreckage they caused will be left in their wake." I swallowed hard, the words catching in my throat. "I'm scared I don't deserve it. I mean... What did I do in this lifetime to deserve that kind of love? What if I'm the one doing the wrecking?"

She reached out, her hand warm over mine. "Honey, love isn't about being perfect or never making mistakes. It's about finding someone willing to stay through the wreckage, because they see *you*, not just the mess around you."

I looked at her. "But we already left each other a wreck once. I spent three years thinking he did all the wrecking. I realize now—we both did. Before I left for New York, I said mean, hurtful things instead of trying to figure out what was wrong between us."

She was silent for a moment, and I thought she had drifted off, until she spoke again. "You know that pond out back? The one I love."

I smiled at her. "Yeah, the one Grandpa dug for you just because you wanted it."

She let out a tiny laugh and looked at me. "Yeah, that's the part of the story we tell everyone. It's cuter that way, without all the messy parts in the middle."

I stared at her, confused. What messy parts? The story I'd always been told was sweet, just Grandpa digging that pond, and her delight when it was finished. I blinked, surprised. It wasn't the whole story? Suddenly, the picture I'd held onto felt a little less clear.

"Your grandfather used to love to gamble. After we bought the house, I thought it would let up, but it didn't. I stayed silent. Then I was pregnant with Scarlett, and I thought it would stop then—but it didn't. By that time, I was at my wit's end. After he got off work, he'd be at the casino until late, and I was home alone. I kept asking myself, *Is this going to be the rest of my life?* Sitting at home with a child, essentially a single mother, waiting for my husband to come home. Struggling to pay bills because he was gambling it all away. The day came when I was done. I decided I wasn't going to put up with it anymore. I called him at work and yelled, telling him I was tired, tired of being alone every night without him. I told him if he didn't come straight home that night, I was done. Oh, and, by the way, he better have fudgesicles when he gets home, because I was mad, pregnant, and craving them."

The story I'd always known was warm, loving, and simple. Hearing it now, painted in such raw, painful colors, shocked me.

"Do you know what happened that night? He showed up with a box of fudgesicles and apologized. Told me he didn't realize how much I hated him being out every night, didn't know I had such a problem with his gambling. He didn't see it because I never said anything. He told me he loved me more than anything and would stop gambling, because I was the most important thing to him. I was annoyed, why would I have to say anything? Didn't he know I was miserable? Didn't he understand we couldn't afford to gamble all the time? I went to bed mad that night, but I didn't leave because he came home like I'd asked. I told myself the moment he went back on his word, I was done. The next morning, I woke up and found him out back, digging that pond."

She smiled a soft, fond smile that seemed to light up the dim room. "He was home every night after that. If he was even going to be a little bit late, he'd call me before leaving work."

I looked at her, a mix of shock and awe washing over me. Shocked that I'd never heard this side of their story before and in awe that despite it all, they had worked through it.

"We had other arguments over the years, of course, it would be unrealistic if we didn't. But we always talked them out, because I learned from that first time that if we didn't communicate, we couldn't fix what was wrong. After every argument, he'd bring me home a box of fudgesicles, that was our way of saying it was over."

I smiled softly, picturing the small but meaningful gesture. I nodded slowly, letting her words sink in. It all seemed so simple—love, communication, forgiveness—but somehow, I'd never thought of it that way before. If I could rewind and do things differently with Nate, I would, in a heartbeat. But time doesn't work that way. I can't take back the things I said, the walls I put up, or the moments I pushed him away.

"Besides, I don't want to worry about Nate and me right now. I'm more focused on spending time with you and taking care of you."

She scoffs, then suddenly starts coughing, her breath coming out ragged and uneven. I quickly grab the oxygen mask and hold it gently to her face. She takes a shaky breath through the mask, her eyes watering. As she takes shaky breaths through the mask, I can feel my heart pounding, helplessness twisting in my chest. I hate seeing her like this, so fragile and struggling for air. Every cough feels like a punch to my gut. After a moment, she manages a weak, "Thanks..."

I squeeze her hand, desperate to give her some comfort. "You okay now?" She nods, looking at me with tired but steady eyes.

"Sweetie, I'm sorry to say this, but we both know I don't have a whole lot of time left. That's just the unfortunate truth." Her voice softens, but there's a weight behind it that sinks deep into my chest. "Whether you think you deserve to be happy or not—which you do—I want you to have someone there for you when I'm gone. Nate is a good man. I mean, he's going to school just to impress you, and he's done so much for me." She pauses, searching my face. "You don't have to figure everything out right now. Just... don't close yourself off. Let him in, even if it's scary."

I nod, tears falling freely now, the thought of losing her hurting more and more every time I hear it. No matter how gently she says it, no matter how much I try to brace myself, it never stops feeling like the ground is slipping out from under me.

"I'm not ready," I whisper, barely able to get the words out. She squeezes my hand with what little strength she has left.

"No one ever is sweetheart."

I blink back fresh tears, my chest tight. I can't tell if she's talking about losing someone or loving them.

I stay sitting with her until she drifts off, her breathing slow and shallow, the room wrapped in a hush that feels sacred. I feel myself starting to nod off too, but I force myself to stand, planning to crash on the couch, close enough to hear her if she needs anything.

When I step into the living room, I stop short. There's Nate, asleep on the couch, slightly slumped to one side. His textbook is open on his lap, one corner hanging dangerously over the edge, about to hit the floor. His laptop rests on the armrest, long gone into sleep mode. He looks completely worn out, like he fought off sleep until it won. The sight of him warms something deep in my chest.

I grab a blanket from the hall closet and gently drape it over him, careful not to wake him. His textbook slips into my hands as I lift it off his lap and set it on the coffee table. He doesn't stir, completely knocked out, his mouth slightly parted, his brow finally relaxed. I settle onto the other end of the couch, pulling my legs up and curling into myself. The space between us feels smaller than it used to. Safer. I watch him sleep for a moment, the soft rhythm of his breathing lulling me into calm. I fight the urge to shift closer, to rest my head on his shoulder, to give in to whatever this is trying to become between us. I hear him mutter, his voice soft and muddled by sleep. For a second, I think he's waking up. I glance over, but he's still out, his face peaceful.

"Sloan," he murmurs, just above a whisper. "I love you… don't leave."

I hold in a gasp, my chest tightening. All this time, I thought I was the only one haunted by what happened between us. But this… this wasn't just a one-sided ache like I convinced myself. He'd been carrying it too. I blink back tears, his voice echoing in my head as it brings me back to what my grandmother said earlier about love, about communication, about staying even when it's hard.

I lean my head back against the couch and whisper, *"I love you too, Nate."*

Then I close my eyes and let the weight of the day finally pull me under.

CHAPTER 33

I wake to the sound of clinking dishes and soft movement coming from the kitchen. Blinking the sleep from my eyes, I glance over, expecting to see Nate gone—but he's still there, curled into the same spot, the blanket slightly askew, his chest rising and falling in a steady rhythm. Still fast asleep. Panic jolts through me as I shoot up, heart suddenly pounding. If it's not Nate, then...

Either we have an intruder or my grandmother is up, alone.

I move quickly but quietly, careful not to wake him. Every creak of the floorboards under my feet feels like a warning bell in my ears. My mind races with possibilities, worst-case scenarios threading through every breath. She wasn't steady last night. What if she fell?

I reached the kitchen and let out a breath I hadn't realized I was holding. She's standing at the sink, hands in soapy water, slowly washing dishes. The stove is off, and there's no sign of anything dangerous. Just the familiar clink of plates, the sunlight cutting soft patterns through the curtains.

"Good morning," I say, trying to mask the panic in my voice with casual cheer. She glances over her shoulder and smiles faintly.

"Morning, Scarlett." I freeze. My mouth goes dry, and the room suddenly feels too quiet. I stand there, caught completely off guard by the slip, by the time warp her mind's dragged us into.

"Do you want anything before you head to school?" she asks, still looking at me like I'm someone else. Like I'm her daughter. Like we're years into the past where nothing has gone wrong yet. I don't know what to say. I open my mouth, then close it again. My heart cracks a little under the weight of her confusion, under the ache of what she's remembering. I force a small smile.

"No, I'm okay," I whisper, my voice barely audible over the sound of the water.

"Are you coming home after school today or staying out again?" she asks without looking up, still washing dishes as if everything in the world is right where she left it. I pause, watching her back, the way she was moving, steady and sure, like this is any normal morning and she's just a mother with a child headed out the door.

"Straight home," I answer softly, praying it's the right response, that it won't shatter whatever gentle place her mind is in. She turns to me then, her face lighting up with something that looks so much like joy, it nearly undoes me.

"Well, that's so great. We can have dinner together; it's been a while." I nod slowly, swallowing past the lump rising in my throat.

"Yeah… that sounds nice." She smiles and goes back to her dishes, humming a tune I half-recognize from my childhood, and I stand there in the kitchen doorway, torn between heartbreak and something that might be gratitude, for this small, borrowed moment where she gets to believe nothing ever went wrong.

Nate walks in, rubbing the sleep from his eyes, still groggy, his hair slightly tousled. The floor creaks under his step, and at the sound, my grandmother turns. Her whole demeanor shifts in an instant. Her shoulders stiffen, her smile fades like it was never there. The warmth drains from her eyes, replaced by something colder. Wary and defensive.

"Scarlett," she says, her voice sharper now, "what's he doing here?"

I freeze, my pulse quickening. I glance at Nate, whose brows furrowed in confusion. He looks between us, unsure whether to speak. I lift a hand, palm out, signaling him to stay quiet. He obeys, trusting me, though he looks concerned.

"Don't worry," I say gently, stepping closer to her. "He's not staying long."

Her eyes flick between us, still uncertain.

"I don't want him in this house, not after what happened last time," she mutters, turning back toward the sink. Her voice trembles, not with fear, but with anger. "I don't trust him. You shouldn't either." I can only think of one person she would have this much distaste for.

"Who, Mom? Kent?" I ask cautiously. She looks at me sharply, eyes narrowing.

"Scarlett, I told you a thousand times, I don't want you seeing that boy. He's no good for you, and I don't understand why you can't see it." Her voice cracks with frustration, maybe even a little pain. "He's the reason you crashed your car. The reason you skipped all those classes. He's poison, Scarlett. I'm trying to protect you."

I smile to myself, the word *poison* echoing in my mind. It's strange how both my grandmother and I see Kent the same way: toxic, draining, a danger that needs to be kept far away.

"It's okay, Mom. I won't see him anymore, *I promise.*" I pull her into a soft hug, guiding her toward the table.

"How about some coffee?" I say, settling her into a chair. She nods, still a little agitated, rubbing her temples.

"I couldn't find the Tylenol... I have a headache," she mutters. I glance back at her as I pour the coffee, careful not to let my concern show too much. I've hidden all her meds so she can't take any without us knowing. I set the coffee down in front of her.

"Okay, Mom, I'll go find you some. Just wait here." I grab the pills she's been refusing, and in her confusion she doesn't notice. I breathe a quiet sigh of relief, finally she'll have a few hours where the pain isn't so sharp. We sit in silence for a few moments, sipping our coffee. Waiting for her to come back to the present. I finish my coffee and stand up, stretching my arms a little.

"Do you want some more?" I ask her gently. She looks up at me, her eyes a bit heavy, tired, but she nods slowly.

I smile softly, feeling the warmth of the coffee cup in my hands as I pour a fresh cup, the rich aroma filling the quiet kitchen. The steam curls up, fogging the cool air between us. When I set the cup down gently in front of her, the ceramic feels smooth and solid against the worn wooden table. She looks up at me.

"Thank you, Sloan" she says, her eyes heavy but clearer now, and offers a small, grateful smile. The faint clink of the cup against the table seems louder in the stillness. For a moment, the soft hum of the fridge and the distant chirp of morning birds outside are the only sounds. It's a fragile truce, but she's really here, back to the present with me.

"I'm tired, hun." I stood to help her, but before I could move, Nate appeared quietly at my side, he must've been listening, making sure everything stayed okay.

"I'll help," he said gently, reaching out to steady her. She took his arm and gave him a grateful smile, her eyes lighting up just a bit.

"Thank you, Nate." I start folding the blankets on the couch, the soft fabric rustling beneath my hands. From the other room, I catch their voices drifting through the quiet house. "

You know, you should just talk to her again," Grandma says gently to Nate. "People change all the time."

Nate chuckles softly. "I'm not sure she'd change her mind that fast, and I don't want to pressure her into anything."

A quiet *tsk* from Grandma. "You're such a good man, Nate. I hope she does change her mind. I want her to be with someone as great as you."

I let out a soft sigh, feeling the weight of her words, knowing she means well. They sit and talk for a while longer, their voices soft and steady, filling the quiet house with a fragile warmth. Then, gradually, the room falls silent, I can only assume she's drifted off to sleep. Nate walks into the living room. I glance at his textbook and laptop neatly placed by the couch.

"Did you get a lot of studying done?" I ask. He comes over, picking them up as he sits down.

"Yeah, I did... uh, thanks for covering me up last night. You could've gone to your bed; I was planning to sleep on the couch for the night shift." I nod, my eyes fixed on him, feeling a sudden pull, as if I could just fall into him right now, if only I let myself.

"So... you never said what's up with the college classes?" I ask, trying to keep my voice light, even though the question has been sitting heavy in the back of my mind. Especially since my grandmother mentioned he was doing it to impress me.

Nate looks down, running a hand over the back of his neck. "I've been taking classes for about a year now... just a few here and there. Trying to find my footing." His voice is quiet, careful—like each word might break if he says it too fast. "At first, it was just something to focus on. But eventually, I realized... if I ever got a second chance with you, I didn't want to still be the same guy you left. I wanted to be better. Someone you could actually picture a future with."

He lets out a shaky breath, his eyes flicking up to meet mine. "So, I started with this. A few classes. It might be stupid—I know a couple of credits won't fix the past—but I needed something. Something to show you, if you ever asked. Proof that I'm not just standing still." His voice softens. "When you left, you said this town was holding you back, that *I* was hold-ing you back. If you ever decide to give me a second chance, I want to be someone who moves with you, not someone you have to leave behind."

His words hit me like a wave, impossible to ignore. I wasn't sure what I expected him to say, but it wasn't that. Not the quiet way he laid himself bare, not the thought that he'd been silently working to become someone better, not for show, not out of guilt, but for the *slim hope* that I might come back. I felt a tightness in my chest, part grief, part something softer. The same kind my grandmother talked about when she told me about the fudgesicles—quiet, deliberate gestures of love that said more than words ever could. He wasn't asking me for anything. Not forgiveness, not a relationship, not even an answer.

"Nate... I need you to know, *I do* love you. I meant what I said the other night." His eyes flick up to meet mine, and in them, I see hope, raw and aching, like he's been holding his breath for years waiting for this moment. "But you also need to know... I don't know if I'm staying here. Not after my grandmother is gone."

I watch the hope shift in his face, like he's bracing for something he knew deep down might be coming.

"This town... there's just so much weight here. People look at me like I'm the problem, like I stirred up things that should've stayed buried. The article didn't help. And Kent..." My voice tightens. "He's going to corner me every chance he gets over and over again."

I pause, swallowing hard. "It's like I can't breathe here."

Nate opens his mouth, probably to protest, but I lift a hand, gently stopping him.

"I'm not going to ask you to leave with me." The words come out softer than I expect, but steadier too. "Even if you said yes—even if you swore you wanted to—I know you. You'd hate New York. The noise, the pace, the people. You'd shrink in a place like that. I couldn't live with knowing I dragged you somewhere that made you feel small, just to be with me." The silence that follows hangs between us.

"It's not 'just to be with you,'" he says, his voice low and tinged with frustration, but not anger. "You don't get it, Sloan. You don't seem to understand how much I love you. I'd do anything for you. I'd go anywhere. I should've followed you three years ago. I should've fought harder. Should've begged you to tell me why you left the way you did."

He runs a hand through his hair, frustration turning into desperation. "But I didn't. Maybe I was scared. Scared of what I'd hear. Scared that you really didn't want me anymore." His eyes searched mine, raw and pleading. "I've spent all this time trying to fix myself, not because I'm some perfect guy now, but because I want to be the kind of man who deserves you. The kind of man you won't have to question."

He exhales slowly, as if letting go of a heavy weight. "I'm not asking you to decide anything now. I just need you to know... I'm still here. I'm still not giving up on us." He leans a little closer, voice soft but steady. "So if I went anywhere with you, it wouldn't be *'just for you.'* It would be for us."

I stay quiet, words caught in my throat, my heart pounding loud in the silence. Part of me wants to lean in, close the space between us, just to feel that connection again.

"Wait, what do you mean Kent cornered you?" Nate's voice shifts—edges sharper, a mix of concern and something fiercer beneath it. I freeze, realizing I just let something slip I'd been holding back. I'd been keeping it from him, knowing how he might react. I clear my throat, trying to play it cool.

"I... um, was just being dramatic," I say, waving it off like it's no big deal. Nate leans in, eyes locking onto mine with an intensity that makes my heart skip.

"Sloan, tell me."

Were his eyes always this green when he was upset? And why did it suddenly feel kind of... hot in here?

Get it together, Sloan, I think desperately. *He's looking at you.*

I take a deep breath and finally admit, "Okay, fine. I ran into him at the store... and we exchanged words. They weren't exactly nice. Not to mention, the guy's still a grade-A creep."

Nate's jaw tightens, his fingers clenching into a fist at his side. He takes a slow, steadying breath, then reaches out, brushing a stray lock of hair behind my ear with a gentleness that contrasts sharply with the tension in his voice.

"Why didn't you tell me sooner?" he asks quietly, eyes searching mine, a mix of concern and frustration. He stands up, pacing a bit, running a hand through his hair. "That guy's not going to keep messing with you. I swear, Sloan, I won't let him."

His voice is firm, protective, a promise and a warning all at once. Then, he stops and looks back at me, softer now. "You don't have to deal with this alone. Not ever."

I reach out and gently take his hand, squeezing it softly. "Nate, please… just leave it alone." I look up at him, hoping he'll trust me enough to let this go—for both our sakes.

He leans in closer, so close our faces almost touch. His breath is warm against my skin as he says quietly, "I won't do anything for now… but no promises if it keeps happening." There's a fierce protectiveness in his eyes that makes my heart skip. I swallow hard, trying to steady my voice.

"I can take care of myself," I breathe out, feeling weak with him so close makes me want to melt into him. The effect he has on me should be illegal.

He holds my gaze, his voice low but firm. "I'm aware you can hold your own, Sloan. I'm telling you, that you don't have to do it alone."

I close the distance between us and kiss him, rough and unhesitating, like the tension between us had finally snapped. It's messy and charged. He responds without hesitation, his hands gripping my waist, pulling me closer. When he bites my lip, sharp and deliberate, it jolts something in me, heat curling low in my stomach. I gasp and force myself to pull back, barely. My breath is ragged, my heart pounding. Our eyes lock, and I see the raw need, untamed and hungry reflecting right back at me.

"Downstairs," I murmur, voice low and certain. He doesn't question it, just follows.

Chapter 34

I brush against the rough texture of the wall as I pull him close, my breath coming in short, eager gasps. The room downstairs was dimly lit, the soft glow of the lamp casting long shadows across the space. It felt as if the world outside had ceased to exist. I could feel the tension in his muscles, a tightness that mirrored my own. This wasn't like the other night, this was raw, unfiltered, and undeniably rough. It was exactly what I needed. Every touch, every press of his body against mine, felt like a release, as if he were pulling the stress from my veins and leaving me lighter, *freer*.

I slipped my shirt off and he pressed me against the wall, his hands firm on my hips, his lips finding the curve of my neck. I tilt my head back, exposing my skin to him, a silent invitation. His teeth grazed my collarbone, light at first, before he found my breast, his lips parting to suck gently before he bit down. It wasn't hard, but it was enough to make me hiss, my nails digging into his back as if to mark him as my own. The sensation was electric, a jolt of pleasure that shot through me, grounding me in the moment.

"Fuck," he mutters, his voice thick with desire.

My hands moved of their own accord, clawing at his shirt before sliding down to his pants. I pulled at them aggressively, my fingers trembling as I sought the warmth of his skin. My touch was desperate, needy, and when I hand closed around the length of him, he gasped, his head falling back as if the sensation was almost too much to bear. His nails dug into me, sharp and insistent, surely leaving faint red marks that would fade all too soon.

"Sloan," he groaned, my name a plea and a warning all at once. I wasn't stopping. I wanted this—wanted him—with a ferocity that surprised even myself. Before he could say another word, I was on my knees, my hands pulling his pants down further, my lips brushing against the head of him. His hands tangled in my hair.

I took him into my mouth, slow at first, savoring the taste of him, the way he shuddered beneath my touch. I swirled my tongue, my lips moving in rhythm, and with each stroke, his groans grew louder, more desperate. I quickened my pace, my confidence building with every sound he made. His hands tightened in my hair, guiding me, urging me to continue, but I didn't need the encouragement. I wanted to make him lose control, wanted to be the one to push him over the edge.

When I finally stood, my lips wet and swollen, he looked at me like I was the only thing in the world. His eyes were wild, his breath ragged, and for a moment, I felt powerful, untouchable.

"Lay down," I say, my voice steady despite the storm raging inside me. He didn't hesitate. The sight of him there, on my bed for the first time in years, was almost too much to bear. He was a mess of desire, his chest heaving, his eyes dark with need. I climbed onto the bed, straddling him, my hands on his chest as I positioned myself above him. His hands found my hips, squeezing tightly as if to anchor me to him. When I lowered herself onto him, he groaned, his head falling back into the pillow.

I began to move, slow at first, savoring the way he filled me, the way he made me feel whole. His hands tightened on my hips, urging me faster, and I obliged, my rhythm increasing as my pleasure built. The room was filled with the sounds of our bodies moving together, the creak of the bed, ragged breaths, and the occasional moan that escaped our lips. I threw my head back, my hair cascading down my shoulders as I rode him, my body moving with a desperation I couldn't deny.

"Fuck, Sloan," he growled, his voice thick with need. "You have no idea what you do to me."

His words were like a spark, igniting the fire that I felt building inside me. I could feel my orgasm approaching, a tightening in my core that threatened to consume me. I moved faster, my hips snapping against his, my nails digging into his chest as I clung to him.

"Tell me again," I whispered, my voice a breathy command. He looked up at me, his eyes wild, his lips parted as if to speak, but all that came out was a ragged groan. I could feel the tension in his body, the muscles coiled tight.

"Tell me or I'll stop," I threatened, my voice low and dangerous. He looked at me like I was crazy, his eyes wide with surprise.

"You have no idea what you do to me, Sloan," he gasped. "Please, don't stop."

I smiled wickedly, my body moving faster as I rode him. I could feel the pressure building inside me, a wave of pleasure that threatened to overwhelm me. I clung to him like my life depended on it. Nate groaned in response as he approached his own release. I moved with wild abandon as a wave of pleasure crashed over me like a tsunami. I cry out as it rips through me like a wildfire. I could feel Nate's body shudder as he released right after me. It couldn't have been more perfect if we had actually planned it. I'm breathing hard, collapsed on top of him, our breaths loud and ragged in the silence that follows.

"Well, that was... unexpected," he says, a crooked smile tugging at his lips.

I laugh softly, still trying to catch my breath. "You think?"

"Sloan?" he says, gently playing with my hair.

"Mhmm?" I reply sleepily, eyes closed, knowing full well I need to get up soon. His fingers were tracing soft circles on my skin, and it was not helping my motivation to get up.

"I meant it when I said I'd follow you anywhere. Don't leave me behind this time, wherever you decide to go."

I look into his eyes, and they're filled with nothing but sincerity. I knew wherever I went, I'd let him come with me. I'd let him follow me to the ends of the earth. Hopefully, he wouldn't regret it.

Chapter 35

We forced ourselves back upstairs, because if we'd stayed down there any longer, we both would've fallen asleep. I check on my grandmother, thankfully still sleeping. We settled on the couch again, the room wrapped in that early-morning stillness. He sits beside me, quietly studying my face as I work, and we slip into a peaceful silence that feels perfect.

We keep this up for several hours. Once I'm done with my work, I start looking up people in town with prior drug arrests, specifically those close to Scarlett's age. I jot names down, one after another, groaning as the list grows longer. Finally, I glance over at Nate.

"We're never going to be able to talk to all these people," I say, pushing the notebook away in frustration.

"If anyone could get through that list, it's you," Nate says, like it's the simplest truth in the world. I glance at him. He's not teasing, not trying to lift the mood. He just believes it—completely.

Time passes and the list keeps growing. My eyes begin to gloss over, the strain setting in until the names blur together on the page. A sudden knock at the door jolts me upright. It takes a second to process, it's been so long since we've had a visitor. I realize we haven't had one since I came back to town.

Nate looks at me, just as confused as I am. I stand, slowly making my way to the door. If anyone had asked me who I thought would be standing at our front door, Doctor Tucker wouldn't have even made the list. But there he was. I can't form words, because what the hell was he doing here? Better yet, how did he even get my address? Behind me, I see Nate looking up, trying to catch a glimpse of who it is. I step outside and pull the door shut behind me.

"Doctor Tucker, it's great to see you," I say, feigning politeness, because what the hell else am I supposed to say? Silently, I pray Nate doesn't come outside.

"Sloan," Doctor Tucker says, smiling like this isn't strange at all. Like showing up unannounced on my doorstep is the most natural thing in the world. He clears his throat, clearly unsure of what to say. The silence between us stretches just long enough to start getting weird, so I decide to be the adult.

"So... what brings you all this way?" I ask, squinting and raising a hand to block the sun, which has decided now is the perfect time to blind me. He shifts from foot to foot like a kid caught somewhere he shouldn't be.

"Well, I haven't seen you—I mean, *you guys*—at the hospital in a while," he says, his voice pitching up like he's not even convinced. "I just wanted to, you know... check in. On you. I mean—on *everyone.*"

I nod slowly, squinting at him like that'll somehow make any of this make sense. *This doctor could not possibly be here to ask me out again.* Not only would that be wildly inappropriate, but he didn't even know me. I sure as hell didn't give him my address. Which means he must've pulled it from her paperwork. Cool. Totally normal. Not weird at all.

"Well, we're as good as we can be," I say, trying to keep my tone even. "You know... she's not getting treatment anymore. Nate called and notified all her usual doctors at the hospital."

My lips tingle slightly as I say Nate's name, and I feel a blush creep up before I can stop it.

"Right, yeah, I know that. It's just... you never called me," he says.

I blink. *Was he serious right now?* Even if I *had* been interested—which, spoiler: I wasn't—my grandmother is still very sick. I've been juggling stress, grief, and guilt like it's a full-time job. The last thing on my mind was calling some guy I barely knew, who I met during some of the worst moments of my life. I mean, yeah—*the stuff with Nate* happened. But that was different. We've known each other for years. We had a long-term relationship before, with history, trust, complications I actually care about. This guy? I didn't owe him anything.

I don't feel the need to be overly nice to this man anymore. He's not her doctor now. That line was crossed the second he showed up here uninvited, fishing for something I never offered. Honestly? I've had it up to *here* with certain men thinking they can act however they want around me—like basic boundaries were just optional.

"Doctor Tucker..." I start, trying to keep my voice level.

He cuts me off with a smile. "Eugene, remember? Call me Eugene."

Good lord. The audacity.

"Right—no thanks," I say flatly. "I'm not going to call you that."

He looks confused. In what world would anyone be okay with this? *In what world is it okay to come to your patient's house to ask her granddaughter out? Seriously, does he think this is normal? Is this guy completely unhinged, or just socially clueless?*

"I really don't know why you came all this way, but my grandmother is still very sick, whether you're still her doctor or not. To be blunt, this whole situation? It feels really unethical. Showing up unannounced, fishing for something personal, it's very inappropriate." He looks taken aback, like no one's ever called him out on his shit before.

"Not only that, I'm happily with someone," I add, a small smile tugging at my lips as I think of Nate. We haven't officially labeled it yet, but if Nate heard me say that, I'm pretty sure he'd agree. Doctor Tucker looks shocked again, like he actually expected me to be free and waiting around for his second invitation.

"With who?" he asks, his voice tightening, annoyance creeping in. The audacity just keeps rolling in with this man.

Before I can answer, the door behind me opens. I spin around, bracing myself for how mad Nate is going to be. But instead, I'm shocked to see him smiling.

"With me," he says, answering the question as nicely as possible. He grabs my waist, pulling me closer, still smiling.

Doctor Tucker's lips tighten, his mood visibly darkening. "Didn't you tell me you couldn't be with anyone while your grandmother's sick? Were you guys together when I asked you out? Because you made no indication of that."

For a second, I almost apologize. Maybe I did give him the wrong impression? Maybe I somehow led him on? But I remember I was clear when I told him I was focused on taking care of my grandmother. That I wasn't in a place for anything else. I remember the way he kept trying to touch me while we were there. The way he ignored every signal that wasn't a green light.

No. I didn't owe him anything. I sure as hell didn't lead him on. What made my blood boil wasn't just this moment, it was the clear pattern. This was yet another man who didn't understand when he was being told to quit. Didn't understand that he was a *menace* to the people around him. A man who walked through life thinking he was some kind of gift to the damn planet. I silently wonder to myself—what makes people like this? What twists someone up so much that they walk through the world with this kind of *gall*? This bold, clueless entitlement. Like boundaries are suggestions. Like decency is optional.

I inhale, my thoughts fueling the anger simmering just beneath my skin.

"I wasn't with anyone at the time," I say, calm but firm, "but Nate and I are together now."

He glances at Nate, and I see it in his eyes— *why him?* Nate has a vast amount of everything I need. This man? None of it. It was never even close. Not a competition. Not even in the same league.

"I'm sorry you drove out here for nothing," I add, my tone clipped, my patience gone. I'm eyeing him now, wondering why he hasn't left. This entire interaction is already painfully awkward, and he's just *lingering,* dragging it.

"I just feel a little led on here," he says, his voice tight and wounded. "I mean... you took my card. You implied you'd call me."

I feel Nate tense beside me, and I speak before he can. "Look, I was being polite. Honestly, you put me in a weird position—hitting on me while you were my grandmother's doctor. That has *got* to be some kind of unwritten rule."

I cross my arms, unwilling to give this sad excuse of a man even a sliver of satisfaction. "So let me get this straight, your first move after finding out my grandmother is too sick to continue treatment is to show up at our house… to ask me out *again*?"

His mouth opens, but nothing comes out.

"Yeah. I'd like you to leave now," I say, voice steady. "If you don't—or if you come back—I'll report you to the hospital. And honestly? I'm almost *positive* this isn't the first time you've pulled something like this."

He looks at me, and for a second, there's nothing. Then I see it—rage creeping into his expression, tightening his jaw, his eyes narrowing. His face flushes red, like he's about to go off on me. Like he's not used to women telling him no. Like this little performance he's been putting on was always just seconds from fading. Nate takes that moment to step forward, his hand gentle as he moves me slightly behind him.

"I suggest you leave," he says, voice low but steady. "And don't come back."

He stomps back to his car, muttering something under his breath that I don't bother trying to make out. We stand there, watching as he pulls out of the driveway and disappears down the road. Neither of us moves until his car is completely out of sight. I glance over at Nate, who's still staring down the empty road, jaw clenched tight. The tension lingers in the air, heavy.

"Well, that was eventful," I say, glancing at him, trying to lighten the mood. I reach out letting my hand brush against his. He doesn't pull away. The simple contact feels like a small anchor after everything that just happened.

"So, we're together, huh?" I say softly, a small smile tugging at my lips as I gently prod him. He looks at me for a moment, all serious and quiet. I tug at his arm.

"Hey," I say, trying to get him to meet my eyes. Finally, he shifts his gaze to me.

"It's okay," I whisper softly.

Without another word, he pulls me into a tight hug, pressing a kiss to my forehead. He holds me there on the porch for what feels like hours, though it's probably only minutes. The world around us fades away, and all that exists is the steady beat of his heart against mine.

Chapter 36

My grandmother finally wakes up around dinner, and I make us fried chicken—hoping she'll be able to eat some of her favorite food. She thanks me for cooking, and to my relief, she eats more than she has in days. It warms me in a way nothing else has lately. After dinner, I bring her a small handful of circus peanuts, and her face lights up like I just gave her gold. I can't stand the candy, but she *loves* it. She takes her time with the candy, chewing slowly, savoring each one like it's the best thing she's ever tasted. I sit beside her on the edge of the bed, just watching. Not needing to say anything. Her hand finds mine, warm and soft and a little shaky, and she gives it a light squeeze.

"You always take such good care of me," she murmurs, her voice a little tired, but full of that familiar affection.

"I learned from the best," I say, my throat tightening a little.

She smiles, eyes crinkling at the corners. "You were always my strong girl."

I lay beside her in the small sliver of bed that remained. Suddenly, I felt like a kid again, when I used to crawl into her bed after a bad dream. I pressed my forehead gently to her shoulder and let the quiet settle between us. For a moment, time felt kind.

We sat there like that for a while, my head against her shoulder and her hand wrapped around mine. The television hums softly in the background, but neither of us is paying much attention. She hums under her breath, a tune I half-recognize from when I was a kid. I used to sit in the kitchen while she cooked, swinging my legs and listening to her sing over the sound of pots clanging. It hits me how many little pieces of me are stitched together from moments like this. Her voice. Her hands. The way she always found sweetness in the simplest things.

"You okay, sweetheart?" she asks, not opening her eyes. I nod before realizing she can't see me.

"Yeah," I whisper, "I'm okay."

Not entirely true. But close enough for tonight. She pats my hand gently, like she knows the difference.

"I know it's hard," she says after a pause. "But you're doing right by me. You really are."

I bite the inside of my cheek, trying not to cry. I just nod again, because if I speak now, I won't stop. I watched the sky change colors as the sun began to set, wishing we could stay in this in-between place forever.

"Do you remember when you were younger and used to perform Taylor Swift songs on the front porch?" she asks, her voice light, touched with amusement. I smile at the memory, still resting against her shoulder, not moving.

"Yeah," I murmured.

"You used to beg me to watch you. Over and over again. Same song. Same dance. And I did," she says, chuckling softly. "Every time, like it was the first time."

I laugh too, a small tear slipping free as I do.

"Then you found that old video camera," she continues, her voice warmer now, caught up in the memory, "and insisted Nate record you so you could make a *music video*. You think any young boy would rather be doing *anything else* than listening to Taylor Swift on a loop while being bossed around by a little girl making *multiple* outfit changes?"

We both laugh, and this time the tears that come feel lighter somehow.

"I made him retake it, like, ten times," I say through a laugh, wiping at my face.

"You made him re-shoot an entire scene because your hair didn't 'flip dramatically enough,'" she says, doing little air quotes with her free hand. "Poor boy looked like he was going to melt in the sun."

"Oh my god, and I made him use the broom as a boom mic," I add, laughing harder now. "Like we were filming some kind of blockbuster."

She shakes her head, smiling. "He never even complained. Just followed your directions like a lost little puppy." My heart tugs a little at that.

"He always did what I asked," I murmur, softer now.

"Even when it made no sense," she adds gently. "He was wrapped around your finger, and you didn't even know it."

I look up at her, and her smile is still there, touched now with something tender. I swallow, blinking fast.

"We were kids."

"You're not kids anymore, but here he is still following you around."

I nod slowly, unsure what to say to that. I look at her, and she's staring out the window now, the last sliver of sunlight painting her face in gold. She's smiling, soft and faraway, like she's remembering it all as clearly as I am.

"He'd do anything for you," she says quietly. "Even now, if you asked him to make another ridiculous music video, I think he'd grab the broom and start filming."

I let out a small laugh, pressing my sleeve to the corner of my eye.

"Yeah," I whisper. "He would."

She turns back to look at me, her eyes gentle but sure. "That kind of love doesn't show up every day, Sloan. You don't need to chase it away or explain it away. Just let it be what it is."

I lean my head back onto her shoulder, not saying anything. She sighs, and I watch the rise and fall of her chest.

"You've always had a big heart," she says after a moment. Her hand squeezes mine again, gentle yet firm. "Don't forget, your heart is yours first. The people who love you will hold onto it like it matters."

I close my eyes, more tears slipping down without permission. We sit like that until the light outside is nearly gone, and her grip on my hand begins to loosen. All I can think, once she's asleep, is that my days with her are numbered. We only had so many sunsets left, and I wanted every single one of them, and then some.

CHAPTER 37

The days pass in a blur. I work, I sit with my grandmother, day after day, hour after hour. Even when she tells me to go, I always say the same thing: "I have nowhere better to be." When she gets truly irritated, insisting I need space or rest or 'a life,' I move to the couch and pretend I left. I stay quiet, just close enough to hear her breathing, just far enough to keep her pride intact.

Lately, she's had to use the oxygen more. The sound of it fills the house, soft and constant, like a quiet reminder that things are changing. Each day it feels a little harder to breathe right alongside her. I try—over and over—to find someone who knows more about Scarlett's last day.

But every lead turns cold. Every conversation goes nowhere. Every night, I stay up too late, combing through notes, revisiting emails, rereading the same names like they'll suddenly reveal something new. Nothing does. Some people don't answer. Others give vague half-truths or pretend they barely knew Scarlett. A few look nervous just hearing her name, like it still haunts them. I start a fresh notebook. I try color-coding by connection, by location, by likelihood. None of it matters. The lines never connect.

Meanwhile, the world in this house gets smaller. The air feels thinner. My grandmother sleeps more and talks less. The damn oxygen machine keeps humming like a countdown I can't stop. I don't know what scares me more: that I might never find out what really happened to Scarlett... Or that I'll figure it out just a little too late.

I sit at the kitchen table, staring at my notes like they hold the answer if I just look hard enough. My hands tremble slightly, exhaustion weighing down every breath. Nate comes up behind me and rests a hand on my shoulder. It's steady, grounding.

"You're doing everything you can," he says softly. "Sometimes, that's all anyone can do." I don't look up.

"It feels like I'm just spinning in circles." I say as he squeezes my shoulder gently.

"You're not alone in this. I'm here."

I meet his eyes as he leans down slowly, his hand still resting lightly on my shoulder. For a moment, I hesitate, unsure if I have the energy to reach back. His lips brush mine, soft and steady. The world blurs around us for a heartbeat, and in that simple kiss, I feel a flicker of calm. When we pull apart, Nate's eyes hold mine, full of patience and love. The one thing that's improved over the past few weeks is our relationship. It's not just the sex, which, yes, is amazing. My grandmother was right; he would do anything for me. At his core, he's still that kid who lets me take the lead, even now. The feeling of being loved by him is so grounding, so real, that for a moment, it almost makes me forget the reality we're living in.

"I'm going to head to bed," he says softly. I know that means the couch. I've told him he doesn't have to sleep there every night with me. He could sleep in his own bed, but he refuses. I nod, already knowing I'll stay up a little longer.

"Don't stay up too late," he says, kissing my forehead before he walks away.

I stare at my notes until they blur, groaning in frustration. I'm missing something; I can feel it. My eyes drift to the door off to the side of the kitchen, the only other room upstairs besides my grandmother's. It's rarely walked into; it was an unspoken rule, forbidden. I stand and open the door.

It creaks softly as I flip on the light, dust particles swirling. The walls still hold old posters of Prince, The Cure, and faded magazine clippings taped to the wall. An old dresser sits against one wall, its surface scattered with faded makeup and trinkets. It feels like stepping back in time.

My grandmother never changed Scarlett's room. It stood frozen in time, untouched. Even as a kid, I wasn't allowed in here. Her old futon sat where a bed would usually go. Grandma told me Scarlett begged for it, insisting it was more comfortable than a bed.

I sit down on it, nearly tipping over. I wonder what went through Scarlett's mind in this space, the dreams she dreamed, the fears she hid, the secrets she kept. A small ache blooms in my chest, a mix of sadness and longing. I never really knew this part of her. The Scarlett I knew was always agitated and on edge.

I open her nightstand, the top drawer smaller than the rest. Inside, I find small bits of crushed weed scattered at the bottom, along with a few loose, old cigarettes. My grandmother really hadn't changed a thing. A strange mix of emotions washes over me. I wonder how many nights she sat here, smoking quietly, lost in her own world while the rest of the house slept.

The room feels even more alive now, filled with silent stories I wish I could hear.

I close the drawer softly, careful not to disturb anything. Moving to the next drawer, I pull it open and find an old yearbook tossed inside, its edges worn, pages yellowed with age. It's her senior yearbook. I run my fingers over the cover, a quiet invitation to step even deeper into her past. I open it and gasp; it's filled with so many signatures from her classmates. The messages seem genuine, full of warmth and memories.

I page through, until I reach a section at the back where the owner filled out a cheesy questionnaire. What were your hopes and dreams? Plans after graduation? The last question catches me off guard: *Who's your hero and why?* If you had asked me yesterday, I wouldn't have known how she would answer. I barely knew her, and what little I did know was tangled and messy.

The passage read:

"My mother. She is one of the strongest people I know. My dad died young, and she carried on with fierce determination, never blinking at the fact that now she was stuck with me, someone who repeatedly let her down and acted so ungrateful. Someone who broke her heart more times than I can count. Someone who told her I'd be home for dinner, only to leave her sitting alone at the table. Yelling at her for trying to control my life. And yet, she still tries to help me after all of that. She never gives up on me, even when she should have. I want to be that strong one day just like her."

The words settle heavy in my chest. I blink back tears, feeling a tenderness for both Scarlett, and my grandmother. I move to place the yearbook back in the drawer but pause—it's resting on top of a black purse I hadn't noticed. I glance around, like I'm sneaking into forbidden territory, then pick it up carefully. It's light, but not so light that it could be empty.

Hesitantly, I unzip it and peek inside. There's a wallet and two pill bottles nestled within. I pick up one and squint at the label, *Lithium.* The other reads *Quetiapine.* A quick Google search confirms my suspicions, both medications are commonly used to treat bipolar disorder. Specifically, they're often prescribed for people who also experience manic depression. I sit back on the futon, the weight of the purse still in my lap, letting this knowledge sink in.

I gasp when I notice the dates on the bottles. *May 2000.* My fingers tighten around the plastic. Scarlett was last seen in *June* of 2000. These pills were filled just weeks before she disappeared. Suddenly the room feels colder. This was close. Close to when everything unraveled. Why were they here? Why didn't anyone mention she was taking medication? My mind races with questions.

From what I can remember, we did spend time here on and off. She'd show up sometimes, ask my grandmother for food or money—mostly money. It's possible she left the purse here, swapped it out for another without thinking, and forgot the pills entirely. If she wasn't taking her meds consistently to begin with, it's not hard to imagine she didn't even realize they were missing. Or maybe she did. Maybe she looked right at that drawer and left them anyway. I stare at the bottles, my thoughts spinning.

I drop the pill bottles back into the purse and reach for the wallet, expecting it to be empty. The zipper scrapes against the dust that's settled over the years, catching slightly before it gives way. I gasp as I find her driver's license, along with a twenty-dollar bill folded neatly beside a few worn ones. My fingers tremble as I pull the license out, staring at her face frozen in time. This wasn't a discarded bag. This was *left.* Intentionally or not... Scarlett never came back for it.

I look up, a sudden unease curling in my gut. I glance out the window, but there's nothing. Just pitch-black pressing against the glass. Still, something in me stirs, an instinct, a chill crawling up the back of my neck. I move quickly, placing everything back where it was: the license, the money, the pill bottles, and the yearbook. Trying not to make a sound. Trying not to breathe too loud. I step out of the room and close the door behind me, but even as I walk away the feeling clings to me. That unmistakable sense that something—*someone*—was there. That I wasn't alone. That I was being watched.

CHAPTER 38

I didn't feel the need to tell Nate about being in Scarlett's room, or the feeling that I was being watched. I told myself I was just psyching myself out after finding her purse. It was nothing. Not a big deal. Even still, I couldn't shake the feeling. I felt on edge, and maybe it was time to admit that looking into Scarlett's disappearance was affecting me more than I thought it would.

So, I decided to take a step back, just for the day. No staring at my notes for hours on end. I'd do something else. Anything else. I tucked my notes away in my desk. Since it was Sunday, I decided to grab the paper from outside for my grandmother. On the way, I passed Nate, still asleep on the couch, breathing steadily, completely at ease. I, on the other hand, could barely remember the last time I slept through the night. I sighed, a little jealous, as I reached for the door.

I stepped outside, scanning for the paper which of course, was in the yard and not on the porch. As I bent down to pick it up, something caught my eye. I froze. Straightening up, I gasped. Spray-painted in jagged red letters across the front of the house were the words:

KEEP YOUR MOUTH SHUT

I felt a scream building deep inside me, but I shoved it down. I hurried back into the house, the weight of unseen eyes still pressing on my back. Nate was sitting up on the couch now, rubbing his eyes as I rushed past him, not meeting his gaze. In the kitchen, I grabbed a bucket, filled it with hot water and a generous squeeze of Dawn dish soap. Would that even take off spray paint? God, I hoped so. I had to get it off the house fast. My grandmother didn't go out much anymore, but if she saw that... she'd not only ask questions, she'd be understandably upset. I rushed back toward the door.

Nate called after me, his voice sharp with confusion, concern, but I couldn't speak. That scream was still sitting in my throat, trembling on the edge, and I knew if I opened my mouth, it would tear its way out.

Nate yelled after me, his voice growing louder with every unanswered call. "Hey! Sloan, what's going on?" I didn't stop. I couldn't. I stood in front of the wall, dunking the sponge in the soapy water, and started scrubbing furiously at the red letters. They didn't budge. Nate stopped beside me, breathless and staring.

"What the hell is this?" His voice was lower now, edged with something dark. I still didn't answer. My hands were shaking as I scrubbed harder, desperate, like maybe if I could erase the words fast enough, everything would go back to normal.

I could feel my whole body trembling, every nerve on edge, and I couldn't make it stop.

"Sloan, stop." Nate's voice was firm, cutting through the chaos. He grabbed my wrist, halting my frantic scrubbing, and I finally turned to him. His eyes searched mine, wide and full of questions, but steady. Grounding.

"What is going on?" he asked, quieter now. "Talk to me."

My hand trembled in his grip, the sponge dripping soapy water between us. I shook my head, my lips parted but no words came out.

"I... I don't... know. I just... came out here and it was here..." The words stumbled out between shivering breaths. My teeth were clacking together like I was freezing, though I wasn't cold.

I turned back to the wall, scrubbed harder. Why wasn't it coming off? The letters seemed burned into the siding, mocking me with every stroke. I gripped the sponge so tightly my knuckles turned white. I didn't care. I couldn't stop. Nate was still behind me, silent now. Watching. I could feel his hesitation, like he didn't know whether to pull me away or let me keep going.

I felt hands wrap around my waist, and I screamed. The sound burst out of me before I could stop it. The contact shattered my trance. I jerked forward, instinctively trying to escape. He gently pulled me back, away from the house. The sponge slipped from my fingers and fell into the grass. Nate guided me a few steps from the house, then turned me to face him.

"Sloan," he said, his voice low but urgent, "what's going on? You're scaring me."

"I think it was Kent," I said, my voice shaky but steadier than before. The words came out slowly, like I was hearing them for the first time myself. It *had* to be him. He told me to keep my mouth shut. He'd been furious. Kent wasn't the kind of man who let things go. He lived just three houses down. Close enough to watch. Close enough to act. I met Nate's eyes, finally really looking at him.

"I think I really pissed him off." I left out the part about feeling watched last night. It didn't matter now. This was why

I felt it, because someone really *was* watching. Nate stared at me, his eyes narrowing just slightly.

"What exactly did he say to you... when he cornered you in the store?"

I blew out a slow breath, stalling. I didn't want to repeat it—not out loud. Part of me was already eyeing the house, thinking about finishing the job. Scrubbing the wall until the letters were gone, until this whole thing felt smaller somehow. Until I could pretend none of it was real.

"Sloan!" I could hear the frustration in Nate's voice, sharp and urgent now. "What *did* he say to you?"

I looked at him, swallowing hard.

"He told me to... stop running my mouth... or he'd put something in it to make me shut up." I winced as the words left my lips. Saying it out loud made it feel even more brutal, more real.

Nate cursed under his breath, the sound rough and angry. Nate's jaw clenched tight, his eyes darkening with anger. "Goddamn it, Sloan..."

I looked up at him, realizing I should've told him everything the moment it happened. But now he was already turning away, his steps heavy and fast, heading toward the road.

"Nate, where are you going?" I called out, panic creeping into my voice. He didn't stop.

"To kill him," he said, cold and steady, like that was the only answer. I grabbed his shirt, tugging hard.

"Stop, Nate. Please." I stood in front of him, searching his eyes—and all I saw was pure rage. "You go over there, and who knows what happens. Say you *do* kill him... then what?"

Nate's jaw tightened, his eyes flickering with a storm I'd never seen so clearly before. For a moment, he looked like he wanted to storm off anyway, to let the rage consume him. But then his shoulders slumped slightly, and the fire in his gaze softened, just a fraction.

"I... I don't know what to do, Sloan," he admitted, voice rougher, less sure. "That bastard scared you. Threatened you. All I want is to make it stop. To make him pay."

He ran a hand over his face, frustration etched deep in every line. His eyes met mine, raw and vulnerable.

"Go back inside," I said firmly, my voice steady despite the chaos inside me. "I'll clean the spray paint. You go... calm down."

Nate hesitated, his eyes searching mine like he was weighing the storm inside him. After a long beat, he finally nodded, stepping back slowly. I watched him walk away, shoulders heavy but retreating, giving me a chance to catch my breath.

I started scrubbing again, wondering if I was even making a dent in the paint. No matter how hard I pressed, no matter which way I scrubbed, it felt impossible. It wasn't coming off. My grandmother's beautiful house—the one she'd bought with the love of her life —now bore its own scarlet letter. A mark that felt like it was burning into the walls. I felt the tears burning behind my eyes. If my grandmother saw this... it might actually kill her. And to make it worse, it would be my fault. I was the one who brought this darkness back into our lives. Maybe she was right, I should have just left it alone.

Footsteps sounded behind me. I turned, and there was Nate again, holding a power washer. I couldn't help but marvel at him, always coming to my rescue, always knowing just what to do. He motioned for me to move out of the way, and I stepped beside him as he sprayed the siding. Slowly, the red paint began to fade, dissolving under the powerful stream. I let out a breath, relief flooding through me.

"Oh my god, you're getting it off!"

He glanced at me and smiled. "I got you, sweets."

My cheeks flushed, he hadn't called me that in three years. It was a little pet name he'd made up when we first started dating. 'Sweets,' because I loved dessert and always needed a little something sweet after dinner. To be fair my love of desserts wasn't self-taught; my grandmother passed that bad habit down to me.

"You head inside," he said. "I'm sure she's up, and we don't want her coming out here. If she asks, just tell her I'm power washing the whole house because it needs it."

I nodded, heading inside. I glanced back at him and smiled, a quiet moment of relief amid the chaos.

CHAPTER 39

My grandmother was particularly irritable today; everything seemed to set her off. It was so unlike her. She'd always been patient with me, so the sharpness in her tone caught me off guard. I tried not to let it get to me. I'd done some reading, and I knew this was common. Especially when someone was in a lot of pain. She still hated taking her pain meds. There were a few times she got confused, and I gave her medication, telling her it was just Tylenol. But she didn't fall for it every time. Even Nate annoyed her today with the power washing, something she'd usually love. She kept muttering about it being too loud and unnecessary. I just kept trying to comfort her—getting her water when she needed it, handing her the oxygen when she struggled to breathe. She refused any food, barely eating, at this point it was maybe once a day *if that*. This was something I wouldn't wish on my worst enemy. Well, almost no one.

My thoughts drifted to Kent, wishing I could get even with him, wishing I could make him pay for everything he'd done. Not just for Scarlett, but to the long list of people he'd hurt. I was starting to think maybe he *did* have something to do with

Scarlett going missing. And the only reason he got away with it was because no one ever tried hard enough to find her.

Even as I thought it, something didn't quite feel right. I was missing something important. I stared at my grandmother, watching her shift uncomfortably where she sat propped up in bed. My heart ached, knowing I'd probably never be able to bring her the closure she deserved.

"Grandma?" She looked at me, a little caught off guard. "I just wanted to say... um, thank you. For raising me. For taking such good care of me. For being there, you know... even after Scarlett left."

The word *left* hung in the air, tasting wrong on my tongue. Because deep down, I didn't really believe she *left* anymore. I didn't want to speak that truth to my grandmother, not now. What good would it do? She was already in pain, already carrying the weight of so much. Telling her what I really believed wouldn't bring Scarlett back. It would only break her heart all over again. So, I swallowed the words. I smiled instead, even though it felt heavy on my face.

"Why do you only ever call her *Scarlett*?" The question hit me like a sudden gust of wind. Of all the things I thought she might say, that wasn't one of them. I blinked, caught off guard.

"Sloan, I'm not getting on to you," she added gently. "I'm just asking a question. She *is* your mother. But ever since you came to live with me you started calling her *Scarlett*, and you never stopped." She paused, her tired eyes watching me closely. "I've just always wondered why."

I looked at her, unsure what to say. Because the truth was... I didn't really know. I *knew* I used to call her 'Mom' when she was still around. I could hear it in the handful of memories I had, the way it sounded coming out of my small voice. But once she was gone, she stopped being *Mom.* She became *Scarlett.*

Somehow, that name stuck. Maybe it was my way of creating distance. Maybe it was easier than saying *Mom* and feeling the ache that came with it. I shrugged slightly, eyes falling to the floor.

"You know," my grandmother said softly, "I think she cared about you very much. Even if she didn't always show it. Even if... she struggled to be a mom."

I scoffed before I could stop myself. It wasn't loud, but it cut through the air between us. I didn't mean to be rude, but I couldn't help it. Most of the memories I had were bad ones. Yelling. Slamming doors. Being left in places she forgot she brought me to. It was hard, to give her any kind of credit. I looked at her, my voice low but steady.

"You know, one time she forgot to enroll me in school? She sent me on the bus like everything was normal. I wandered around for hours, trying to figure out where I was supposed to be. Somehow, no one noticed until I ended up in the library, reading. I stayed there for most of the day." I let out a short, bitter laugh. "School was almost over when the librarian finally came over and asked me to come to the office. It didn't take long for them to figure out that she never filled out the back-to-school paperwork. They called her up there, and when she showed up, she looked like she'd just rolled out of bed. Messy hair, no bra, annoyed like *we* were the ones who inconvenienced *her*."

I shook my head. "She acted mad that she even had to be there."

I bit my tongue. That really wasn't necessary. What did that solve—hurting my grandmother's feelings? Just to prove a point? I mean, I was the one advocating for Scarlett writing that article, telling the whole town she was a person who deserved compassion, deserved to be remembered. Yet here

I was... still carrying all this bitterness. Still dragging around the weight of every awful memory. Still struggling with how to hold space for both truths: that she was *hurting*, and that she *hurt me.* I took a breath.

"But you're right," I said softly. "She did care about me. I know she did—in the best way she could." I glanced down at my hands, a flicker of memory warming my chest. "Like on my last birthday with her, she surprised me with this pink shirt that said *'Birthday Girl'* on it. She was so excited to see my face when I opened it."

I smiled, just a little. "She made me breakfast that day... or, well, she bought donuts. But still...it was nice." I paused, letting the next memory come. "There was this make your own float parade at school. Every kid had to make their own float, and I remember being so stressed out. I couldn't get mine right. When she saw me struggling, she actually helped me with it. When the day came and all the parents were invited to the parade... she showed up." I

felt my throat tighten a little. My grandmother didn't say anything. She just watched me, her eyes soft, like hearing that healed a small part of her. The memory floating between us. She reached out, her hand settling lightly over mine. I could hear her breathing heavily in the quiet between us. Her chest made a faint rattling sound with each breath, fragile and un-even. It was a harsh reminder of how much time was left.

"I'm sorry," I said, looking at her with all the sincerity I could muster. "I'm sorry I couldn't help find her for you. I wanted to so badly... I wanted to..." I trailed off, the words slipping away because I wasn't even sure what I wanted anymore. Closure? Answers? Maybe just peace for both of us. It all felt just out of reach.

"Sweetheart," she said softly, her voice steady despite the crackling breaths, "that was never something you had to do. If you're putting that on yourself, you need to take it off. It's too much to carry."

I wanted to tell her everything I'd found in the past few weeks. All the clues, the dead ends, the things that were missed. But even with all those pieces, none of it felt real unless I had the answer. Without it, it was just noise. It was just a reminder that her daughter was gone.

"I need you to know something, Sloan," she said quietly, her voice fragile but steady. "When I'm gone, all my important papers are in my filing cabinet. In the bottom drawer... there are letters for you. I've been saving them for you." I didn't tell her I had already found and read them.

"Sure, I will," I smiled softly at her. She winced, pain flashing across her face, more intense than before.

"I think I'll take some of that pain medication now." That should have made me happy, knowing she'd get some relief. But instead, I felt sadness wash over me.

I handed her the pills, watching as she struggled to swallow, her throat catching. After a few coughs, she settled back against the pillows, trying to get comfortable.

"You need me to get you anything?" I asked gently. She waved me off with a tired smile.

"You do enough, hun. Just sit down." So, I sat beside her, ready to stay here all day. Then, out of nowhere, she said hoarsely, "You should marry him, you know." I blinked, caught off guard by the suddenness of it.

"The pills are already kicking in, huh?" I joked softly, trying to lighten the mood. She looked at me seriously, the most lucid I'd seen her in weeks.

"You and Nate... you've been through a lot. But you need each other." She paused, then added with a smirk, "You should get married, live here. I mean, the house will be yours after all. Where else is a broke 25-year-old going to go? I'm not leaving you millions, you know."

She laughed softly at her own joke, and for a moment, the heaviness in the room lifted.

"You should raise kids here. Be happy here," she said, her voice soft but certain. "Redecorate this place—God knows my taste must be dated by now." She chuckled quietly, then grew a little more serious. "I know you don't care much for this town, but it can be better than you think, sometimes it can surprise you."

I nodded at her, not wanting to argue. I didn't want to start naming the million reasons I didn't want to stay here. The countless ways this town had let me down. How, when it did surprise me, it was never in a good way. But I didn't say any of that. Sometimes silence was easier.

"I'll think about it," I said, offering her a smile hoping it looked convincing. She seemed satisfied with that, her eyes softening as she looked at me. She drifted off shortly after, her breathing evening out as the pain meds settled in. I sat there, watching her chest rise and fall, memorizing the rhythm. I decided, I was going to sleep right here every night, until she wasn't here anymore. Not because I could stop what was coming, but because I didn't want her to face it alone.

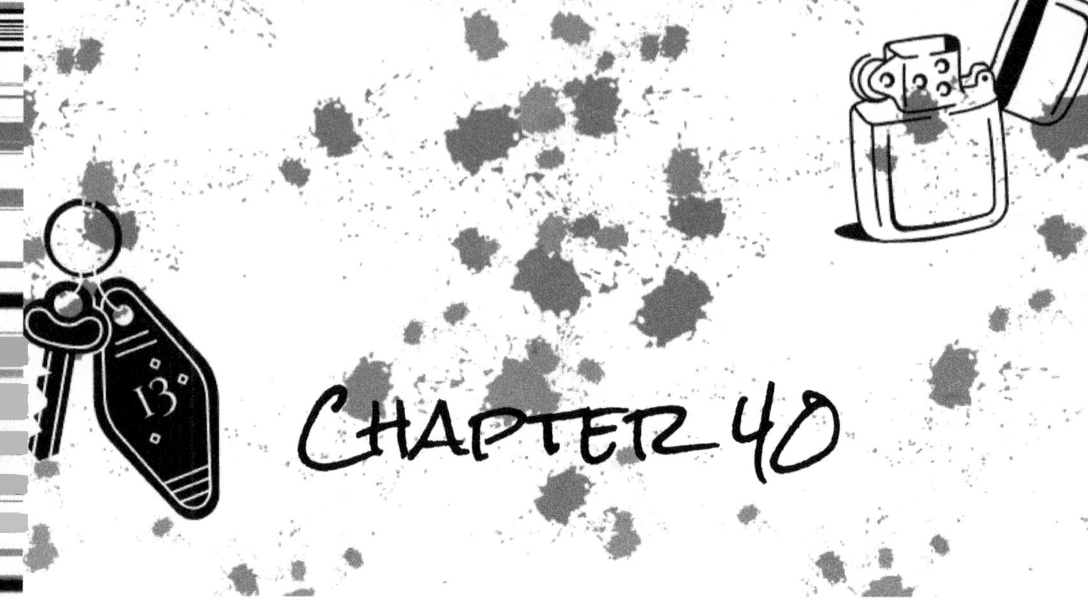

CHAPTER 40

I woke up with a start, heart pounding in my chest. That feeling was back, like I was being watched. I sat up slowly, eyes scanning the room, but it was pitch black. Nothing but darkness stretching along the walls, shaped by the soft glow of the hallway light filtering in under the door. All I could hear was my grandmother's rough, crackling breathing beside me. It should have been comforting—proof that she was still here. But the chill crawling up my spine told me something else was near. Something I couldn't see.

My heart was racing as I got up, stepping quietly to my grandmother's window. I pulled the curtain back just enough to peek out. Nothing out of the ordinary. I turned around—"*Oof!*" My foot hit something solid, and I froze, breath catching in my throat. Then, from the dark;

"*You kicked me,*" Nate whispered.

Relief surged through me, my shoulders sagging as my breathing began to slow. Just Nate.

"What are you doing on the floor?" I whisper-yelled, trying to keep quiet but unable to hide the surprise in my voice. I reached for him in the dark, trying to find his hand, and instead accidentally jabbed him right in the eye.

"Cease fire," he whispered, wincing as he slowly got up. I covered my mouth, a mixture of shock and that wild, sleep-deprived laughter bubbling up in my chest.

"Oh my God Nate, I'm so sorry! I didn't mean to—" I grabbed his arm and pulled him toward the living room so I could see him in the light. He was already grinning, even as I gently tilted his face up to examine his eye.

"It's not a big deal, Sweets," he said with a soft laugh. "I've survived worse."

I blushed at his nickname for me yet again. The way he said it made something in me ache and warm at the same time. I hadn't realized how much I missed hearing it until now.

I touched lightly around his eye, careful not to press too hard. "So... why were you on the floor?" He looked at me, and something about the way he did made me squirm a little.

"Well," he said, voice low, "I wanted to make sure you two were okay." I smiled, trying to hold back how much that meant to me.

"You know, that could've been done easily from the couch." He smirked.

"Okay, Sweets—you got me." There was a pause, just long enough to make my heart skip. "I also didn't want to sleep in a different room than you."

I didn't say anything, and I reached up on my tiptoes and kissed him lightly. The second our lips touched, something shifted. His hand moved to the side of my face, warm and steady, anchoring me there. I leaned in, deepening the kiss, my fingers curling into the fabric of his shirt. His other arm wrapped around my waist, pulling me closer until there was no space left between us. The world outside faded, the worry, the weight, even the question of what came next. I pull away, looking into his eyes.

"I don't want to sleep away from you either, but you know my grandmother might freak out if she wakes up and finds you on the floor with no explanation."

"Then I guess I'll just have to come up with a better explanation," he says, brushing a loose strand of hair from my face. I smile.

"Promise me you'll try to get some rest, though," I whisper. His gaze softens.

"Only if you promise to let me stay close."

I nod, feeling a deep affection for him. "Deal."

I slip back into the room and curl up in the chair, my mind wandering—wondering what it would be like to wake up with Nate beside me every day in this house.

Chapter 41

I stopped looking for Scarlett altogether. As painful as it was, I knew my time could only be stretched so far. Weeks pass. Nate goes to work, mows lawns, studies, and takes his finals. Me? I'm stuck in a constant state of paused grief and guilt, mourning someone who wasn't gone yet.

Our conversations dwindle more and more. Some days, she barely wakes up. When the hospice nurse comes by, she gently lets me know it doesn't seem like it will be long. She gives me instructions, but I can't hear them over the ringing in my ears. Since she's struggling to swallow more and more each day, the doctor prescribes morphine drops to help with the pain. My days feel both too short and endless all at once. I cry silently when she's asleep. Sometimes, when she's awake, she calls me Scarlett, and it takes everything I have not to break down.

Sometimes, I wished I was Scarlett; those were the days I felt the guiltiest. I wish she were here, taking care of her, so I wouldn't have to watch the person I loved most in this world slowly fade into nothing. When she thinks I'm Scarlett, she asks about me—how I am, where I am. I tell her Sloan's at school, and she smiles. Sometimes she gets mad at Scarlett, telling her she needs to be a better mother. Other times, she repeats sorry over and over—for failing her, for not being a better mom, for not trying hard enough. I tell her she did a great job, that I'm fine now, that she helped me enough. Even though I know it's a lie, it makes me feel good, if only for a moment, to see her believe Scarlett is okay.

The days begin with her not waking up at all. Sometimes, I can't even remember the last thing she said to me. The nurses encourage me to keep talking to her—that she can likely still hear me. So, I hold her hand, squeezing it lightly. Sometimes she squeezes back. I tell her that Nate and I are really happy, because I know she'd love to hear that. I turn on *Dateline* and keep up the usual commentary, even though it's not the same without her chiming in. I tell her Keith Morrison is still as handsome as ever and pretend I can hear her laugh. I imagine it just to fill the silence. I sing that Taylor Swift song—the one I used to make her listen to over and over again—completely out of tune. I hope, against all hope, that she'll wake up and tell me *that's enough.*

I feel my heart slowly hollow as I watch her fade. Nate isn't handling it much better. Sometimes, when I'm in the other room, I hear him talking to her. He tells her he misses her. Thanking her for everything she's done for him.

"No one else would've done what you did for me," he says softly. "No one ever cared the way you did. You didn't have to, but you did anyway, and that means the world to me. I hope you knew—*know*—that I stayed because I care about you, too. Not just to drool over your granddaughter."

He chuckles softly at his own joke. "I want to marry her, you know. If that would be okay with you. I didn't get to properly ask you... before..." His voice trails off, and I feel my breath catch in my throat at his words. "I'll take care of her, but even without me, she'll be just fine. You raised a smart, stubborn, headstrong woman. She's amazing, but you already know that."

That night, I fell asleep in the chair with my hand resting on top of hers. When I wake up, she's gone, and my world shatters. I cry hot, ugly tears, unable and unwilling to move. It feels like I'll never breathe again. Like someone reached in and carved my heart out with a paring knife. Slowly. Carefully. Leaving me here, hollow.

I can't even speak to call Nate, eventually my wails grow so loud I don't have to. He comes in, and the moment he sees me, he knows. As always, he takes care of everything. He calls the funeral home. They show up all too soon. When it's time, Nate has to pull me away; he has to drag me into another room as I fall apart, hysterical. He tries to get me to eat, but I won't. He tries to get me to move from the chair, but I can't. So, he carries me to the bath and cleans me up while I sit there, silent and still. I don't say a word. I just let him take care of me, because I can't imagine doing anything anymore. I can't imagine existing in a world where she's gone. In the back of my mind, I knew this was going to be hard. I knew that losing her would crack something inside me. But I don't feel cracked—I feel *shattered*. Grief hasn't just touched me; it's paralyzed me. It shocked my body, slithered in, and took me over.

She planned her own funeral, and as heartbreaking as that was, I was eternally grateful. I didn't have to make a single decision. Even near the end, she was still protecting me. I wrote her obituary before she passed, because I knew I wouldn't be able to do it afterward. The idea of putting her in the past tense made me feel physically sick. I lay in bed, the document open on my phone, reading it one last time before sending it off to

Diane. My hands were shaking. My chest felt hollow. I sent it off, my eyes blurring as I did.

I knew I couldn't lay there forever; there was her funeral to attend in just a few days. The thought of it made my stomach turn. I couldn't imagine anything worse. I felt the bed dip beside me. I didn't need to look, I knew it was Nate, checking on me again. I can feel his worried gaze on me. As sweet as he's being, and attentive as he's been, all I want to do is scream. I want to tell him to leave me alone. Every instinct is telling me to push him away. I knew those feelings weren't fair, so I stayed quiet. He's talking to me, but his voice is muffled and distant.

"Okay, Sloan?" he asks. I nod, not even sure what I just agreed to. He kisses my temple and leaves the room. I breathe a sigh of relief, glad to be alone with my grief again.

I sleep for hours on end because when I sleep, she's still here. She's in my dreams, and it feels so real. In those dreams, we play cards, cook together, and watch *Dateline*. If I could sleep forever, I would—just to live in a world where she never disappears. It takes all of me to get up on the day of the funeral.

Nate, as helpful and loving as ever, has to help me get ready. Practically having to dress me himself. He tries to get me to eat again, and I appease him with a bite of bread I didn't even bother to toast. He helps me out of the car at the funeral home, and the closer we get to the doors, the heavier I feel.

I feel my stomach twist and for a moment, I want to run—this can't be real. I can't be attending my grandmother's funeral. The one person who was always there for me, even when I was at my worst. The one person who always had my best interest at heart. Nate is practically holding me up as we walk in. An employee greets us and reaches out a hand. I just stare at it, not taking it. Nate starts talking to him, but I can't make out the words. Am I going deaf? It's like I can't hear anything lately. They lead us back to see her, and I know there's no way this is going to go well. I freeze in the doorway. Nate turns to look at me, his eyes full of quiet worry.

"I don't know if…" I trail off, my voice barely there, as my eyes lock on the casket ahead of us.

He holds his hand out to me, and I take it as we walk forward. Everything goes in slow motion. When I reach her, I hear an awful, guttural sound, and for a moment I'm confused. It's just us in the room, but I realize it's me. I'm sobbing over her, and I feel like I can't breathe. She looks like she's sleeping. I lean over her, noticing the shirt, one of her favorites from her closet. Nate must have picked it out. She's holding her rosary, just like she asked. I pause when I see her nails. They're painted. I turn to Nate.

"Why are her nails painted?" He looks at me, confused.

I ask again, a little louder this time. My crying has stopped, and now I just sound angry. "Nate, why are her nails painted?" I feel crazy—like no one is listening, no one is answering me. Nate opens his mouth, stuttering. I turned to the funeral director instead. He doesn't look nearly as concerned as Nate does. "No one asked me if her nails could be painted," I say. My voice is too loud, but I can't contain it.

"Ms. Mercer," the funeral director says gently, "you sent Mr. Reed in your place to drop off her clothing and finalize the remaining details. We asked him about the nails, and he told us to proceed as we normally would."

I blink stunned and my mouth opens, but nothing comes out at first. I turn slowly to look at Nate, who's already looking at me with guilt etched all over his face.

"You said to do what?" I ask, my voice quieter now, tighter. "Nate, she *hated* nail polish."

He starts to explain, stumbling over his words. "I—I didn't know what to say. I just thought—"

"You *thought*?" I cut in, my voice cracking. "She planned everything. There were only a few small details left, and you let them do something she would've hated?"

I know it's not fair. He looks like I've slapped him. I turn away before I have to watch him try to answer. Suddenly the casket feels like it's glowing, too bright, too wrong. I want to reach out and wipe the polish off her fingers myself. Instead, I just backed away. I feel the tears rising again—hot and bitter. Not just grief now, but guilt. Guilt for not being the one who went. Guilt for letting someone else speak for her when she'd spent her whole life taking care of me.

The service starts, and it's all a haze. People come in—so many people—offering condolences, telling me how sorry they are, how wonderful she was. On and on, until all the words start to melt together.

When it's time for the eulogy, I snap to attention. Nate leans in, gently trying to ask if he should do it. If I *can* do it.

"No thanks," I snapped. "You've done enough."

I stand, willing my legs to carry me forward, telling myself that after everything she did for me, this is the least I can do. I reach the podium clearing my throat seeing a sea of people.

"As many of you know, I'm Marilyn's granddaughter. She raised me for most of my life. She was unlike anyone I will ever know. I know people say that a lot, but in her case, it's the truth. She was the best person I've ever known. In a world full of uncertainty and cruelty, she was my light in my dark. She was my best friend. She lived her life caring for others, right up until the very end. In her lifetime, she endured one of the hardest things anyone could go through. Her daughter going missing was one of the greatest losses of her life. And yet, she raised me. She looked at me every day, seeing a copy of her missing daughter. I can't imagine how much that must have hurt. She was *always* there for me. Through everything. She never made me feel like a burden. She never asked for anything. She never took—she only gave. I can't imagine the weight she carried. What she felt every single day. It would have broken most people. I wanted to bring her closure before she died. I wanted to find Scarlett. But I failed her. I don't know if I'll ever forgive myself for that."

My vision blurred as I felt myself go off script, the composure I'd managed to muster slipping away, slowly but surely. I couldn't keep going. I walked back to my seat, leaving the rest of what I had to say unsaid. The service continues, and I stand as the casket is carried out to the hearse. We walk to the gravesite, where her headstone is already in place. The only thing missing is her date of death. My grandfather was already buried there; his name and information etched on one side.

As the service comes to an end and people begin to leave, I stay seated, watching as the dirt is shoveled in. Nate sits beside me, silent. He hasn't said much since I snapped at him.

"Sloan... are you ready to go?" I look at him like he's lost his mind. I wasn't leaving, not until every last bit of dirt was in place.

"No, thank you. But if you feel the need to leave, I'll find my own way home." I've clearly hurt him, but I can't stop myself.

"Sloan... about the nails," he says softly. "I'm sorry. I tried to get you to go in, to make the final decisions, but... I couldn't get you out of bed."

I clench my jaw, staring straight ahead at the grave. I want to tell him it wasn't his decision to make. That it mattered. That *every* detail mattered because it was the last thing I could do for her.

"Maybe you should have tried a little harder, Nate. I mean... how many times did you actually ask me?" Even as I say them, I know the accusation isn't fair. I bite my tongue before I make it worse, before I say something I can't take back. I close my eyes and exhale shakily.

"I know," I say, my voice low. "I know you tried." There's a long silence between us, but it doesn't feel tense anymore, just heavy.

"I just wanted everything to be perfect," I whisper. "It was the last thing I had left to give her." My eyes stay fixed on the dirt being shoveled in. "I'm not going until it's done."

Nate doesn't leave. He just sits beside me, silent. I'm sure we're the only two left, until I turn around and see Diane standing a few steps back, watching quietly. I stand up slowly, not wanting to leave. The crew is packing up, and I can feel Diane behind me, waiting patiently. I feel Nate trail behind as I reach her. She gives me the *I'm sorry for your loss* smile and I can't quite bring myself to smile back.

"The service was beautiful," Diane says softly. "I just want you to know, your grandmother was a close friend of mine. I know I haven't been around much since you've been home. I couldn't bear seeing her sick. It was so hard. I know that sounds ridiculous."

I looked back at her, not quite sure why she waited until the service was long over to say this—or why she felt the need to say anything at all.

"We bonded over the fact that our daughters suffered from addiction," she says quietly. "While Scarlett has been missing for a while, talking to someone who didn't judge me—or my daughter—was always nice." She hesitates, then takes a breath. "She loved you more than you know, Sloan. She would have done anything for you—I mean, she *did* do anything for you."

While I knew she loved me and would do anything for me, it was something else entirely to hear someone else say it with such certainty. Tears welled up in my eyes, and a few slipped down as I looked at Diane.

"I just wanted to come here to tell you that, and make sure I reminded you of one more thing. Your grandmother asked me to remind you about her paperwork in her filing cabinet. The usual stuff: wills, policies, deeds. I'm sure you know about them, but I promised her a long time ago I would tell you anyway." I'd been meaning to deal with those things, but I just hadn't been able to. "She also asked me to tell you there's a drawer at the bottom of the filing cabinet full of things she saved just for you. She said it was important that you have all of those things."

I couldn't help but smile at how sentimental she was.

"Thanks, Diane," I say quietly. She steps forward and envelops me in a hug, and I surprise myself by hugging her back. As Diane leaves, it's just Nate and me.

"Let's go home," I say softly.

CHAPTER 42

I went right back to wallowing in my bed after the funeral. Weeks stretched by, and I barely got up. Nate and I spoke very little. I mean, it's hard to talk when all I want to do is sleep and watch old reruns of Dateline. He tried every day to get me out of bed, to eat, to smile. None of it worked. I silently wondered how long he would keep trying.

"Sloan, maybe you should go through her paperwork now," Nate says hesitantly during his usual morning check-in before heading to work.

"Maybe," I reply, my eyes fixed on the TV, not really watching it I hear the front door close a few minutes later. The silence settles over the house like a weighted blanket. The credits of the episode roll. I don't bother changing it. It'll auto-play the next one anyway. I should get up. I should do a lot of things. Instead, I sink deeper into the mattress, letting the familiar drone of crime narration wash over me like static.

Nate comes home, and I'm in the exact same place I was when he left that morning, curled up in bed TV still humming in the background.

"Sloan, I have some good news," he says, a little too upbeat for the fog I'm still buried in. "I contacted your old boss at *Ink Ever After*; they said they'd take you back. You could even start soon, if you wanted. I was thinking... Maybe we could move. I could take classes anywhere. I'm sure I could find a place to work in New York once we get there."

I looked him in the eye for the first time in weeks. Was he speaking a different language, or did he really just say what I think he said? I sit up slowly, my body stiff from disuse, my mind struggling to catch up.

"What?" I snap, my voice sharper than I intended. "How in the hell did you even get my old boss's contact information?"

I can feel the anger rising in my chest, how *dare* he do this without asking me. How dare he move pieces of a life I haven't decided I even want back. He looks shocked

"Sloan, I think this is what you need," he says, his voice strained. "You haven't done anything in weeks. You're not eating, you're not writing, you're wasting away. I can't just sit by and watch it happen." I get out of bed, my voice rising before I can stop it.

"Nathan, no one asked you to watch. You don't like how I choose to grieve? Then you're free to leave. But you have no right to contact anyone on my behalf. You don't get to decide what I need. I wake up every day feeling like I've been crushed by something I can't see. I can barely breathe most of the time, let alone *plan a move* or go back to work like everything's fine. You think I want to be like this? You think I *chose* to lie here every day and rot?"

I can feel my chest tightening, tears burning behind my eyes, but I don't stop.

"You're trying to fix this like it's a problem with a clean solution. But it's not. She's gone, Nate. *Gone.* And no job, apartment, or escape plan is going to make that okay." Nate runs his hands through his hair, looking frustrated for the first time in weeks.

"Sloan, I love you," he says, his voice tight. "You need to understand, I lost her too. I'm trying to be patient, trying to give you space, but we still have to live our lives. We *have* to. You're lying around like you're the only one who's lost something, and I know it hurts, but we can't stay stuck here forever. You need to go through her paperwork. We need to figure out what comes next."

I let out a bitter laugh, one that doesn't even sound like me.

"Figure out what comes next?" I repeat, shaking my head. "Next is what, Nate? A new city, a new job, us starting our lives together? She was the only person in my life who really knew me—who *really understood* me." I catch the flicker of hurt in his eyes, but I'm too far gone to stop. "I'm sorry if I'm not grieving on your schedule. But I don't need a plan. I need time."

He leaves the room without another word, and I hear his door open and close behind him. I let out a shaky breath. What did he want from me? I have no clue what I'm supposed to be doing. Every time I get out of bed, I feel unsteady—like I'm walking on fragile glass. I lie in bed alone, doubting Nate will come lay with me tonight. I can't help but think—this would be easier if I'd figured out what happened to Scarlett. If I could have brought her some small piece of closure. I drift asleep, hoping to see her in my dreams again.

We're sitting at the table, cards in hand, her smiling at me. We play, and even in my dreams, she's beating me. Her laughter fills my dream, soft and familiar, like a warm embrace. For a moment, the weight of the world lifts. She looks at me and says,

"Sloan, you need to get up." I reach out to touch her hand, but it slips through my fingers.

I woke up, the room pitch black. My breath comes heavy and ragged. I get out of bed and head upstairs, straight to her room. Opening the door, I'm hit with the sting of absence—the bed is gone, just an empty space where she used to sleep. I find the key where I did last time and kneel in front of the filing cabinet. The bottom drawer creaks open, revealing all the school projects she saved, my old articles, every little piece of me she thought was worth keeping. It's all still there, exactly how I left it.

I reach toward the back where the letters from Scarlett were. Something catches my eye. A letter I hadn't noticed before. My name is scribbled across the front but not in Scarlett's handwriting like the others. It's my grandmother's. Unmistakable. I open the letter, and the first few sentences blur in front of me. I read them again. My hands are shaking. Was this some kind of joke?

Sloan, *If you're reading this, I am no longer a part of this world. I knew I couldn't tell you this any other way, no matter how hard I tried. Scarlett isn't missing. She's dead, and I'm the one who killed her.*

CHAPTER 43

June 17, 2000 – Marilyn

I wake up to noises in the kitchen and jolt upright. I wish I could say this is the first time this has happened in the middle of the night, but it's not. My daughter, Scarlett, even now that she's grown and has a place of her own, still shows up here when she needs something or when she's nearby, running around with that no-good boyfriend of hers. Just in case it's not her, I grab the bat from beside my bed and walk slowly into the kitchen. As I suspected, it's Scarlet, she's throwing cold leftovers onto a plate like she owns the place.

I look at my daughter, *really* look at her. She's a shell of the person I raised. Addiction has hollowed her out, stealing parts of her body and mind, piece by piece. Tonight, she has a split lip and what looks like the beginnings of a black eye. She glances up at me and grins, like it's not one in the morning.

"Hey, Mom," she says casually. "Just came to crash in my room for a sec and grab a bite."

She sounds high right now; it would surprise me more if she *wasn't*.

"What about Sloan?" I ask, my voice sharper than I mean it to be. "Where is she tonight?"

Scarlett rolls her eyes like my concern is just background noise. "She's fine, Mom. Geez. She's taken care of."

Scarlett always says that when she wants me to stop asking questions. But I can't. Not when it comes to Sloan.

"Scarlett, you're a *mother*. She's your *daughter*. You need to take care of her, not run around all hours of the night. She needs stability. She needs *you*." I sigh, turning to put on a pot of coffee, hoping we can actually talk.

"Look, Scarlett," I say, gently. "Maybe we can have Sloan come live here for a while. You could go to rehab. I'll pay for it—we'll find a good one. You can get clean and come home. Start fresh. Be the mom she needs."

For a second, she doesn't say anything. Just staring at me with that same blank look I've come to dread. Then her mouth twists into a tight, bitter smile.

"You think it's that easy?" she snaps. "You think rehab's some magic switch that's gonna fix everything?" She laughs, cold and joyless. "Why don't you just say it, Mom? You think I'm a lost cause."

I sigh, already feeling the shift in the air. "Scarlett... have you been taking your meds?" The words are barely out of my mouth before I realize what I've done. Her eyes snap up, sharp and furious.

"Oh my God," she says, voice rising. "There it is. There's the real reason you want me in rehab, because you think I'm *crazy*, right? Not just an addict, but a whole damn disaster." She slams her plate down on the counter, and I flinch at the sound. "Why do you even bother pretending to care?"

My stomach sinks. It doesn't matter what I say, everything seems to set her off.

"Scarlett," I say gently, trying to hold my ground without lighting a fuse. "You *know* you need them. It's important that you take your meds. There's no shame in it." She scoffs and turns her back to me like she can shut me out just by not looking.

"You don't get it," she mutters. I take a deep breath, my heart breaking for the millionth time.

"I want you *alive,* Scarlett. I want you well. Running around with Kent and whoever else, getting high—that's not living." I pause. "I want Sloan to have her mother."

She's pacing the kitchen now, voice rising with every step.

"Sloan, this, Sloan that," she snaps. "She's *my* daughter, Mom—*not yours.* You're just trying to send me off so you can have her and get a do-over. I'm not an idiot."

Her words cut deeper than she realizes. I want to reach out, to make her see I'm only trying to help, but the distance between us feels too wide to cross right now. "Scarlett, let's sit down, you can eat at the table." She snatches her plate, shooting me a glare, but follows anyway.

I pour her a glass of water, watching as her mood shifts again. The sudden change scares me and I wonder what she's like at home with Sloan. How does Sloan handle it? How does Scarlett manage? The silence between us is heavy, filled with things left unsaid. Then she breaks it.

"Kent asked me to marry him," she says happily. I balk, the words catching in my throat. Kent, the same guy who got her hooked. The one who dragged her deeper into that dark world.

My voice is barely steady when I say, "Kent?" She nods, smiling like it's the best news in the world. I want to scream, to shake her and make her see what he really is. But instead, I swallow the fear and pain and try to keep my voice calm. "Scarlett, are you sure that's what you want?"

Her smile fades just a little. I sit back, helpless, realizing this is going to be harder than I thought.

"Scarlett, I got a call from Diane tonight."

She scrunches her nose, skeptical. "Diane?"

I nod, keeping my voice steady. "Yeah, Emily's mother."

She stares at me, eyes narrowing. "What did she want?"

I take a sharp intake of air preparing me "She wanted to call and let me know my daughter is going around collecting drug debts." Scarlett freezes, her fork halfway to her mouth. The words hang heavy between us, sharper than any knife.

"I—I don't know what you're talking about," she stammers, eyes darting away.

I lean in, voice steady but firm. "Scarlett, this isn't just about you anymore. It's about Sloan. We have to get you out of this before it's too late."

Her face crumples, anger and fear flickering across it. "You don't get to come in here and act like you're in charge of my life—or hers." The kitchen feels colder now, the silence growing heavier than before.

"Someone needs to do something, Scarlett, because you're not. You're not taking your meds, you're in a relationship with a drug dealer, and you're high almost every day. How is this fair to your daughter?" I swallow hard, fighting back my own tears. "This isn't just your life anymore, Scarlett. Sloan deserves better."

Scarlett sits down, her fork paused mid-air as she looks at me. "Mom, you don't have to worry about her. I'm going to take care of her just fine. Kent and I are getting married, and Sloan will have a father figure in her life." I want to vomit at the thought of that man living under the same roof as my granddaughter. "Anyway, we're moving after the wedding, so you won't have to worry. Kent says he can find better work in Columbia."

I stare at her; surely she's joking. She's planning to move Sloan away from me, to a city two hours away, bigger than either of them is used to. "Scarlett, do you really think it's a good idea to move? Sloan's already settled in school here. She has friends. I can help you when you need it."

She smirks at me, and I see her mood shift again. The mean Scarlett surfaces, the one who laces every word with venom, the one who takes pleasure in hurting others.

"You just can't stand it, can you? I found someone, and I don't need you anymore. I'm taking Sloan with me, and you'll be left completely alone. You sit around here pretending like I'm the one who needs you, but really, you're the one who needs me. Well, guess what? That's done. We're moving, and there's absolutely nothing you can do to stop it. Keep pushing me, and don't expect me to even bother telling you where we're going."

I felt the situation spiraling out of control. "Scarlett, if you leave with Sloan, I swear I'll call the police. I mean it, I've been patient, I've let you run wild, even let you steal from me without a word. If you take Sloan away like this, I won't hesitate to report you both."

She stands up, eyes blazing. "You report me, and what? I go to jail? You think I'm just going to let Sloan stay with you after that? I'll fight tooth and nail; I'll do whatever it takes to make sure you don't get her."

I look at her, and I have no doubt she would. Addiction has turned my daughter into a stranger, someone just wearing Scarlett's face. I miss my daughter so much, who she was before this other person took over. This is the same girl who used to bring home straight As, who drew me pictures and begged me to hang them on the fridge. Now, I can't see a trace of that little girl in the woman standing in front of me. I have to get this conversation under control. I have to make her understand that Sloan staying here is the best option.

"How about I grab us some coffee?" I say, standing up slowly. "Maybe a slice of cake too—to celebrate your engagement."

She stays at the table, launching into a ramble about how great Kent is, how happy they're going to be together. But as she talks, I notice she hasn't mentioned Sloan once. Not once. It's all about them. It hits me, like a cold weight in my chest, Sloan is just an afterthought to her. She'll always be an afterthought if Scarlett has anything to do with it. That's the brutal truth I keep trying not to face. Scarlett won't change, no matter how hard I try, no matter how much I want to help. I've bent over backwards, made excuses, covered for her, prayed she'd find her way back. But the truth is, sometimes unconditional love isn't enough to fix someone. Change doesn't happen just because someone needs it, it only happens when they want it. Scarlett has shown me, time and time again, that she doesn't want to change. Somewhere along the way, the daughter I knew disappeared.

She's still rambling, going on and on about Kent, their future, how "everything is finally falling into place." Her voice feels far away, muffled, like I'm underwater. In my hand—almost like it appeared there on its own—is a bottle of pills. My fingers are curled around it so tightly, the label is creased. I blink at it, my mind scrambling. *When did I grab this?* I try to replay the last few minutes in my head, but everything is a blur. I don't remember going to the cabinet. I don't remember reaching for it. It's an out-of-body experience—the way my hands move without instruction, crushing the pills, stirring them quietly into her coffee. Not all of them. Just enough. Just a few.

She keeps talking, still rambling about her engagement, about Kent's 'connections' in Columbia, about the future that sounds more like a delusion than a plan. I nod along, pretending this is all the best news I've ever heard. We eat. She drinks. Eventually, she wanders off to her old room, laughing at something she said that I didn't hear. I don't follow her. I stay in the living room, settling into the old recliner that creaks beneath me.

I stare at the wall, going over the plan again and again. I'd wait a few hours. Call 911. Tell them I think she's overdosing. They'll have no choice but to step in. Sloan will come live with me. Scarlett will go to rehab, or jail depending how much I tell them. While she's there, I'll hire a lawyer. I'll do everything I can to protect Sloan. Someone has to. I close my eyes—just for a moment. Just to rest. But the moment stretches too long, but I forget one critical thing as I drift off. I left the bottle of pills out on the counter.

CHAPTER 44

Sloan, *If you're reading this, I'm no longer a part of this world. I knew I couldn't tell you any other way, no matter how hard I tried. Scarlett isn't missing. She's dead. And I'm the one who killed her. I've carried this weight for years. The guilt has been relentless. When Scarlett was younger, she was brilliant, smart, artistic, and full of potential. Somewhere along the way, that light began to dim. I remember the shift so clearly. It started when she met Kent. Suddenly she was staying out late or not coming home at all. Her straight A's vanished.*

As a young widow raising a daughter, I'd love to say I did everything I could to help, but the truth is, I didn't know how. So, I punished her. I grounded her. I banned her from seeing Kent and anyone else I thought was dragging her down. Sometimes it worked, but most of the time it didn't. She'd sneak out. Skip school. Steal from me. When she became an adult, it didn't get better. I kept trying. I paid for rehab, for apartments, and cars. Each time, she swore she'd change. Each time, I believed her. I wanted to believe her. I wanted so badly to have my daughter back.

Then she told me she was pregnant, and I was terrified. Until that moment, she had only been hurting herself, but now there was someone else involved. You. She came home to live with me while she was pregnant. For nine months, she stayed clean. She was different—better. I started to hope again. When you were born, I held you in my arms and cried. I thought maybe this was it. Her turning point. She was clean, she was calm, and she was trying.

For a while, things were good, but it didn't last. She started slipping again. Staying out too late. She couldn't handle being your mother for more than an hour at a time. The only silver lining was that she always left you with me, and I didn't mind. I loved you so much, but at some point, Scarlett noticed and the cruel part of her resented it. Resented me. She moved out, took you with her, and refused to tell me where you were. I was wrecked with worry.

Eventually she called because she needed something. That was always the pattern. You came over again. I could see she wasn't taking care of you. You were always tired and quiet. I begged her to let you stay with me. I gave her everything she asked for just so I could see you, so I wouldn't lose you. The time came when she got arrested, and she sobered up. She got a place nearby. For a while, she was the version of herself I always hoped for. You probably don't remember those days. You were too little to remember, but when she was truly herself, who she was meant to be, she was nothing short of amazing.

Somehow Kent slithered back into her life. I didn't notice at first. The changes were so slow. I wanted to believe she was fine, but she wasn't. She started to unravel again, and I got scared. Scared she would take you away for good. Scared of who she might become again. That night she disappeared, she showed up high. Rambling. She told me Kent proposed. She told me they were moving to Columbia. I panicked. I tried to reason with her. Told her you could stay with me. That she didn't need to move, but she was set on her decision. Said she was taking you, whether I liked it or not. I couldn't let that happen.

I want you to understand, I never meant to kill her. I know that might not matter now, but I need you to know. My plan was to make it look like she was overdosing. I thought if I called 911 in time, they'd take her in, and I could get custody of you. I crushed up a few pills and stirred them into her coffee, just enough to make her sleep. But I fell asleep and mistakenly left the bottle of pills on the counter. When I woke up... it was too late. She had taken more. I found her on the floor, and I knew it was my fault. While it wasn't my intention, it was something I couldn't undo.

Looking back, I know logically that if I had just called 911, it would have been believable. Scarlett was already high, no one would have questioned an overdose. I panicked. I spent an entire day inside that house, mourning the loss of my daughter, paralyzed by guilt and fear, not knowing what to do next. I was spiraling. I wasn't in my right mind. Before I even realized what I was doing, I was outside in the middle of the night, digging a hole. Praying no one would see me. I placed Scarlett in the hole, and I mixed a bucket of cement and poured it in before covering her with dirt. I slept for days after that—partly from exhaustion, but mostly from grief and shock. I lost Scarlett twice. Once to addiction, and once again when she died. It wasn't until almost a week had passed that the haze started to lift.

That was also the day I got a call from your school. That was when it hit me—you were alone. That was the moment everything changed. I knew then that I had to live. I had to survive this so I could be there for you. I had to find a way to carry what I did and still give you the life you deserved.

That summer, I had the front porch extended over where Scarlett was buried. I kept having nightmares that Scarlett would crawl back out of the ground. That someone would find her. I was terrified every day. If anyone ever discovered the truth, I'd lose you. Then what would all of it have been for? I raised you. I watched you become this beautiful, kind, brilliant young woman. I watched you fall in love with Nate. I watched you chase your dreams. You were everything I thought you could be and more.

Even still, I lived in fear. I waited for a knock on the door, for a phone call, for someone to say they knew. The day came when you asked me to move to New York with you. I wanted to. God, I wanted to. But I couldn't. I know I hurt you by saying no, but I need you to understand, I couldn't leave her. I couldn't risk someone buying this house.

All these years, I wanted to tell you, so many times. But I just couldn't. I was too afraid of what it would mean for you, and what it would cost me. I also couldn't stand the idea of you hating me, and I know that's selfish. Now I'm sick, and I know I don't have long.

And I want you to know—need you to know—Scarlett did **not** abandon you.

I wish you had known that as a child. I wish I could have helped you understand that her love for you was never the problem. If not for addiction, she would have been an amazing mother. I saw glimpses of it, those beautiful, shining moments where she showed up, fully present, full of love. You were her light, even when she was drowning in the dark. She was lucky to have you as her daughter.

I took that away from both of you. I took away what she could have been. So now, the choice is yours. Everything that was mine is now yours. You are free to do whatever you need to do. You can tell the truth. You can go to the police. You can have Scarlett's body exhumed. You can sell this house, leave, and never look back. You can hate me.

I do have a few requests. I know I've lost the right to ask anything of you, but I'm going to anyway. If you choose to have Scarlett reburied, please bury her near me. I know it's more than I deserve, but it's all I can hope for now. My last request is this: Please make sure Nate receives something from my estate, a sizable amount. He's earned it in more ways than one. If there's any part of you that still *loves him, I truly hope you've found your way back to him by the time you read this. That boy would walk through fire for you, Sloan.*

You need someone in your corner now that I'm gone.

Love you always and forever, **Grandma**

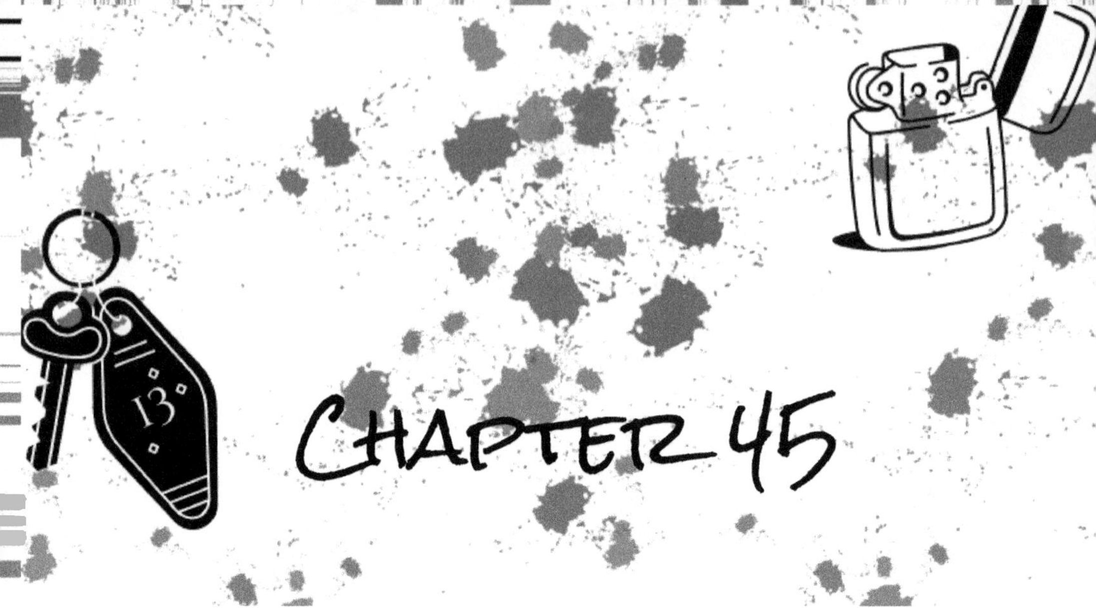

Chapter 45

I must've fallen asleep on the floor, curled around the letter like it could anchor me to the earth. When I woke, the sun was just starting to rise, casting soft, golden light across the room. I blinked against it, still clutching the letter. I got up, folded the paper with shaking hands, and placed it back exactly where I'd found it. I locked the drawer again. Then I did the only thing that made sense, something I'd been avoiding for weeks. I went through her paperwork.

I found her will first, confirming what I already knew: everything was left to me. There was a thick folder with her life insurance policy, and tucked behind it, an envelope. Inside was a single silver key and a note in her familiar handwriting: **Safe Deposit – Bank of Summit Grove**. She had laid everything out for me, piece by piece, like a final act of care. As I sifted through her bank statements, my eyes widened. The dollar amount on the policy was staggering. Even her savings account held more than I ever would've imagined.

I was confused at first; she worked long after retirement age, often taking on more than she needed to. I thought she had to work. But now I see it differently. She didn't need to work. Not with what she had saved. My heart sinks and swells all at once as the truth settles in. She must have been punishing herself all these years, trying to make up for what she'd done the only way she knew how—by quietly building a life for me. A safety net. A future. Every hour she worked, every penny she saved, it was her penance.

I gathered the paperwork in shaking hands and carried it to my room, closing the door softly so I didn't wake Nate. I sit on the edge of the bed, the stack of documents spread out in front of me like puzzle pieces to a life I thought I understood. I try to summon the anger I thought I'd feel, the righteous justified rage at what she did to Scarlett. But it doesn't come. All I can feel is love. She wasn't trying to hurt Scarlett. She was trying to protect me, and it got out of hand. Even if I wanted to be furious, it wouldn't matter. She punished herself enough for both of us over the years. The guilt had carved itself into her like stone, and I saw it so clearly now, in the long hours she worked, the sleepless nights, and the way she clung to me like I was the only thing keeping her afloat.

No, the rage I feel isn't for her. It's for him. Kent. I can't prove it, but deep down I know—if it hadn't been for him, Scarlett would've been different. She would've had a chance. Without him, she might still be here. Kent didn't kill her, but he lit the fuse. He killed Scarlett slowly, quietly, turning her into someone else. And no matter how much time passes I don't think I'll ever stop hating him. As long as he was out there, free and unbothered, I knew I'd never sleep soundly again. He didn't just break Scarlett. He hollowed her out. He would do it again. To someone else's daughter, someone else's mother. I couldn't let that happen. I wasn't going to let this go.

I left the house just after sunrise, the silver key clenched tight in my fist like it might vanish if I let go. The plan was simple—go to the bank, open the safe deposit box, get whatever it is she left for me. But as I drive, the familiar curves of the road lead me somewhere else, and I find myself three houses down. Before I can stop myself as I into the driveway. The tires crunch over gravel, the early morning sun casting soft light over the chipped siding and overgrown yard. I kill the engine. The silence swells around me. I don't know why I'm here. Maybe I thought I'd feel something, fear or clarity. But all I feel is the way my pulse thrums in my ears. I grip the steering wheel so tightly my knuckles ache. I put the car in reverse, foot hovering over the pedal, telling myself to back out. But I can't. Something roots me there, like I'm supposed to be here.

Before I know what I'm doing, I throw the car into park and open the door. I get out with no plan. Just this wildfire of emotion crackling in my chest. I step over a pile of garbage bags that reek of sour food and cigarettes, making my way toward the porch. The boards groan under my weight, brittle and warped. The whole thing looks one strong gust away from collapsing. Still, I move forward. I raise my hand to knock, but before my knuckles meet the door, I hear footsteps approaching. The door flies open, and I'm face to face with Kent.

He looks worse than ever. Gaunt. Greasy. Eyes bloodshot and sunken like he hasn't slept in days. He smells like old beer and stale smoke, even from a few feet away. He looks me over, top to bottom, and I have to force myself not to recoil. That same sleazy, smug appraisal he gives all women, like we're all just inventory he gets to inspect.

"What do you want?" he asks, voice low and scratchy.

I open my mouth, nothing comes out. I didn't come here with a script. I didn't come here with anything but anger and grief, and now it's all catching in my throat. He sneers, the corner of his mouth curling.

"Oh. I see. You finally figured it out, huh? Realized you need a real man." He leans one hand on the doorframe. "Nate's not doing it for you?"

His words hit me like a slap, ugly and disgusting. My mind goes startlingly clear. Like the fog that's been choking me for weeks finally lifts. I know exactly why I'm here. I smile at him, sweet and easy.

"Yep. You guessed it." He blinks, surprised.

"I just wanted to come over," I continued, batting my lashes, "and see if your offer was still good." His eyes light up in that sick, familiar way, like he thinks he's won something.

He grins. "Well, hell. Took you long enough."

He swings the door open wider, stepping aside to let me in. I step over the threshold, and every instinct in my body is screaming. I keep walking forward with a smile on my face, because now I know exactly what I'm doing. The door shuts behind me with a quiet click that sounds more like a lock than a welcome. The air inside is stale and heavy with cigarette smoke and that god-awful sewer smell. Kent moves ahead of me, smug and unaware, like he thinks this is a victory. He talks as he walks, tossing a beer can onto an already-crowded table.

"I always knew you'd come around. Girls like you, always come running to guys like me." My heart pounds, not with fear this time, but with purpose. Rage coils beneath my ribs, sharp and steady. I came here to finish what he started.

CHAPTER 46

I pull up to the bank feeling lighter than I had in weeks. The weight of uncertainty that had been crushing me seemed to lift, replaced by a cautious hope. Inside, I approach the teller and request access to the safe deposit box. I slide my ID across the counter, hands steady. She leads me through the quiet halls to a small room tucked away from the main floor. They place the cold metal box in front of me and give a gentle, "Take your time," before quietly stepping out and leaving me alone. I take a deep breath, fingers trembling as I lift the key, ready to see what she left behind. As I open the box, my eyes fall on a ring first, small, worn, it was unmistakably Scarlett's class ring. I pick it up carefully, feeling the weight of memories it carries. Next, I find another ring set with three small diamonds, one I've never seen before. Nestled beneath them is a small, folded piece of paper. I unfold it slowly and begin to read:

Sloan,

This is your mother's class ring. You should have it. The other ring was my engagement ring from your grandfather. It's yours. Please make sure the envelope in here gets to Nate.

All my love, Grandma.

I look down, my eyes welling with tears as I realize she saved these for me. Despite everything, through all the years and all the silence, she was always thinking of me. I pick up the envelope marked for Nate and study it, curiosity pulling at me. I don't open it. It wasn't mine to read. If Nate wanted to share it, he would. If he didn't... Well, I'd respect that.

I carefully placed everything back inside the box and tucked the rings into my bag, the envelope held gently in my hand. I close the safe deposit box, thank the employee, and step outside. In the parking lot, the sun is higher now, warming the pavement. I pause, drawing in a deep breath that should have calmed me. But that feeling is back, that prickling sensation along my spine. Like I'm being watched. I scan the parking lot. Cars roll by and horns go off in the distance, the buzz of everyday life playing out like normal. I don't see anything out of place. Still, the unease lingers, refusing to leave. I shake it off, clutch the envelope a little tighter, and head to my car.

I stop at McDonald's on the way home, grabbing breakfast for Nate and me. For the first time in weeks, my hunger is back in full force, a quiet signal that something inside me is beginning to shift. I can feel the toll the last few weeks have taken: the hollowness in my limbs, the weakness pressing down on my chest. So, I order more than I should—hash browns, sandwiches, pancakes, coffee—enough to feed ten people. Still, that prickling feeling lingers. Like there are eyes on me. I glance around the parking lot one last time before taking the long way home, telling myself there's nothing to worry about. Not anymore.

It's around ten a.m. when I pull into the driveway. As I step inside, I see Nate pacing the living room, looking frantic. His head snaps up when he hears the door, and the look on his face guts me—he's wrecked.

"Sloan," he says, rushing toward me. "You didn't tell me you were leaving. I woke up and you were gone, no note and your car missing. You can't keep doing this, running off every time we disagree."

He's rambling, frustration and worry bleeding into every word. Then he stops, staring at the McDonald's bags in my hands. "Wait... you went out to get food?" He blinks like he doesn't quite believe it.

"Well," I say, setting the bags down on the dining room table, "and to run an errand. I ordered way too much food." He follows me into the dining room, speechless. I glance back at him and offer a small smile. "You're going to have to help me eat some."

He just stares at me like he's still trying to figure out who I am this morning. I sigh, stepping closer, placing my hand gently against his face.

"I'm sorry," I say quietly. "I acted like I was the only one hurting, and that was selfish. You were right, we need to figure out what comes next. *Together*." I lean in and kiss him. He kisses me back immediately, grounding and tender. I pulled away reluctantly, suddenly self-conscious I hadn't brushed my hair or my teeth. He looks almost disappointed when I break the kiss, and I laugh under my breath.

"I take it I'm forgiven?" His smile is the only answer I need. We eat, and the whole time we can't stop smiling at each other.

Nate finishes eating before I do, but instead of clearing his plate, he moves behind me and leans down, pressing a soft kiss to the side of my neck. I freeze—not because I don't want it, but because it's been so long. Weeks have gone by without a touch, without a kiss. No gentle hand on my back, no late-night reach for mine under the covers. Now, here he is—his lips lingering, brushing against my skin in a way that makes my heart flutter. I tilt my head, giving him silent permission, and he takes it. One of his hands comes to rest on my shoulder, the other brushing a strand of hair away as his mouth moves lower.

"Nate," I whisper. He pauses but doesn't say anything, waiting.

"I should really shower," I say, my voice barely above a murmur. "I've missed this... I have but let me clean up first and we can pick this back up after."

He groans playfully against my neck. "Maybe I could join you in the shower?"

I laugh, nudging him with my elbow. "Not this time. I feel gross. Besides—" I gesture toward the table littered with wrappers and empty containers, "you've got cleanup duty."

He grins, backing away with his hands raised in surrender. "Deal, but don't take too long."

I head to my room, grabbing a clean towel and some clothes. As I toss them onto the bed, I suddenly remember the letter tucked away in my bag. My chest tightens a little. I wasn't sure when the right moment would be, but that wasn't my decision to make. I jog back to the kitchen, where Nate's still picking at the last of our breakfast mess.

"Hey," I say, catching his attention. "I went to open the safe deposit box this morning. There wasn't a whole lot in there, but one of the things was this." I handed him the envelope, slightly crumpled at the edges now, but still sealed. Still private. I hold it out to him.

He takes it slowly, his brows pulling together. "What is it?"

I shrug, trying to sound casual even though my heart's thudding. "It's from my grandmother. She left it for you, and no, I didn't read it."

He looks down at it in his hands, turning it over once, then again. His lips part, like he's about to speak, but he closes them again, giving a tight nod instead.

I shower for what feels like forever. I wash my hair three times, scrubbing until my scalp tingles. I lather my skin again and again, like I'm trying to peel away the past few weeks. I don't stop until the water turns cold. Even then, I linger, letting the chill ground me. When I finally step out, the bathroom is thick with steam, curling around me like fog. I brush my teeth three times, until my gums sting and the sharp taste of mint leaves no room for anything else. By the time I'm done, I feel lighter, like I've shed something. I slip into clean sweats and one of Nate's shirts, soft and worn at the collar. I open the bathroom door slowly, quiet enough that I can listen for him before I see him. My heart skips, not from nerves, but from wondering if he read the letter. If it said something that might break him. Something that might make him pull away.

I stand at his closed bedroom door for a moment, my hand hovering uncertainty over the wood. Should I knock? Say something? Instead, the door swings open, and there he is with that easy, familiar smile that feels like home. With no trace of anything being wrong.

"You shouldn't have bothered getting dressed," he murmurs, his hands sliding around my hips, pulling me close. Before I can say a word, his lips find mine. The kiss is urgent, desperate even, like we're both trying to make up for lost time. I sigh into him, relief flooding through my chest as I melt into his arms. He guides me gently but with undeniable urgency toward his room. Every step feels charged, like we're both finally answering a call we've been ignoring for too long. I go willingly, my hunger matching his, craving the closeness we've both been starved for.

The door clicks shut behind us, and the world starts to fade away—until the sharp wail of sirens cuts through the air, growing louder by the second. I freeze, heart pounding, as a faint, acrid smell drifts inside. Fire.

Chapter 47

We sprint upstairs, hearts hammering, checking every room and corner. No smoke, no fire here. When we step outside, the source becomes chillingly clear. Three houses down, flames are still being doused, the blackened skeleton of Nate's old home standing in stark contrast against the smoky sky.

"Nate... I'm so sorry," I whisper, my voice barely steady. He stands there, shoulders slumped, staring at the ruins like a wounded animal. For a moment, I'm terrified he might break. Then he lets out a slow, heavy sigh and turns to me.

"Sloan, that house stopped being mine a long time ago," he says quietly. "Even if I somehow got it back, it would never be what it used to be."

His words hang in the smoke-filled air. I wrap my arms around him on the porch as we watch the fire finally die down, the firefighters sifting through the rubble like they're searching for more than just ashes.

"You know," he says quietly, "the only downside is Kent was probably not home. Would've been nice for that guy to finally get what's coming to him."

I stiffen slightly but don't say anything. He continues, bitterness edging his voice, "Now he'll probably just pitch a tent on the property." Nate lets out a low, frustrated sigh, the anger simmering just beneath the surface, clear in his eyes.

We stand there, just staring, and I see Nate can't tear his eyes away from the ashes.

"Hey," I say softly, and he looks at me. "I decided this morning what I want to do, you know with our lives." He cocks his head, waiting for me to continue. "I want to live here, in this house, with you. I want to start my life with you. I don't know yet what I'm going to do for work, but I do know this—I want to wake up every day next to you and go to sleep every night with you beside me."

I look at him, waiting for a response, my heart pounding in my chest. He stays quiet, his eyes fixed somewhere past me. The silence stretches longer than I expected, and a flicker of nervousness rises inside me.

"Nate, I want you to think of this place as your home. Seriously, this house is as much yours as it is mine. You'll always have a spot here, no take backs." I grin, trying to lighten the mood.

"I want us to redo parts of the house together, make it ours. And hey, maybe even raise some tiny humans here someday—build a life, you know?" I freeze mid-sentence, realizing I just threw in the 'kids' bomb out of nowhere. We've never really talked about that before. If worry this might send him into orbit. I mean, who brings up kids when his childhood home is turning into a pile of ashes just down the street?

A single tear slips down his cheek. Nate, who's been so steady and strong, finally lets his guard down. He pulls me close, still not taking his eyes off the spot where his house used to stand. I sigh in relief, glad I didn't scare him away.

"That's exactly what I want to do," he whispers softly in my ear.

We stay in for the rest of the day, eating the leftovers from breakfast and watching TV, slowly talking about the future. Later that night, we're in bed surrounded by junk food when Nate flips to the nightly news. My heart pounds in my ears as the screen shows footage of our street and the smoldering remains from earlier that day.

"Local authorities report that an accidental fire tore through a residence in a quiet Summit Grove neighborhood earlier this morning," the anchor begins. "Firefighters responded quickly, but the house was not salvageable. Sadly, one local man died in the blaze. Officials have confirmed there will be no further investigation, stating the fire appears to be accidental with no signs of foul play." The report moves on swiftly, the fire not even a blip on their radar.

We sit in silence, the news filling the room with cold and detached facts. Only one person could have been in that house. Only one life lost to the flames. Nate's eyes meet mine, and for a long moment, we say nothing. Suddenly, a bitter, jagged laugh breaks free. It starts low, broken—like a crack in a dam—before spilling out uncontrollably. We laugh at the irony: the one person we wished dead, the one who ruined so many parts of our lives, will never bother us again. Nate falls asleep before I do, and I watch him, marveling that I get to stay with this man for the rest of my life. I knew he would walk through fire for me, but that went both ways. I'd *gladly* start one for him.

Chapter 48

Even with Kent long gone, I still felt like I was being watched. Maybe it was just my nerves, edged sharp from everything I'd done, from knowing Scarlett was buried somewhere here on the property. If this was the kind of weight my grandmother carried for years, I wasn't sure how she managed it.

I sorted out her affairs and had the house put in both of our names. He protested at first, but I told him, "If one day you get sick of me, I don't want you thinking you have nowhere to go." He laughed, called it absurd, but eventually relented.

He was hesitant to accept the 'sizable' amount of money I was instructed to give him. Holding the check, he shook his head. "I can't take this, Sloan. How do you even have anything left?"

I smiled. "I don't have a choice. I was told to give you that."

He narrowed his eyes. "Told to?"

I nod, eyes drifting over him—fully aware that I could have him wrapped around me like a weighted blanket in under five seconds if I so much as crooked a finger. The thought makes me bite my lip, zoning out into what can only be described as a rated R daydream.

"Earth to Sloan," he says, waving a hand dramatically in front of my face like he's guiding an aircraft. I blink, pulling myself out of the fantasy.

"Sorry, were you saying something, or were you just being distractingly hot again?" I tease, a slow smile tugging at the corner of my lips.

He rolls his eyes, but there's no hiding the warmth in them and that, *you're ridiculous but I like it* look. "You said you were 'told to' give me the money. What's that about?"

I take a breath. "Well, you weren't the only one who got a letter," I say, smiling as I lean in to kiss him softly on the lips.

I never asked him what was in his letter, if he wanted to tell me, he would. And I didn't want to be asked about mine. I didn't want him to think my grandmother was a bad person, because she wasn't. She was simply the same woman she had always been. I understand that now more than ever.

I stayed around the house most days. I wasn't in a rush to find a job just yet, not that I would never work again, but now I had more time and more money than I ever had before. I didn't have to settle. That was the whole point of her leaving all of this to me: so I wouldn't have to. Besides, it's not like I was doing nothing. I may or may not have been working on a book. Nothing official yet, but it's happening. When it's done, I'll definitely release it under a pen name, no way I'm putting my real name on the cover.

Nate still goes to work. He says he can't just stop, not when so many of the older residents of Summit Grove rely on him for their landscaping. He's adamant about not letting them down, no matter what. I smile every time I think about it. Somehow, it makes me love him even more than I already did.

I was staring at my laptop when something out the window caught my eye—a car creeping slowly past the house. One

I didn't recognize. My stomach tensed, but I forced myself to shake it off. It was nothing. Just nerves. I turned back to the screen, still browsing real estate listings—stopping at the one I've been looking for. What do you know? It was for sale. Practically a steal. I couldn't help the twisted little smile that tugged at my lips. Or shall I say... fire sale?

Chapter 49

Nate - present day

I'm up early almost every day waking up next to the love of my life, and each morning I'm still amazed we found our way back to each other. I never thought it would work out like this, or that we'd end up staying in our hometown. I meant it when I said I'd go anywhere for her. So, I was surprised when she told me she wanted to stay. There was a time, when grief had her so lost, I wasn't sure she'd ever be the same. I thought I might lose her for good. She fought her way back, stronger than ever. I look down at the woman I want to spend the rest of my life with as she sleeps peacefully. She's beautiful, even when she snores, though she'd never admit it. I lean in and kiss her forehead, about to leave for the day.

One of her eyes pops open, and she murmurs a sleepy "good morning." She turns to me, catches my lips with hers, and snakes her arms around my neck. I feel her hands tangled in my hair, and a low moan slips out as her kiss deepens.

"I have to go, sweets," I murmur, but she groans softly against my lips.

"Just stay in today, come on," she pouts, and somehow that pout makes her even more irresistible.

I press soft kisses to her temples, trailing slowly down the curve of her neck, taking my sweet time like I've got all day.

"I'll be back later, and we can pick this up right where we left off," I whisper between kisses, making my way to her shoulder. She lets out a shaky gasp, pulling me closer.

"You're such a tease. This is emotional sabotage."

I flash her a grin, the kind I know drives her nuts, stealing one last kiss, slow and sweet, just enough to make her miss me. "See you tonight, sweets. Try not to miss me *too* much, and hey—get some rest. Doctor's orders."

I head upstairs, grab a few bottles of water, and load up the work truck. As I back out of the driveway something catches my eye, a car I don't recognize, rolling slowly past our house. Too slow. My gut tightens. It could be nothing... or it could be something. Either way, I make a mental note of the make and color before turning onto the main road, watching in the rearview mirror a little longer than usual.

I start my rounds, making it to all my customers right on time. The work is grounding steady and familiar. Most of them are more than kind to me, offering hellos, cold drinks, and the usual small talk. But a few still haven't let go of that article Sloan wrote about people in town. I can see it in the way they purse their lips or throw out a passive comment meant to sting. I don't let it slide. I tell them politely that if they've got a problem with Sloan, they've got a problem with me. If they can't let it go, they're welcome to find another landscaper. They usually don't say much after that. Sloan told the truth in that article. It might've made some folks uncomfortable, but that's on them—not her. I won't let anyone make her feel small for it, not on my watch.

I didn't need to keep this many clients anymore, not since Sloan insisted on giving me that check. She swore it was Marilyn's wish, stating her grandmother had made it clear she wanted me to have it. It felt like too much. More than I deserved. Sloan wouldn't take no for an answer, and honestly, arguing with her is like trying to stop a train with your bare hands. So, I did the only thing that made sense. I opened a savings account and tucked it away, for *our* future. For home renovations, for vacations, for a wedding... maybe even for our future kids. I wanted to give her everything she's ever wanted. Everything she deserved, and more.

I sighed, thinking of Marilyn. About how she'd included me in something so big, so meaningful. It wasn't about the money. It was about what it stood for. It was about the way she always made me feel worthy of her affection. She took me in when I had no one, and for that I would be forever grateful. That, and the fact that her granddaughter just so happens to be the absolute love of my life.

My mom tried. She really did, but her love always seemed to fall short. She picked herself over me, again and again, and Marilyn saw that. She saw what I needed, and she gave it to me. She made me feel like I was worth loving. Without her, I honestly don't know where I'd be. Her last words to me are burned into my memory. I had every single one memorized:

Nate,

I've watched you grow from a quiet young boy into an amazing, strong man. I know life hasn't always been easy for you. I knew your mother was close with Scarlett, and the first time I saw you walking home alone, I knew I needed to take you in. It helped, of course, that you were the same age as Sloan. You two grew up together, side by side, and I knew—long before either of you did—that you were meant for each other. As I write this, you still haven't found your way back to each other. But I have no doubt you will.

I'm sorry your mother couldn't truly see how great you really are. I know how badly you wanted her to. You tried so hard to impress her, to be the kind of son she'd finally notice. You were even willing to give up Sloan to stay behind and take care of her. I'm sorry your mother battled the same addiction that took hold of my daughter. It's a cruel disease. It makes people lie, manipulate and makes them into versions of themselves they would never otherwise become. Like a mother lying to her son... telling him that his girlfriend of five years came by to break up with him—when she didn't. Just so she could keep you around, paying her bills, wasting your potential.

I had a feeling she had something to do with your breakup from the start. It didn't make sense. I'd seen the way you looked at Sloan. There was no way I was wrong about that. That day I confronted her... she was high. Of course she was. I was angry, I couldn't help it. All I could think about were the times you came to my house hungry because there was no food in yours and how she tore the two of you apart.

I didn't mean to push her. The porch had loose steps, and when she backed up, she lost her footing. I heard her head hit a rock and I knew right then it was bad. I'm not proud that I left. I'm even more sorry that you were the one who had to find her.

For a while, I tried to see the silver lining. Maybe now you'd finally have the house to yourself. Maybe now, you could live your life for you. When I found out the house was going to Kent, I was livid. Kent. Ruining lives. Again. When you had nowhere to go, I was glad to take you in. But the damage was done. You lost your house and your mother in one blow.

I know this letter won't change anything. I know it doesn't give you back what you lost. But I've instructed Sloan to give you a sizable amount of money after I'm gone. Maybe you hate me, and I wouldn't blame you. All I ask is that you don't let this affect how you feel about Sloan. Don't let it ruin what you two have. You've always been willing to walk through fire for her, just don't stop now.

She needs someone in her corner. Especially now that I'm gone.

Marilyn

I only read the letter once. The only thing that truly upset me was the idea that any part of her believed I could ever hate her. By the time I held that letter in my hands, I already knew the rest. I knew my mother had lied to me just to keep me under her roof. I knew Marilyn was the one who had pushed her, leading to her death. Just like I knew Scarlett was buried somewhere on the property. I didn't know all along. If I had, I would have never let Sloan keep looking for her. I would've told her the truth. By the time I figured it out, Sloan had already given up the search.

It was near the end, one quiet evening, I sat with Marilyn while Sloan made dinner in the next room. She turned to me, tears already slipping down her cheeks, and confessed every-thing. I don't even think she realized she was saying it out loud. Maybe part of her had been waiting for someone to tell the truth to. I doubt she remembered doing it later. But in that moment, once I told her it was okay, that she wasn't alone, something in her loosened. Like she'd been holding her breath for years. I told her Sloan would understand too. She asked me, over and over again, to look out for Sloan. She told me I was the only one who would go to the same lengths for her. That no one else loved Sloan the way we did, and she was right I'd do anything for her.

CHAPTER 50

Nate - present day

I finished work early, eager to get back to Sloan. The whole drive, there was that familiar lightness in my chest, the kind I only felt when I knew she was waiting for me. I swung by the store and picked up some flowers, and of course a cinnamon roll. She couldn't resist anything sweet, and I couldn't resist the way her whole face lit up when she took that first bite. But the second I turned onto our street, that warmth vanished.

That same car was parked just a few houses down. It was half-hidden between some trees, something I wouldn't have normally noticed. Our houses were spaced out, far enough apart that most people wouldn't notice something like this. On a weekday, on this quiet stretch of road, it didn't belong. My stomach clenched. This wasn't bad timing anymore. It wasn't a coincidence. I eased the truck down the road, heart thudding, keeping one eye on the rearview mirror. The car didn't move. Something about it made my skin crawl. Something was off. I pulled into our driveway and killed the engine, but I didn't move. I just sat there, gripping the wheel. Then I checked my phone.

No new messages.

No sweet midday texts from Sloan. No memes. No *'I miss you already'* or *'I'm making something weird for lunch again.'* Nothing. She'd been home alone all day. I glanced back at the car. I got out and jogged toward it. When I reached it, I peered through the driver's side window—and froze. There was a stack of photographs on the seat. I squinted, trying to make out the ones on top. My blood ran cold. Sloan. They were pictures of Sloan, clear as day. It was clear she had no idea they were being taken. I bolt back to the house, heart pounding, legs moving on instinct. I slam through the front door, shouting her name.

"Sloan!" No answer. I take the stairs two at a time—*please let her be downstairs, please let her be okay.* Maybe she's in her room, maybe she's just writing, earbuds in, completely unaware of everything going on outside.

Panic claws at my chest as I race downstairs, and I'm welcomed with destruction. Chairs overturned. Picture frames shattered. The coffee table knocked on its side. A lamp lying in pieces. I find her curled into a ball on the floor. I stumble toward her, a breath of relief escaping me just to see her there, breathing, alive, but it's short-lived. I drop to my knees beside her. Her lip is split and bleeding. The collar of her shirt has been torn. There's the faint, ugly beginning of bruises rising on her neck and eye. She flinches when I touch her shoulder.

I pick her up slowly, careful not to jostle her too much. She winces, biting back a sob. I try to soothe her, whispering soft reassurances she barely hears. I settle her into the only chair that's still standing. She curls up, trembling, and soon the sobs spill out, the sound of them raw and heartbreaking. I sit beside her, unsure what to say, my hands just resting gently on her knees. She looks up at me through tear-blurred eyes.

"Nate… this is all my fault," she whispers, voice cracking. I furrow my brow, searching her face.

"What are you talking about?" I ask, voice tight with worry. She only sobs harder, shoulders shaking uncontrollably. My heart races as she struggles to breathe.

"Sloan, breathe," I say firmly, leaning closer. "*Please*, tell me who did this to you."

Her eyes flicker with pain and fear, but she stays silent, tears streaming down her cheeks.

"He's dead," she whispers, barely audible. I blink, confusion twisting in my gut. *Dead*? There's no one here. No signs of anyone else.

"Who, Sloan?" I press gently, though my mind races. "There's no one here. Just you and me."

Her eyes lock on mine, wide and trembling. She doesn't say anything. Just lifts a shaking hand and points toward her bedroom door. My stomach sinks. I rise slowly, every step toward that door heavier than the last. I don't know what I'm expecting as I push it open. Lying on the floor. Still. Doctor Tucker, blood pooling underneath his head. I hadn't even given him a second thought since the last time I saw him. Now… he's in Sloan's room, and he's definitely dead.

Shit, I mutter under my breath.

CHAPTER 51

Sloan - present day - that morning

I was already awake when Nate left for the day. His touch, even half-asleep, could raise me from the dead. Now I'm curled over my desk, typing away on my current work-in-progress. My playlist is blaring in one ear, the other earbud dangling loose—half listening to the music and half lost in my words.

That feeling is back. The one I hate. The one that wraps cold fingers around my spine and whispers *you're not alone.* I glance around the room, telling myself I'm just being paranoid. Still, I get up and walk upstairs, just to be sure. I check each room—empty. No one's here. I peer out the windows. The street is quiet. No cars, no neighbors.

My heart jumps as I hear a knock at the front door. I move toward the window near the door, but from this angle, I can't see who it is.

"Damn it," I mutter. *We really need to get with the times and install a doorbell camera.* I unlock the door and pull it open, already bracing for some delivery or a neighbor. The man standing there isn't either. I freeze.

"Doctor Tucker?" The name stumbles out of my mouth before I can stop it. He stands there calmly, like this is normal, like he belongs on my doorstep. My mind spins. Why is he here? Does this man ever quit?

"Sloan, may I come in?" he asks, like this is just a casual visit. I squint at him. *Was he serious?* There was no way I was letting him in. Not now. Not ever. And especially not while I was alone. Something about him felt... off. He was too calm, too sure of himself. I didn't care what excuse he had. Whatever he wanted, he wasn't getting it *inside* my house.

"Um... no?" I say, though it comes out sounding way less confident than I meant it to. *Why did I sound unsure?* I *didn't* want him to come inside. Not even a little. He laughs. Actually laughs—like I'd just told the world's funniest joke.

"I think you'll want to reconsider," he says with that smug smile of his. God, he was starting to annoy me. I was almost certain he had this effect on a *lot* of people.

He digs into his back pocket and pulls something out. A photo.

"Here. Take it," he says, holding it out like it's nothing.

I hesitate, unsure, but grab it quickly from his hand anyway. As soon as I look at it, my breath catches in my throat. It's me, walking into Kent's house. The image is grainy but clear enough. At the bottom—stamped in black—is the date and time. Undeniable. My heart starts to pound. What the hell is he doing with this?

"Oh, you can keep that one," he says casually. "I have copies." I glared at him, my grip tightening around the photo.

"What do you want?" I snap. He smiles like he's already won.

"Like I said, Sloan... can I come in?"

I exhale through my nose, jaw tight, then step aside and hold the door open. He walks in like he owns the place. His presence instantly changes the energy in the room. I shut the door behind him, already regretting it.

"Have you been following me?" I ask, watching him closely. I glance out the window, scanning the street. His car isn't visible. *Where the hell did he park?*

"I wouldn't call it *following*," he says smoothly, turning to face me. "More like... admiring from afar."

A chill creeps up my spine. I force myself not to shudder.

"I'll ask again, what do you want?" I say, cutting through the silence, done playing around. "Is it money? I can write you a check."

He chuckles softly, eyes locked on me like he's savoring the moment. In the back of my mind, I already knew that this wouldn't be that easy.

"No, Sloan," he says, voice low and deliberate. "I don't need money. I simply want you."

My eyes go wide, heart pounding in disbelief. *Was he serious?* A cold wave crashes over me. I scoff, disbelief dripping from my voice.

"You can't be serious. That's not a real request." He steps closer and I can't help but take a step back. He leans in, eyes cold.

"The way I see it, you have two choices. You can do what I ask... or I can turn you in." I balk, my mind racing. *What the actual fuck?*

"If I do what you want," I say, voice shaking but steady, "what stops you from coming back again?"

He smiles, like this is some kind of pleasant chat.

"Well," he says slowly, "I guess nothing does, and I never said I wouldn't."

I hold my breath, the weight of the choice pressing down like a bad idea in progress. Then I exhale slowly.

"Fine," I mutter, barely above a whisper. "Let's go downstairs."

I turn and head for the steps. Naturally, he makes me go first, because nothing says "trustworthy man" like forcing a woman to lead the way into a potential crime scene. He's a looming shadow behind me. Every instinct I have is screaming at me to run... but I kept walking. I had no idea what the plan was. If he thought I was just going to roll over and become his creep-of-the-week fantasy, he picked the wrong girl.

We reach the basement, and I just stand there like an idiot while he takes me in, like I'm something he already owns. He steps closer and I freeze. His hot, sour breath hits my ear.

"Don't worry," he whispers. "You'll like it. I promise."

My stomach twists violently. Then I feel his mouth on my neck. Sloppy. Greedy. Right where Nate kissed me this morning. I want to vomit. He wasn't gentle. He wasn't anything but *wrong*. For a second, I think about shutting down, and just letting it happen, dissociating, surviving. But if I let this go, he could keep coming back. He could take and take, and he would always hold this over me. My chest tightens, my heart breaking at the thought of Nate. The way he touches me, holds me, sees me. The way no one else ever has. This man didn't get to ruin that. He didn't get to ruin *me*.

I start to shake with fury, and I see red. I see Kent, ruining lives like it was nothing. I see the cops who didn't care. Everyone who looked the other way. I think of every woman who was ignored, blamed, and diminished. Every woman who was told her past defined her. That *she* was the problem, and something inside me *snaps*.

His hand brushes across my chest, and I decide *I was done*. I rear my head back and slam it into his face with everything I've got. Pain explodes through my skull, stars burst in my vision, but I hear the satisfying crunch, and then a *curse* as he doubles over clutching his nose.

"You bitch," he growls, voice low and wild. He lunges toward me, and I dodge. He crashes into a chair, sending it toppling with a sharp *bang.*

His anger is unfiltered now—no more manipulation, no more fake charm. This was never about turning me in, he was never going to let me walk away, no matter what I said. This was never just about blackmail. He'd made up his mind before he even walked through the door. It makes something burn hot in my chest.

He lunges, and I move fast—sidestepping him just in time. He crashes into the wall, knocking down a handful of framed pictures. Great. Not only is he after me, now he's tearing apart my home too. I bolt for the hallway, desperate to make it to my room, but his hand catches in my hair, yanking me backward. A cry escapes me before I can stop it. He pulls hard, spinning me around, and the next thing I know, I'm on the floor. The impact knocks the air out of me. My head swims. Blood runs warm from my nose.

Get up, I tell myself. *Move.*

He's already reaching for me again, grabbing the front of my shirt and pulling me halfway up. The fabric tears at the seam. His expression is twisted and vile. It disgusts me. He grabs at me, and the moment his hands touch me, tears spring to my eyes—unwanted, but impossible to stop. He smiles at my reaction, and I can see it clearly now: he enjoys this. That twisted satisfaction in his eyes makes my stomach turn. I snap forward and bite down on his neck, *hard.* He yells, reeling back in shock, doubling over as pain overtakes him. I run, breath ragged, vision blurry. My room is just ahead. If I can just reach my phone, just one call can end this.

I feel him behind me again. I reach for the doorknob, but before I can grab it, he catches me. He pulls me back and shoves me against the wall, forearm pressing hard across my collarbone, trying to pin me. My breath catches in my throat, panic flaring as I struggle to pull in air. He swiftly wraps his hands around my neck, and suddenly everything narrows. My vision blurs at the edges, black spots blooming like ink in water.

I claw at his arms, struggling to pull in even a shred of air. Is this really it? After *everything*—after finding my way back to Nate, after finally deciding who I wanted to be, what I wanted my life to look like—*this* is how it ends? It feels like some cruel, cosmic joke. As the pressure builds, as my limbs grow heavy and the panic tightens around my chest, a voice cuts through the fog—clear, firm, and impossibly familiar.

Fight, Sloan. I must be worse off than I thought, because it sounds exactly like my grandmother. With the last ounce of strength I can find, I drive my knee upward, hard. He gasps and suddenly, his grip loosens. I drop to the floor, gulping in air like I've never needed it more. My lungs burn and my head spins

I scramble to my feet, still gasping, every breath sharp and ragged. My hand fumbles with the doorknob before I finally wrench it open. I stumble into my room, mind racing, trying to remember where I left my phone. He's still on the floor behind me, recovering slowly, his face twisted in rage. That look alone tells me I don't have long. My strength is draining fast, and I know I can't hold him off again. I grab the phone and unlock it, hands shaking.

Even as I open the screen, the truth crashes down on me like cold water. Even if I call someone—*anyone*—they won't get here in time. The cops in this town hated me. Most of them wouldn't rush to help me anyway. Not after everything. They'd take their time, maybe even blame me. I look toward my bed and remember I only had one option. My grandmother's old bat, the one she kept by her side every night. I moved it down here weeks ago, when I first started feeling like I was being watched. I reach for it now, hand steadying.

He's closer now, that awful smile back on his face like he's already won. As I grab the bat, he *laughs*. For a second, doubt creeps in. Maybe this was a terrible idea. He steps forward, grabs the end of the bat and the sock I'd slipped over the top slides right off.

Now it's *my* turn to smile. The moment he looks down at the sock in confusion, I swing—and I swing *hard*. Adrenaline surges through me as the bat connects, the shock of impact jolting up my arms. He staggers back, the smug look vanishing from his face, replaced by something I haven't seen in him until this very moment. Fear, and it's almost *liberating*, seeing the fear on his face. He's on the floor now, clutching his head, and the sound of him groaning in pain fills me with a sharp, undeniable satisfaction. I'm breathing hard, adrenaline pounding in my ears. A smile creeps across my face before I can stop it.

For a brief, flickering second, I wonder if there's something wrong with me for feeling this way. I shove that thought aside, now is *not* the time to unpack that. *Leave.* You can leave now, I tell myself. *Run.* Get out of the house. You'll make it. My legs won't move. Instead, my fingers tighten around the bat.

I take a step forward, looking down at this sad excuse for a human being, and I don't just see *him*. I see all the lives shattered by men like him. His eyes are dazed, his body barely conscious, but I grip the bat tighter, and I swing. I swing for Scarlett, whose life was changed forever by someone just like him. I swing for Karrie. I swing for Emily. I swing for my grandmother. I swing for every woman who was ever made to feel small, invisible, or afraid—because a man decided she was less than. I pulled back one last time. This time, I swing for *me*. My breath comes hard and ragged with each blow, my arms shaking, my chest heaving.

When it's over, the bat slips from my hands and hits the floor with a dull thud. I drop to my knees. Tears burn in my eyes, hot and relentless, as the weight of it all crashes down. My neck throbs, every breath scraping against bruised muscles. My body feels heavy, leaden. I look down at him—and I know. There's no calling anyone now. Blood pools beneath his head, dark and final. I don't need to check for a pulse, I *know* he's gone. I can't look at him anymore. With legs that barely hold me, I rise—unsteady—and step out of the room, closing the door softly behind me. I sink to the floor in the next room, my back against the wall, my mind slipping into blankness. Silent. Still. The tears come. Not for what I did, but because I didn't feel bad for doing it.

CHAPTER 52

Nate present day

I'm holding Sloan, and I'm not sure I'll ever be able to let her go again—not after hearing what she just went through. Her body is tense in my arms, still too pale. The bruises on her neck, the swelling around her eye, every mark makes my chest tighten with helpless anger. She's not crying anymore, and she's now silent, still. That terrifies me more than the tears ever could. She's here, but something in her eyes hasn't fully come back yet.

She begins to shiver, and I don't think twice as I rush to my room and grab the first blanket I can find. When I returned, she hadn't moved. It's like she didn't even notice I left her side. I kneel down and gently wrap the blanket around her shoulders. She flinches. Her breath catches in her throat, sharp and shallow.

"Sloan... hey. It's me. Nate." She turns slowly, eyes wide and distant, like she's just now remembering I'm still in the room. "I'm so sorry I wasn't here, sweets... to protect you."

Silence. She just sits there, staring at nothing, her eyes glassy and far away. I just watch her, memorizing the shape of her face, the way her hands tremble slightly beneath the blanket.

She finally speaks, her voice barely more than a whisper. "I'm not sorry." Then the tears spill over again, tracing silent paths down her cheeks.

I gently wipe the tears from her cheeks, careful not to hurt her. Without a word, I lift her into my arms and carry her upstairs to the bathroom. I start the bath, the warm water running as I undress her slowly, tenderly, making sure she doesn't protest. I settle her into the water, letting it wash away the blood. When I'm done, I gather her clothes and toss them into the trash without hesitation. I dry her off, brushing her hair softly, all while she stays quiet, lost in her own world. I gather blankets and pillows and bring her to the couch, settling her down gently. Before she lies back, I hand her two Tylenol PM, hoping they'll help ease the pain.

I lean down and kiss her cheek. It doesn't take long for sleep to claim her, I can see her fighting it, but her body's too worn down. Eventually, she slips under. I don't want to leave her. Not now, but time is slipping away, and I have no choice.

Quietly, I head downstairs, jaw clenched as I reach into his pocket. My skin crawls as my fingers close around the keys. I shut the door behind me, soft and slow, then pause to scribble a quick note for Sloan. I slide into his car and take the back roads toward Columbia, doing everything I can not to attract attention. Every turn feels like a risk. I keep one eye on the gas gauge, silently praying it'll hold long enough to get me there. By the time I reach the city, the sky is starting to darken, the last of the light fading fast. I pick a parking lot on the edge of town—run-down, half-abandoned, barely lit. No security cameras in sight. At least, I *hope* not. I can only pray I'm right, that no one cares enough to comb this place for DNA or ask too many questions about a car left behind. I grab the pictures of Sloan from the passenger seat and shove them into the backpack I brought, my jaw tightening. I searched the car for anything else that could come back to her. His phone is next. I wipe it down carefully, smudging away every print, then toss it into the back seat, right out in the open. To finish the scene, I reach into my bag and pull out a bottle of pain pills I took from the house. I pour most of them into the cup holder, the rest scattering onto the floor.

With any luck, this would work. Columbia was a big city. People disappeared all the time. Maybe a guy like Eugene Tucker wouldn't be missed—at least not right away. I groan, dragging a hand down my face. Of course he'd be missed. He was a doctor. Someone *would* come looking. I give the scene one last look under the dim streetlight—pill bottle spilled, phone in view, pictures gone—and turn away.

I walk casually, head down, keeping my pace steady until I reach the edge of the lot and slip into the shadows. My phone's back at the house, right where I left it. No GPS, no digital breadcrumbs. That meant I had two choices: walk the whole way or hope a stranger was feeling generous. I start walking toward the highway, thumb out when a car passes, but no one stops. Not at first. Thirty minutes in, just when my legs are starting to burn and doubt creeps in, a semi slows down and pulls over.

The driver leans across the cab and opens the door. "Where are you headed?"

I hesitated. No way I'm saying *Summit Grove*.

"Jefferson," I say instead. He nods.

"I can take you that far. I'll pass through there anyway." I climb in without another word.

I silently pray I make it back before Sloan wakes up. The driver tries to make small talk—where I'm from, where I'm headed—but I keep my answers short. Just enough to seem polite. Not enough to be memorable. If anyone ever asked, I didn't want to stand out. We reach Jefferson, and the night swallows the town whole. He drops me off at a gas station without asking too many questions. From here, it's about an hour's walk back to Summit Grove and that's still better than walking all the way from Columbia. By the time I reach our street, it's nearly 2 a.m. Every muscle in my body aches, but I exhale a shaky breath of relief the second I see her— still curled up on the couch right where I left her. I step closer, careful not to wake her. The bruising on her neck has darkened, the edges turning a sick shade of purple. My chest tightens as I stare at the woman I love and my heart twists. I wasn't here when she needed me. Marilyn asked me to protect her, and here I am already failing.

I head straight downstairs. I open the door that leads to the back of the property, the cool night air hitting my face like a slap. I have to get Sloan's room cleaned up. I have to get the body out before she wakes up. There's no way I can dig a deep enough hole before sunrise. The shed will have to do. It takes everything I've got to drag him there, silence pressing down on me with every step. By the time I shut the door and lock it behind me, I'm gasping for breath, sweat soaking the back of my neck. I head back inside and hurry to Sloan's room. I strip the bed, gather the blood spattered sheets, and roll up the rug—stained, heavy, reeking of copper. I shove everything into a garbage bag and tie it shut. Out here, burn piles are just part of life and soon enough we'll burn it. I know there's no way I'll get every trace of evidence out of here tonight. I cleaned up the worst of it, the parts that would shake her all over again. Once

I'm done, I shut the door to Sloan's room and lock it behind me.

I gather everything we'll eventually burn and stash it under the stairs, locking that door too. My mind spins, raking over every detail, searching for anything urgent that I might've missed before Sloan wakes up. My body's starting to give out. My eyes are heavy, limbs dragging. I head to the bathroom, knowing I need to shower before I collapse right where I stand. The water hits me, hot and punishing. I sway on my feet as I scrub the day off of me, forcing myself to keep moving. If *I* feel like this, I can only imagine what Sloan must feel. It's in that moment, under the steady rush of water, that I let myself fall apart. Just for a minute. A short, quiet breakdown while I still have the space to have one.

When it's done, I shut off the water, towel off, and dress in clean clothes. I take my dirty ones and head back downstairs one last time, stuffing them into the bag under the stairs. By the time I reach the couch again, my legs are trembling from exhaustion. I don't sit next to her. I sit on the floor beside her instead, watching her sleep, letting the quiet hold us both. As much as I want to pull her into my arms, I don't. She needs rest more than anything, and I won't take that from her. So, I stay close. *Finally,* I let my eyes close, as exhaustion pulls me under.

CHAPTER 53

Sloan present day

I wake with a sharp intake of breath. My body jolts, muscles screaming in protest as I force myself upright. Every inch of me aches. For a moment, I'm confused. I'm on the couch. I look down, Nate, he's asleep on the floor beside me. I blink at him, then glance up at the old clock hanging above the door frame, it's 1 p.m. How long have I been asleep? Everything comes rushing back. All of it and my hands start to shake. My breath catches in my throat. There's a body in the house and his car has to be somewhere nearby. Panic twists in my chest, fast and tight. I need a plan. I need to *move*. Why didn't I stop at one hit? Why did I just keep going?

As if he senses my distress, Nate jolts awake, his eyes wild and body tensed like he's ready for a fight. But the moment he sees me he exhales and the tension leaves his shoulders. He sits beside me without a word and wraps his arms around me.

Nate says softly, *"Don't go downstairs."*

I don't need to be told twice. What strikes me most is what he *doesn't* ask. He doesn't ask me if I really set Kent's house on fire. He doesn't ask why I didn't stop after the first swing.

I wondered, for a moment, if he was worried I was on some kind of scorched-earth, get-even spree. He just looked *worried about me*, like I was the only thing that mattered. He told me he was taking care of everything, and if anything else happened or went wrong he'd take care of that too. No hesitation. No judgment. He told me we could start remodeling the house right away, and suggested we start downstairs. My heart warmed. This man was literally covering up murders for me without a second thought.

Later, I caught my reflection in the bathroom mirror. The bruises were dark and harsh, painting my neck with the truth of what happened. I thought they'd scare me. But the longer I looked, the more empowered I felt. Yes, he did this to me, but *I* won. He would never ever do this to anyone again.

I think about the flames swallowing Kent's house. Burning down Nate's childhood home was never part of the plan. But the truth is, it stopped being his home the moment Kent poisoned it. I picture Kent inside, the fire crawling up the walls, smoke thick in his lungs, unable to move, trapped by the pull of the morphine I slipped into his drink. The world is better without men like Kent and Eugene. I wasn't going to lose sleep over killing them. What *would* keep me up at night was the possibility of getting caught. The memory of their eyes and hands on me, and the sickening truth that wiping these two men off the planet barely made a dent. They were just a small blip on a map full of monsters hiding in plain sight, wearing smiles and titles and respect they never earned.

Nate finds me in the bathroom, standing in front of the mirror, staring at the bruises that mark my skin like shadows. He doesn't say anything at first, he just comes up behind me and wraps his arms around my waist—solid, warm and steady. His chin rests lightly on my shoulder.

"Everything's going to be okay," he murmurs, his voice low and sure. *"I've got you. I'll take care of you."*

I lean into him, letting his warmth anchor me. I stay quiet, but my thoughts are loud. I wonder what he'd think if I told him that, given the chance to do it all over again... I wouldn't change a thing. That I'd still lace Kent's drink with morphine. I'd still light the fire, still swing that bat. That the feeling of wiping men like them off the map didn't haunt me—*it freed me.* I wonder if he'd still hold me like this if I told him I didn't need him to take care of me. That I could take care of myself. The fractures that had shattered through me over the years—I felt them melt and meld together. I felt myself becoming whole again. Some of the soft edges turned sharp, the cracks were paved over with steel. Nate breaks the silence, interrupting my spiraling thoughts.

"How do you feel about building a new porch out back?" I look up at him and smile knowingly.

"Let's do it."

Chapter 54

Nate 3 weeks later

I stand watching the flames engulf the trash, breathing a long sigh of relief as the last of the evidence burns away. I threw all of Sloan's old bedroom furniture onto the fire, and the blaze roars, swallowing it whole. We couldn't risk anything ever coming back to her. I glance back and see Sloan on the new deck, opening the grill to flip the burgers she's making us for lunch. The bruising was almost gone now, fading into faint shadows. I was relieved, soon I wouldn't have to see them anymore. I wouldn't have to be reminded that I wasn't there when she needed me most.

She looked beautiful as always, the sun casting a warm glow across her cheeks, her hair catching the light just right. The shorts she was wearing hugged her in all the right places, and it took everything in me not to cross the deck and pull her into a kiss so fierce it would leave us tangled up, forgetting everything but each other. I turned back to the fire, watching the last of her old furniture collapse into ash. The past reduced to smoke.

Fuck it.

I stride toward her. She catches sight of me and smiles, like she already knows exactly what I'm about to do. I scoop her up, lifting her off her feet. She lets out a surprised yelp, laughing, her arms instinctively wrapping around my neck. I kiss her feverishly, and she giggles in my arms.

"Nate, you're going to make me burn the food," she laughs, her voice light and happy. God, I'd do anything to see her like this every day.

"Screw the food," I murmured, holding her tighter. She wraps her legs around my waist, fingers threading through my hair as she pulls me into another kiss. I groan against her mouth, the sound low and desperate. I trail kisses down her neck, making her arch into me.

"You don't seem too worried about the food now," I whisper against her skin. She only moans in response, and I keep going, pressing my lips further down until I reach her collarbone. She groans, frustrated, and reluctantly pulls back.

"We better stop," she says with a pout that somehow makes her even cuter. "The neighbors already don't like us."

I roll my eyes. "Let them file a complaint."

She throws her head back laughing, looking so carefree, so gorgeous it makes my chest ache.

"Fine," I sigh, rolling my eyes. "Let's hope the food hasn't burned. Come on, let's eat."

I set her down, already missing the feel of her in my arms. She grabs the plates, moving toward the grill, sliding the burgers onto them with practiced ease. The smile never leaves her face, and I don't take my eyes off her. Not even for a second.

Sloan had been right; Eugene Tucker had pulled similar stunts long before he ever set his sights on her. When news of his disappearance broke, the reports mentioned multiple complaints from nurses and patients' family members. Several charges had been filed over the years, but nothing ever stuck. No one wanted to believe a doctor could be capable of something like that. With pills found discarded in his car and no sign of him anywhere, people were finally starting to believe it. Most assume he's on the run. No one has come to us with questions. The world feels just a little bit lighter without him in it. The only downside is that the women he hurt will never feel real justice.

Sloan saunters over to the table and sets my plate in front of me. She scoots her chair close, close enough that her knee brushes mine under the table. Instead of digging in, I just watch her. Watch the way she carefully builds her burger, adding toppings with a little hum under her breath. The happiness on her face is so plain, so effortless, it makes something twist in my chest.

For a split second, I wonder. What really happened inside Kent's house the day it caught fire? What led her to swing a bat so many times she cracked a man's skull open? She told me when she went to Kent's house that day but swore she didn't start the fire. She was just trying to convince him to sell her the house. For me. She told me the day Eugene Tucker showed up, he was blackmailing her. Said he threatened to go to the police, to tell them he saw her coming out of Kent's house the morning before the fire. She swore to me that all she remembered from that day was him trying to force himself on her, and the next thing she knew, she was standing over him, the bat in her hands. I believed her. I swore to myself I did. Because after everything we've been through... after everything we've survived together— wouldn't she tell me the truth?

I stare down at my plate, untouched, appetite gone. I want to believe there's nothing more to the story. I need to. But there's this voice in the back of my head asking me if she's holding pieces of it back. If there's more I don't know. She stares at me, eyes narrowing in concern.

"Oh no, did I really burn it?" she asks, lifting the bun to inspect her burger. I force a smile, pushing through the heaviness in my chest.

"No, it's fine. I'm just a little tired from the yard work."

She pats my leg affectionately and goes back to eating, like we're just a normal couple having lunch in the sun. Like there isn't a dead body buried ten feet beneath us.

Guilt creeps in, slow and sour in my gut. What the hell is wrong with me? She's been through so much. It's not like she's walking around offing people like it's nothing. This wasn't cold-blooded. It wasn't planned. It was survival.

"Well, I have a surprise for you," she says, grinning like she's about to burst. Whatever weight I'd been carrying a second ago lifts slightly. I raise an eyebrow, leaning in with a smirk.

"Is it that we're skipping the rest of lunch and heading upstairs?" She laughs, cheeks flushing just a little.

"We can definitely do that too if you want," she says, biting her lip, and she knows exactly what she's doing. "But I have something else for you first."

She leans over, lifts the cushion of the chair next to her, and pulls out a manila envelope like it's some hidden treasure. She hands it to me with a grin. I take it slowly, eyebrows pulling together. "What's this?"

"Open it," she says, bouncing slightly, eyes glittering with impatience. I peel the flap open, heart thudding harder than it should. Inside the folder is a slip of paper, and I'm momentarily confused. Until I notice, it's a deed. I blink, then blink again, running my thumb across the print like touch will confirm it's real. I look up at her, stunned.

"Is this real?" She nods, smiles soft and proud, and reaches for my hand. Don't cry, Nate. Jesus, don't cry. But there's a lump in my throat, sharp and sudden. My chest tightens as I stare down at my name on the paper. Because this—this is the deed to the land where my childhood home once stood.

"I'm sorry the house is gone," she says softly, "but I bought the land for you. We can do whatever you want with it. I know how much it means to you, to have this piece of your past."

I look at her, amazed. Completely stunned. I can't even find the words. She squeezes my hand.

"I know you said you'd do anything for me. That you'd go anywhere for me. I need you to know, it goes both ways. I love you so much it hurts, and it scares me, but in the best way. I love you more than all the words I've ever written. I couldn't even put it into writing, no matter how hard I tried." Her voice dips, honest and unflinching. "Words have always been my safe place. My armor. My weapon when I had nothing else. But you... you're better than words on a page. Stronger than any line I've ever written. There aren't words I can put on any page that would ever come close to describing how much I love you."

The guilt that had been gnawing at me suddenly feels heavier, like a weight I've been carrying for no good reason. Here I am, sitting across from her, doubting the woman who's given me everything. I meet her eyes, and I smile, soft, grateful, and full of a kind of awe I can't put into words.

"Thank you," I say quietly, meaning every bit of it. I can't believe how lucky I am to have her, to get to spend the rest of my life with her.

"You know, we should celebrate this nice thing you did." She leans in, eyes sparkling with mischief.

"By going upstairs?" she asks, smirking. I grin back.

"No, you perv. We're going out for a nice dinner tonight." She swats me playfully. I scoop her up, her squeals echoing as I carry her inside. We've got plenty of time before dinner.

Chapter 55

Nate has his hand on my leg as he drives us to dinner, his smile beaming like he hasn't got a single worry in the world. I feel a warmth bloom in my chest, knowing I'm part of the reason for that smile, part of the reason for his happiness. In a world full of vile people, I somehow ended up with one of the good ones. The way just his touch—his hand on my leg—can make me feel like I'm on fire, in the best way... it still amazes me.

"I was thinking about something," he says, breaking into my thoughts. I glance over at him, matching his smile.

"Sounds dangerous," I tease. He chuckles, his hand gently squeezing my leg.

"What if we built a house on the land?" I blink.

"Nate, you can do whatever you want with the land, it's yours."

He shakes his head slightly. "No, not just any house. A safe house, for people in bad situations. Somewhere they can go when they have nowhere else. We'd help them find resources, jobs, support, and community. Summit Grove needs something like that."

I'm speechless. He said it so simply, like building a safe haven in a town as small as Summit Grove was the easiest thing in the world. A place where someone could go without judgment. Where they'd be met with support instead of suspicion. Compassion instead of shame.

"If Karrie or Scarlett had something like that..." I start, my voice catching. "Maybe things would've turned out differently."

Tears spring to my eyes before I can stop them. The idea is perfect. I can see it, the good we could do.

"I was also thinking..." he glances over at me, eyes soft, "we could call it *Marilyn's House*."

That's all it takes for me to break. The kind of sobbing that comes from a place too deep to name. Big, ugly, soul-wringing tears. The kind you don't hold back because there's no use trying. By the time we're pulling into the restaurant parking lot, I can barely breathe.

"Hey," he says gently, putting the car in park and turning to face me. His hand finds mine, his thumb brushing slow and steady across my skin. "It's okay. I've got you."

I look at him, and somehow, I love him even more than I did five seconds ago. I didn't think that was humanly possible. Just by being himself. By turning pain into something purposeful and by loving me in a way that never felt heavy, only freeing.

"You want to go home instead of eating out? We can get takeout," he offers, always so thoughtful.

I shake my head with a soft smile. "No. Let's go have dinner."

He leads me inside, and once we're seated and ordering drinks, a rare calm settles over me. It feels like a real night out. A real life.

We're laughing, relaxed, probably having the best dinner of our lives, when I hear it—two tables over, a man's voice, sharp and cutting. He's berating his date. I glance over and she's staring down at her plate like it might disappear if she focuses hard enough, like if she stays still, maybe his words won't land. He's speaking low, but the venom is unmistakable. I try to look away. I try to focus on Nate, on us, on our perfect night, but no matter how hard I try my attention drifts to them. I know that look in her eyes. As each vile word spills from his mouth, it echoes louder in my ears than it should.

It's then that I hear it. The crack of a bat. The strike of a match. Like a rhythm buried in my bones. A song I didn't ask to learn, but one I'll never forget. His words blend with those sounds until I'm no longer in this restaurant. I'm back there. Back in the blood, the smoke, the heat of rage and revenge. I grip the edge of the table, grounding myself. Nate asks for the check, and I glance over just in time to see the couple stand. He's still towering over her, still talking down to her like she's nothing. She keeps her eyes low, shrinking into herself.

"I'm going to run to the restroom while you pay," I say quickly, trying to sound casual. I move fast toward the restrooms.

As soon as Nate looks down at the check, I veer toward the exit, slipping through the front doors without a second thought. My eyes scan the parking lot frantically. Across the lot, he's still shouting even as they get into the car. She doesn't say a word. She just takes it. He slams the door, starts the engine, and peels out. I burn the license plate into my memory. Every digit. Every letter. I whisper it under my breath like a mantra.

Maybe I could have a pool put in the backyard next, I think to myself. A slow smile spreads across my face, the cold certainty of what comes next settling in my bones.

To all my fabulous readers, thank you for taking the time to read this story. This is something I began writing while my grandmother was sick. While most of this story is fiction, parts of it are, unfortunately, true. My mother did go missing when I was young. She struggled with many things, but she was still a person. Sometimes, as a society, we forget that people who struggle are still people. When my mother went missing, everything changed the moment they found out who she was. It was like she instantly became *less than.* My whole life, I've heard people talk about her as if her struggles erased her worth. But the most painful part? The consensus from many—people who didn't even know her—was that she somehow *deserved* whatever happened to her. That kind of judgment, that dehumanization, isn't something only my family has experienced. Sadly, there are millions of families who have gone through the same thing, families whose loved ones were treated as if their lives mattered less because of addiction, mental illness, poverty, or simply bad luck. I hope one day we realize how easily it could be *any* of us—tossed aside by the world, labeled, and forgotten. I hope one day we do better. That we lead with compassion instead of assumptions. Writing this book was hard, but it was necessary. To anyone who has ever experienced this kind of treatment, who's ever been told, directly or indirectly, that they or someone they love isn't worth the time of day: this one's for you.

Allow me to say, from the bottom of my heart—I'm sorry. You deserved better. You still do.